ARIEL:NANO WOLVES 1

DONNA MCDONALD

WWW.DONNAMCDONALDAUTHOR.COM

Cover by *Black Raven's Designs*

Edited by *AJ Carmicheal* at *Blackraven's Designs*

❀ Created with Vellum

DEDICATION

This book is for all the wolf lovers in the world—both make-believe and real.

ACKNOWLEDGMENTS

Many thanks to S. E. Smith and Eve Langlais for all their encouragement, and for letting me make the leap from fan girl to peer with them. You both rock and fill my ereader with stories I always look forward to reading. May you have continued success in your work.

Special thanks to Robyn Peterman for being my paranormal reading partner and for her steadfast support of my paranormal writing journey. My shifters are not as funny as yours, but I found my sweet spot. Thanks for all the help.

Thanks to my husband Bruce who will never read my shifter book —lol. You still are every hero to me even if you do think zombies are more realistic than werewolves.

Dr. Ariel Jones blinked at the bright lights overhead as she woke. Finding herself naked and strapped to some sort of gurney, she turned her head and saw two women similarly strapped to gurneys beside her. One was weeping steadily. The other was glaring at a fixed spot on the ceiling.

Her scientist brain got busy immediately, trying to figure out what had happened since she'd come to work that morning. Her typical day at Feldspar Research always started at five in the morning to accommodate the light limitations of living and working just outside Anchorage, Alaska.

She had processed the new set of blood samples waiting for her in the lab and instantly reported the unusually rapid cell mutation she had seen happening under the lens of her microscope. Then at about ten o'clock, she'd gone for a direct meeting with Dr. Crane, who had asked to speak with her in person about what she'd found.

One minute she had been drinking coffee and talking with a colleague. The next she was waking up naked in… where was she anyway? Looking around more, she finally recognized the place. It was where they had brought the giant wolf.

Sniffing the air, she could indeed smell the pungency of the trapped animal. It was what had bothered her most. From what she knew, he'd been here longer than she had worked for Crane. The one and only time she'd seen the wolf in person had been more than enough. He was the biggest animal she'd ever seen and bigger than any she could have ever imagined.

Now she was here—in the same room where they had kept him. The discovery brought her back to her own pressing problem of waking up naked and restrained without knowing why. A thousand thoughts raced through her mind, none of them pleasant.

"So good of you to join us at last, Dr. Jones. I've been delaying things and waiting for you to wake up. I didn't want to start the injections while you were still under the effects of the mild sedative we gave you earlier."

"You put drugs in my coffee this morning," Ariel stated, somehow sure of it even before her bastard employer nodded and smiled.

"The sedative was the fastest way to obtain your physical cooperation. Time is critical. We don't know how long the window of opportunity from your findings will remain open. You told me several weeks ago you had come to Alaska because you craved more out of life than sitting in a lab doing research. Well, I'm about to make your dreams come true in a way you have never imagined."

Ignoring her accelerating heartbeat, Ariel decided she wasn't going to get emotionally alarmed until there was a greater reason to do so than simply being naked and unable to free herself. She was used to thinking her way out of bad situations. She just needed to remain calm, ask questions, and figure out what was really going on.

"I would like to know the purpose of your actions. Are you planning to take physical advantage of my helpless condition? Who are the two women next to me? What role do they play?"

Dr. Crane smiled. "So many questions. Of course, I expected someone like you would have them. You're going on a scientific adventure or at least your body is. The three of you are about to become the next step in the evolution of our species. But I guess it's rather bold of me to theorize such a result without any proof yet. Part of the excitement is considering all the possibilities. Now I know your circumstances are a bit alarming at the moment, but if this experiment works, you'll become an extremely valuable asset to our military. Even the most highly trained K-9 units won't be able to compete with your animal skills. Alaskan wolves are quite superior to canines in nearly all areas. Everyone studies their predatory actions for just this reason."

"I still don't understand, Dr. Crane. I thought Feldspar was testing wolf fortitude to glean survival information for living in extremely harsh environments," Ariel said, discreetly testing the restraints around her wrists again.

"Oh come now, Dr. Jones. That sort of work is barely fit for a second year university student. You are here because you personally possess several strands of DNA in common with our latest Feldspar wolf acquisition. He's been rather solemn since we informed him of your findings. He's glaring at us steadily which I take as the highest compliment about your discovery. It's as if he senses what we are about to do to the three of you."

"Dr. Crane, are you saying you're communicating with a wolf? Don't you think that assumption is a bit odd?" Ariel asked.

"Not at all. I sincerely wish we could be communicating with his human side, but we've purposely kept him from shifting back to his human form by the silver collar around his neck. I think it helped greatly to leave the six silver bullets someone put into him too. He was initially impossible to capture in his wolf form. If his pack had been nearby, I doubt we would have. In fact, I don't know who exactly did capture him. I found him both shot and tranquilized with a note pinned to his collar when someone activated the alarm on the back door of the lab."

"I'm sorry Dr. Crane, but you sound like some crazy mad scientist out of a movie. What are you going to do to us? Seriously? You don't have to make up such wild stories. I assure you I won't be reduced to hysterics by hearing the truth," Ariel demanded.

"Still the skeptical scientist, I see. In just a moment, I'll happily explain the rest to you. Since what's going to happen to you is beyond your control, I don't see any benefit from not telling you the whole story." Dr. Crane waved at the man assisting him. "Proceed with injecting the weeping one on the end. I cannot tolerate a weeping female. She is highly distracting. I can't talk to Dr. Jones over her constant whining."

Ariel's head whipped over, straining to see the gurney at the end. She saw the woman's body arch when a plunger was placed at her neck directly on the carotid artery. Whatever was in the injection, they wanted it to hit all parts of her body quickly. To her surprise, the man rolled the woman's head, and shot a second plunger directly into the woman's brain stem. The woman seized, strained at her straps, and then fell silent. If the second injection didn't paralyze her spine, its content would be in every brain cell in less than ten minutes.

"Now administer the sedative and move Heidi to the last cage. Come straight back and process Brandi next. I'll take care of Dr. Jones personally."

Ariel looked back at the man speaking so calmly. He looked at her and offered a shrug.

"The sedative is to help keep you calm during the worst of your genetic transmutation. We're not completely without conscience. I see no need for any of you to suffer more than necessary. Since you're the first of your kind, we don't exactly know how much the transpecies mutation process hurts. Our captive wolf shifter has been quite unwilling to share any information, assuming he can still speak in his wolf form. We haven't been able to ascertain it one way or the other."

The woman directly beside her was still as quiet as ever. So far, she had not made a sound. Ariel listened to the gurney with the now unconscious Heidi being pushed to the far end of the room. She listened to a cage door being opened and straps being undone.

"Please continue your explanation, Dr. Crane. Did I find something important this morning?"

"Yes, you did. I applaud you for being as smart as your resume indicated. People usually lie on those you know. Somehow I knew right away when we met that you were being honest. It was quite the stroke of luck your blood also showed excellent—most excellent—counts of nearly everything required for the experiment. When I personally saw the metamorphosis strand in your DNA, I was literally as giddy as a schoolboy. The strand is missing from your fellow subjects."

"I did my doctoral thesis on the metamorphosis strand. Most in the scientific community don't even think its real. But I've seen it. People who have it tend to die fairly young. It's one of the reasons I left New England and came here. I wanted to explore the world a little before I came down with some disease I couldn't survive."

"Yes. Human subjects with the strand do tend to die young. But extending your doctoral hypothesis, I also believe the strand has a higher purpose in those who possess it. So when I saw from the extensive health exams Feldspar required that you personally had the strand, I just couldn't pass up the opportunity. Roger, I said to myself, what would happen if someone extremely intelligent suddenly became a wild animal? Would the person be able to control their carnal nature enough to use their intelligence in their animal form? The chance to discover the truth was just too much to pass up. Now you get to benefit from the very discovery you made this morning, Dr. Jones. It's too bad the global medical community will never know anything more about you except for the unfortunate accident which burnt your body to ashes today when you went into Anchorage for lunch. Alaskan winters can be terribly challenging on vehicles, as I'm sure your gurney mates can also attest to since they suffered the same fate."

Ariel flinched when she heard the woman beside her hiss and swear at the depression of the plunger at her neck. When her brain stem was shot, the woman shrieked loudly and nearly broke the straps with her arching. The sedative calmed the woman instantly, but it had the opposite effect on Ariel. Starting to panic at last, because she knew the same fate would be hers, Ariel renewed her efforts to escape and twisted against her restraints. Unfortunately, she lacked the strength to break them.

She listened to the second gurney being wheeled down the hall. Again a cage door opened. Moments later, she heard it close and a key turning in a lock.

"Who gave you the right to do this to us, Dr. Crane? I came to Feldspar to do research for you, not to *be* your research. What you are doing is illegal and immoral."

"I know. I do feel a little bad about hiring you under false pretenses, but your discovery this morning stacked the odds in favor of your participation. My benefactor is most anxious to see some evidence that the transpecies mutation process can work. If even one of you survives the change, he will fund me for at least another two years."

"You're the sickest, sorriest excuse for a scientist I've ever met," Ariel declared.

Dr. Crane nodded as he lifted the first injection into the air above her. "Not anymore. Now I'm the scientist who has figured out how to make werewolves. As far as I know, I'm the only one like me on Earth. My services will be highly sought after when I show them a brilliant scientist in her wolf form."

Ariel called out and felt fire crawl under her skin as sizzling hot liquid entered her bloodstream. "*Nanos?* You injected me with nanos? It feels like a billion ants crawling on the inside of my skin." She saw Crane lift an eyebrow at her knowledge, but then so did she. She wasn't even sure how she knew what they were giving her.

"You're very sharp, Dr. Jones, much too sharp to spend your

life doing research. I picked women as initial test subjects because they could be physically restrained the easiest. I did not plan on using a woman who would be able to figure out what was going on. But that's what makes life interesting. Now the next injection has to go directly into the brain stem for best results. I'm sorry for the extreme pain it causes. Judging from your fellow test subjects, the pain won't last more than a few moments."

Ariel fought as the assistant turned her head and held it still while Dr. Crane positioned the plunger. The depression happened quickly. Pain more intense than anything she'd ever known shot through her head and had her calling out. Before her consciousness faded, her last thought was that Dr. Crane had lied to her. She had been spared nothing. Her head exploding from the inside was what dropped the eventual black veil over her thoughts.

She never felt the sedative working at all.

2

ARIEL SHOOK WITH COLD AS SHE CAME UP OUT OF A DEEP, DRUGGED sleep. Naked and shivering, she determined that she was lying on a small cot.

As she struggled to open her eyes, she could just barely make out the forms of Dr. Crane and his white-coated asswipe of an assistant. They were staring into the cages where they'd stashed the other two women who had been captured alongside her. There was a bunch of growling and hissing which kept getting louder as the men talked.

Dr. Crane looked extremely pleased with whatever was happening. The knowledge pissed her off, but her dark thoughts of doing vicious and hideously cruel things to both men surprised her.

Ariel lifted a pale hand in front of her face, which blurred out of focus, but finally came back in. So far, nothing overly unusual had happened to her body, unless you counted the sick headache she had at the moment. She felt strange though—very strange. Her stomach growled with fierce hunger and there was a steady fire burning between her legs. Those two white-coated bastards had better not have touched her. If they did, she was cutting off their man parts and throwing them in the recycler. Later, when she was more alert, she promised herself she would check her body closer.

A loud clanging against the bars of her cage had her covering her ears. Sound—all sound—hurt terribly and increased her headache. A percussion band played in her head as she fought the pain.

"I'm afraid your doctoral thesis is now a complete failure, Dr. Jones. Apparently, the metamorphosis strand is a deterrent to transpecies mutation as well as being something to shorten a person's life. Now I have to decide what to do about you. We can't just turn you loose in society and have you telling everyone what we're up to here. You were certainly a waste of a couple billion very expensive nanos we can't get back. Sadly, you've become the only failure case, rather than the pinnacle of our success."

It took her a lot of effort, but Ariel finally managed to manipulate her hand enough to get her middle finger to stand up alone. Crane's laugh at her silent rebellion grated on every nerve she had, not to mention how much his voice hurt her ears.

"When I get out of here, I may kill you just to watch you hurt," Ariel croaked, her mouth dry as dust.

Crane laughed harder and walked away. At his departure, the growling and hissing in the cages next to her ceased. When the room was totally silent once more, she drifted back into a peaceful oblivion where she could pretend nothing had happened.

———

Dr. Jones—Ariel. Wake now, but do not shift. Wake in human form. Think of yourself as human and you will be one.

Ariel rolled to her side on the canvas cot and tried to pull the scratchy cover she'd found over her naked body. Even with her knees scrunched up, it was far too short. She covered her eyes with a hand as she fought off the nightmares which were now continuously talking to her. There must have been hallucinogens in what they gave her.

I am not a hallucination. I am Reed—a three hundred year old alpha. You are a two day old version. It is very wise of your wolf to hide itself from those who seek to harm you.

Ariel groaned and rolled to the other side. "Head hurts. Stop talking to me."

I know you are in pain, but you must fight off the drugs now. Crane returns soon. He is planning to move you to another facility and dissect your body to find out why conversion failed with you. They have identified another experiment victim and she arrives tomorrow. You must rescue the others and kill Crane before he can turn more.

"Kill Crane? Sure. I'd love to do that," she repeated, covering her eyes with her hands.

Yes. I regret the extremeness of the step, but Roger Crane must not be allowed to continue his work. You will have to destroy the lab as well. Accidents happen all the time in Alaska. I doubt Feldspar Research will fund any other scientist if we completely destroy the proof of Crane's success.

"O—K." she said groggily, working her body into an upright position. Sitting up hurt as much as anything else did. "And I thought my divorce was traumatic. Either my nightmares are getting bossy or I'm hearing real voices in my head."

Putting a hand up to her head, she rubbed the base of her skull where they had shot something into her brain stem.

"Hey nightmare, since we're on a speaking basis, do you know what the hell Crazy Crane shot me with in the back of my head?"

My blood—I believe. He took it at the pinnacle of my wolf's lunar cycle. Since I was already in my wolf form when he caught me, hitting the lunar pinnacle was evidently strong enough to cause a species turning. I had heard the legends, but human turnings have not been done since the middle ages. Packs prefer to propagate organically. Unfortunately, Crane found a way to take the choice from me.

Ariel laughed. Her intuition spoke to her all the time, but it usually didn't announce she was a wolf in human form. "Hey Nightmare, are we going to keep talking in my head?"

Yes. I am your alpha. You are an alpha in training. So yes—we will talk in your head—until we can do so differently. I cannot shift from my wolf until the bullets and collar are removed from me. Silver has a restraining effect.

"Being shot with your blood doesn't make you my dad or anything, does it?" Ariel could have swore her nightmare wolf tried to laugh. He huffed like a dog doing it.

No. But it does make you my responsibility until you take a mate who can look out for you. Being part of a pack is like having a large family. I think you might like it once you understand it.

Ariel snorted. "So I'm an alpha. Does being alpha mean you're top dog or something?"

We are canis lupis, not dogs. Alaska is home to more than eleven thousand wolves. More than half are what humans call werewolves. This is what you have become, Ariel Jones. You are now both human and wolf, as are the other two females. They are your charges and the first of your pack. They are your responsibility and will look to you for guidance on how to adjust to their new lives.

His comments—which she was starting to believe weren't just voices in her head—had Ariel standing on wobbly legs and walking to the bars of her prison. In the cages next to hers, two multi-colored wolves paced restlessly. They were less than half the size of the black wolf, but still real enough to convince her she wasn't just having a nightmare. Oh no—she was living one.

"Brandi. Heidi. Relax. We're going to escape. I promise." When both multi-colored wolves sat and turned to her expectantly, Ariel shook her head. She knew their names and could command their obedience. Though she'd never been a person given to swearing, there were no normal words to express the enormity of her shock. Was she truly going to one day be a wolf as well?

"Un—fucking—believable," she whispered. She turned her

head until she saw the edge of the giant black wolf as he leaned against one side of his cage. "Reed? Is the giant black wolf you?"

Yes, Ariel. The giant black wolf is me. You should see the alpha of the Wasilla Pack. Matt's wolf is even bigger.

She felt like peeing herself when the black wolf turned his head and met her gaze like a human would during a conversation. He had the greenest eyes she'd ever seen on a man or animal. They were filled with a kind of determination she'd never felt before, but had a feeling she was about to get an education in it.

Crane returns. I know it is him. His stench will haunt me for the next hundred years of my life.

"Okay. I'm wide awake now and mostly willing to believe you," she said, hoping all three wolves understood she was working her way to acceptance as fast as she could. She went back to her cot and huddled under the short cover. "Hey Reed, did I get bigger or something?"

Yes. And you are strong enough to kill the men who will be trying to kill you. You have to try, Ariel. It is important to me that you and the other women survive. When they open the cage to take you out of it, call your wolf to help. She will be more than happy to answer. I've been helping you hold her back until the time was right.

"My mind is having a hell of a time trying to believe all of this is real, but I'm sure as hell not ready to die. Let's say I believe you. What does my wolf look like?"

Until she comes, none of us will know. I just hope she's big and strong. Rest now and pretend to be weak. You do not want them to know what you really are until it is too late.

Ariel leaned back on the cot and tried to look as pathetic as possible so her captors would believe she was just as harmless as they assumed she was.

Inside, she was praying that Reed—or whatever inner voice was helping her survive—was right about her being able to free them all.

3

Despite the fact Reed had said he smelled Crane, it was almost a half hour before the two men finally came back into the room. Assistant asswipe walked to her cage immediately and unlocked the door without a thought. He came in and grabbed her arm, forcefully lifting her to her feet. She jerked away from his hold and walked to the door of the cage on her own, staring at Dr. Crane, who was standing just outside, waiting on her exit. Two steps later and she was free of her prison. Something inside her seemed to expand in relief.

"What you did to me sort of negates saying you're the worst employer I've ever had, Dr. Crane. So instead of saying I quit, I'm going to say I'm done being your science experiment."

When both his eyebrows rose at her firm statement, Ariel dropped the insufficient blanket and stood in front of him completely nude. She heard asswipe chuckling behind her. She could smell their lack of concern and hear it in their steady heartbeats. Something in her rejoiced in the knowledge. Their complacency was going to be their downfall.

Assistant Asswipe suddenly smacked her bare ass and made

her yelp in surprise. Crane laughed at his goon's actions, but didn't chastise him for it.

Fire suddenly raced through her unchecked. She felt the nanos scrambling under her skin. In a blink, she was on all fours and leaping on Assistant Asswipe. One minute he was screaming in shock and the next he was silent because it was impossible to talk with your throat ripped out. She wasn't even tempted to eat the man, no matter how much she was starving. Turning loose finally, she turned to Crane who was walking backwards to the lab door.

"Look at you, Dr. Jones. You're absolutely magnificent. To think all this time, you were a giant golden wolf. And almost as large as the acquisition. How were you able to fight off the change for so long?"

Ariel heard him talking, but his words meant nothing. She leapt into the air toward the bastard who had tormented her, only to feel a taser hook attach to her chest while she was still several feet away. She hit the lab floor with a thud, whimpering in pain as Crane sent voltage into her. She struggled at the end of the attached wire.

Writhing, she watched Crane walk to the wall and pull a silver collar off a peg. Ariel blinked her new eyes and recognized it was a match for the one Reed wore. She couldn't let Crane put the collar on her. She couldn't fail them all by letting Crane control her wolf.

Behind her, she heard Brandi and Heidi whimpering, but also growling and snarling.

I know it hurts, but you must fight for us, Ariel. You've killed one. Kill the other and free us all.

At hearing Reed's encouragement in her head, she rolled to a half-sitting position, lifting what felt like massive wolf's shoulders from the ground. It took a lot of effort. Crane sent another shock into her as he reached out with the open collar. Though it hurt to move, she lifted a giant paw and knocked the metal from his hand. He pressed the button on the taser, only to find it was out of juice. Her wolf quivered in relief.

A low growl started in her chest as Crane set the taser aside, casually rose, and headed to the door. He was definitely not leaving, not if she could stop him. She wobbled as she stood and took a couple unsteady steps. Crane's hand was on the access pad. She listened to him enter the exit code. Three – eight – nine – two. Maybe she was going to like having ears that could hear this well.

She braced herself and leapt on the back of him, dragging him to the floor by his white lab coat. He yelled once as she landed heavily on his back, but stopped struggling when she chomped on the back of his neck. She bit down until she felt something crack at the same time she punctured his jugular. Hot blood rushed into her mouth. Mad still, she raised up his body with her bite, which she soon realized covered his whole neck. She shook him back and forth even though the dead man was already totally limp.

Knowing she had indeed stopped Crane was the most amazing feeling. She walked around with the scientist clutched in her teeth, even trotting back to show Brandi and Heidi. They laid down on the floor and put their noses on their paws. Her pride over his death filled her with enormous satisfaction. The crazy scientist would never torture another female.

Enough, child. Let the dead man go. Don't contaminate your body by chewing on him. You need to change back to human form now and free us.

Whimpering, Ariel walked back and dropped Crane's body in front of Reed's cage. Part of her didn't want the cruel bastard to be dead yet. She wanted him to suffer longer—suffer the way she and the women had—the way Reed had. Maybe she shouldn't have bitten so hard. Maybe she should have done it in a way where he would have bled out and died slowly.

Ariel sat on her rear haunches and glared at the black wolf. How was she supposed to become human again? She didn't want to be human. She was happy in her wolf form. Look at what she'd done. Her head turned and she whimpered again at the body of the man who had smacked her naked ass. She dropped her head to look at the other dead man in front of her.

If you change back, the others will follow your lead. You need human hands to unlock my cage... and theirs. You need human hands to gather up the evidence of Crane's experiments. Dr. Jones, I'm begging you to do this. You can be a wolf anytime you want now. I promise.

Her ears perked up. Dr. Jones? Yes. She had always liked being called that. Lying down, she laid her head on her paws and thought about becoming a female again. Fire consumed her once more, but not as much as it had when she had become her wolf. Again she felt the nanos getting busy under her skin.

A tortured groan split the air when she turned and saw a bloody Crane lying next to her, his dead eyes wide with shock.

"Shit. Did I really do that to him?"

Ariel raised to her knees gingerly and stared back at the cages.

"Did I really kill both of them?"

She looked back at Reed. He blinked, but said nothing to her, not even in her head. Of course she had killed them both. The memory of their deaths lived in her brain now. She had been a wolf, but she had been herself too. She just hadn't cared about anything but stopping them. She had no regrets.

When she could stand, she stumbled to Assistant Asswipe and fished the cage keys out of the pocket of his bloody lab coat. She looked at the wolves prowling the cages again. "Think of the women you were and change back. If you do that, I'll let you out."

Brandi laid down immediately and two seconds later, she was her normal self. Heidi still paced and whimpered, reluctant to do what they'd done. Ariel walked to the cage and stared at her. "Yes, it hurts, but it's necessary. Now do it, so we can get the hell out of here."

Whimpering harder than ever, Heidi laid down and moments later screeched as her human form took over. Ariel unlocked both cages as quickly as she could.

"In a minute, I'm going to set off the fire alarm. While that's distracting the building guard, go find us some long lab coats," she ordered. "There are two techs somewhere in the building who are going to stare at you both if they see you naked. They're harmless. Wiggle your fingers and giggle. They'll think you're the party girls Crane orders for entertainment on Fridays."

Brandi glared at her for her comments, but Heidi just hung her head. Apparently, one of them was a party girl. Ariel rolled her eyes at the knowledge and headed to unlock Reed's cage. He barely moved while she searched the key ring for the collar key. "I can't find it, Reed."

Leave me. Find Matt. He'll take care of you.

"No. I'm not leaving you. I'd be dead if it wasn't for you. You told me to save all of us and that's what I'm going to do."

Ariel left the cage open. She bent over Crane's body and ripped a wide swatch of fabric from the back of his blood soaked lab coat. She brought the fabric swatch back and wrapped it around the chain where it attached to the wall. She could feel the metal heat her skin as she tugged on it to test.

"Come on nanos. Get your little fixing asses to work. I've got to do this no matter how bad it hurts." She yanked and tugged and yanked some more. At this rate, it was going to take awhile.

Brandi appeared at her shoulder and without speaking took hold of the chain too. Ariel nodded at her stare. Breasts swinging with every yank, she and Brandi pulled twice and then the damn thing popped free of the wall.

Ariel kept her fingers wrapped around the chain. Even through the fabric it was burning her skin. Not being able to handle silver had to be some kind of metal allergy. She was going to look into it sometime and see what the hell that was all about.

"Okay. You're free now. Let's go, Big Guy."

Reed stood, wavered, and then braced himself for each painful step. Ariel walked slowly as he limped out the door beside her. At the lab exit, Ariel deftly keyed in the code Crane had used earlier.

The doors opened smoothly. She held it wide for the women who followed behind her and Reed.

Just outside the lab, Ariel rammed her fist into the door of a locked case in the wall, the glass cutting her knuckles. She ignored the pain which was already going away by the time the fire alarm filled the air. Her gut was overruling her brain. It was an odd sensation, but something urged her to trust it for the sake of all their lives.

"Go. Find us clothes. Do what I said," she ordered, turning to Brandi and Heidi. "Try to find us transportation too. Our vehicles are all dead. Crane drives a jeep. Let's take that. He's never going to need it again."

"Heidi, hold the door for me," Brandi ordered. She ran back into the lab and stooped to search Crane's pockets, brandishing jeep keys when she found them. Once she was outside the lab, Heidi closed the lab until the lock clicked.

Beside her, Ariel felt Heidi shiver. She turned and gave her a stern look. She had no time to deal with any emotional meltdowns. "Look—I don't know you and you don't know me. But I can tell you for certain that what was done to us can't be undone. All we can do is move forward. Unless you want to be responsible for Crane's backer coming after all of us, get your ass moving and follow Brandi out of here. We need to run while we can."

Both women nodded and ran off ahead. Heidi trailed behind Brandi only by a fraction.

The lab wasn't heavily staffed on Fridays. Knowing Crane, he'd made sure most of them weren't around for a few days during the experiment. She and Reed stopped at Crane's office. His laptop was open and still running on his desk. She took the time to turn off the screen lock before closing the lid and tucking it under one arm.

Next they stopped at her lab where she tugged on a lab coat she'd left there two days ago. She buttoned it up all the way to cover her nudity. Patting Reed on the head, she dropped his chain on the floor for a moment. "Wait here a minute."

Knowing she would heal fast because of the nanos, Ariel walked to the nearest chemical cabinet and repeated her bare knuckled fist pump through the glass. Reaching inside, she drew out the two most volatile chemicals it contained. Dumping both in a glass beaker she'd placed in a nearby sink, she watched the chemical reaction start to happen. She wanted to make sure it was working before they left.

"Come on, Reed. Compliments of my scientific education, that mix is going to have this room in flames in about five minutes. Then the whole building is going to go up when everything else in this lab explodes."

On the way out, she grabbed the largest microscope she could carry and tucked it under her arm. With Crane's laptop and a strong microscope, maybe she could start to unravel what had been done to them. Not that she believed she could ever reverse it. What she had said to Heidi still reverberated as truth. Nanos couldn't be removed once injected into you. They could be killed by extreme radiation, but never removed.

And Reed's blood was part of their molecular structure now. She wasn't sure how she knew that was a fact, but it felt like the same kind of truth as the nanos. Transpecies mutations weren't anything she'd learned in any genetics class. Knowledge of her blood connection to the black wolf who patiently waited for her came from sources she hadn't identified yet.

She picked up the silver chain still attached to Reed's collar, forgetting to wrap the cloth around it first. It burned like fire and stuck to her fingers, but there was no time left to think about the pain. Right now, they needed to vacate the premises before they went up in flames with it. By the time she and Reed got to the front door of the building, her hand was stinging like she'd rammed it into a hornet's nest. She was regretting her haste in leaving the fabric swatch behind.

When Brandi swerved in with the jeep two seconds later, Ariel and Reed both limped over to it. He made a running jump and nearly missed. Ariel caught his backside to push him up the rest of the way into the seat. He immediately curled up into a ball in the passenger's seat and shuddered. The effort to leave had obviously cost Reed the last of his energy. It made Ariel angry all over again. She turned a glare on the male who yelled at her.

"Why did you bust the wolf loose, Dr. Jones? You didn't seem the type. Are you one of those freaking animal lovers?" Feldspars' surly guard demanded.

Ariel glared briefly and then dismissed the speaker. The man and his attitude weren't important. Getting away was. "Yes, Frank. In this case, I am an animal lover. I'm setting the wolf free."

"Well, I hope you got everything you wanted when you got out, because you can't go back now anyway. You know this whole place is about to be blown all to hell, right?"

"Yes, I know, and good riddance," Ariel declared as she climbed into the backseat, plopping down beside Heidi. "Let's get out of here, Brandi."

Brandi shook her head, climbed out of the driver's side, and walked to the guard.

Before Ariel could figure out her intentions, Brandi grabbed and twisted the guard's head until she broke his neck. The man fell soundlessly to the ground. She watched Brandi drag him by one leg and throw him back into the building, closing the front door behind him. The lab techs were nowhere in sight. Ariel decided not knowing where they were was probably the best thing. She imagined they'd suffered the same fate as the irritating guard.

Fire engines were turning into the quarter mile long drive from the main road to the secluded facility as Brandi jogged back to the driver's seat. "The techs we talked to on the way are already headed home. I let them go because they were grieving your alleged death, but the guard recognized you, Dr. Jones. He was a loose end and would have given people way too much to talk about later if he had lived."

"Did you have to kill him? What if the man had a family?" Ariel demanded, biting her lip as Brandi swerved and drove down a side road she said would take them out a rarely used entrance.

"I don't think Frank had a family. He was too good a customer at the place where I worked," Heidi declared.

Ariel rolled her eyes. Seconds later a loud explosion rocked the air behind them. Black smoke filled the sky above a blazing Feldspar Research building.

Brandi kept driving calmly forward like buildings exploding around her happened every day. Ariel suddenly decided she wanted to know why—and why killing the guard hadn't caused her any remorse.

"You both know I worked for Crane, and I think we have a pretty good idea what Heidi did for a living. What's your story, Brandi?"

Brandi shrugged. "I was a federal agent who was investigating Feldspar's unauthorized use of Alaskan wolves for experiments they refused to explain to the National Wildlife Foundation. Before that I was special forces in the military. This NWF investigation was supposed to be a break from this kind of traumatic shit for me."

Ariel nodded. "Reed—the black wolf up there—talks to me in my head. He's the one they used to turn us into werewolves. Head to Wasilla, which is just a short distance from Anchorage. Reed said to look for someone named Matt. We need to get him to some sort of veterinarian too before he gets any sicker."

Look for Matthew Gray Wolf. His pack healer will be able to help me —if it's not already too late.

Ariel nodded, even though Heidi looked at her strangely. "Reed says we're looking for a Matthew Gray Wolf. A werewolf named Wolf. Gee, who's not going to figure that one out? This is some crazy shit 'B' movie we woke up in."

Brandi chuckled. "Whatever they put in your shots must have been better stuff than what I got. You're a lot sassier than the stoic scientist who kept asking all those serious questions yesterday. If I hadn't been strapped down, I'd have stuffed something into your mouth to shut you up. I really didn't want to hear what was happening to us. I wanted my death and I wanted it done quickly. They took me down with a tranquilizer gun when they caught me. I'm still too pissed to talk about it."

Ariel sighed. "My default setting is to gather information. I suppose what they did to me could have affected my personality as well as my molecular structure. Killing those two men didn't even begin to satisfy the urges I had about doing stuff to them. My entire being is on fire every second now. My wolf is there at the edge of the fire just waiting to be let loose."

"I don't want to fight anyone, but I would definitely like to spend time with two or three men. I woke up incredibly horny, and it's as bad in human form as it was in the wolf," Heidi declared.

"I feel a burning need for sex too," Ariel said. Her gaze went to their driver. "How about you, Brandi?"

"I'd jump on anything with two legs and a big Johnson. And I don't even like sex. This isn't normal arousal. This shit is going to drive me crazy soon if I don't get some. I have never had this problem in my entire life."

Ariel nodded and sighed. "The urgent need to have sex is probably part of our change. Our hormones must be running high. When Reed comes back around, I'll ask him about it. In the meantime, it shouldn't be too hard to get the fire put out where we're going. Until I do some research though, make sure the guy uses a condom and don't kiss him. We can't afford to exchange fluids and give away our nanos. That's what was in the first shot we got. If you think the change to wolf and back hurts now, I bet it's nothing compared to trying it without the nanos fixing you each time it happens."

4

As they drove through downtown Wasilla, Ariel looked at the names on the buildings. She saw one with a sign reading Gray Wolf Industries. Could their search really end so easily? Without being told, Brandi pulled over into a parking spot directly in front of the building. Being as careful as she could not to jostle Reed in the front seat, Ariel slipped around him and landed barefoot on the ground.

"Watch out for Reed until I get back," she ordered.

She walked into the front office and found two men. One looked at her curiously. The other leered at her lab coat and bare feet. She walked closer to him and a growl erupted from her throat as she met his stare. The calm guy slapped the leering guy's arm when he started to laugh.

Ariel switched her attention to the calmer one. "I'm looking for Matthew Gray Wolf."

"Why?" he asked.

Ariel paused before answering. If these men weren't part of the Gray Wolf pack, then she didn't want them to know much about her situation. "His friend Reed sent me with a message for him."

"Reed? Reed who?" the man demanded.

Two questions into it and Ariel had asked enough without getting real answers, so she stepped forward and stared into the man's gaze.

"Either tell me where Matthew Gray Wolf is or I'll search the place for myself. I have a dying wolf in my jeep and no time to play twenty questions with two fools unwilling to use their instincts. That burger you had for lunch was cooked well done. It doesn't surprise me your wimpy friend here had chicken salad. Don't make me gut you both for the leftovers."

"Hey," leering guy said.

Ariel glanced at him, but said nothing else as she looked back to the calm guy. "Fine. I'll tell Matt you're here," calm guy said.

Ariel nodded and relaxed, only to go mental again when she heard Heidi scream outside. She ripped the front of her coat open and was in full wolf form by the time she got all the way back out of the door. Several males had surrounded the two women. Brandi was pushing on a chest or two as the men teased and intimidated them.

In one leap, Ariel took down two of the men. Climbing up from that, she leapt at the remaining two. Once all four men were on the ground, she went to the women. Positioning herself between the men and them, she growled as the men shifted into good size wolves. She sent up a howl of challenge that pierced the air with a sound she hadn't known she had the capacity for making. The males growled threateningly in reply, but she didn't care. She was bigger than them, madder than they could ever be, and had an urge to kill which hadn't been sated yet. Truthfully—she'd love nothing better than to have a few more dead bodies to pack around.

"Enough, fools. Leave the women alone. You don't want to take on their alpha. She's full of bloodlust."

Ariel turned in the direction of the tall man who'd stepped outside and barked commands. The other two she'd talked to had followed him out. Their eyes widened as they took in the fight that was about to happen.

"Go home now," he ordered. "These females are under my protection."

Ariel growled as the wolves glared at her before trotting away. She paced in front of Brandi and Heidi. Brandi's hand came down and patted her shoulder gently. "It's okay, Dr. Jones. I think you scared them off. You can change back now."

Ariel felt her wolf shake all over in rebellion. She didn't want to lose the wolf again. She was better as the wolf. What needed to be done was very clear in this form. Thinking was so much easier than when she was human.

Ariel, change and talk to Matt. He is a friend. I'm fading fast and want to know you're safe before I die.

Reed. Whimpering in regret for her selfishness, she lay down at Brandi's feet until she shifted back to human form. Groaning as the nanos scrambled, she took the hand Brandi held out. Back on two feet, she turned to the three males now ogling her completely naked body.

Uncaring of their opinions, she walked forward.

"I have a giant wolf named Reed in the jeep. He needs medical help. There are six silver bullets in him and a silver collar around his neck that I wasn't able to remove. He can't shift to his human form. From what he's told me, I think he may be dying."

Matt took the shredded white coat from his gawking beta's hand and held it out to her. He was not going to be able to talk to the female until she was at least partially covered. Her perfect body was far too distracting. He'd not had that problem in quite a while, and having it now made him want to hear what they had to say.

"Thank you," Ariel said, slipping on the shredded coat. "I heard Heidi scream and didn't take time to save my clothes."

"Because you're an alpha," Matt declared, feeling a little twitch of excitement. Normally, he got antsy around other alphas. He didn't feel that way with her.

"That's what Reed calls me. I have no idea what it entails yet, but if it means I go ape-shit crazy now and again, I guess the shoe fits."

Matt smiled. "Are the women your pack?" He motioned to the two women watching their conversation.

Ariel nodded. "Reed said they were. He's the wolf that… " She drifted off and shook her head over not wanting to discuss it yet. "I guess you could say Reed is my creator. I consider him mine to protect too. Right now, he's the one who needs help."

Matt's eyebrows rose. "I see. Well, he guided you right. I consider him a friend. So Reed bit all three of you?"

Ariel shook her head. "No. He didn't bite us. It's a long story and I can't tell it to you until I know you better. Right now, I just want to save the big, black wolf. He said you had a healer."

Matt nodded, curious as hell about them. "We do, but Eva can't work miracles. How long ago was Reed shot?"

Ariel sighed. "I don't know. He was already captured when I arrived at Feldspar. It was several weeks ago."

"Five weeks," Brandi said tersely.

Ariel looked at her and then nodded. "Brandi would know. She was trying to stop Feldspar from what they were doing to the wolves."

"Five weeks may be too long to fix anything." Matt said, but turned to his second. "Ride with the pack to take Reed to Eva. The alpha and I will follow shortly. I'm going to find her some new clothes. Her nudity would only attract attention we don't want until we get this figured out. See if Eva has some additional clothing for the others."

Ariel heard the calm man agreeing, but she followed his gaze, which had gone to Brandi and remained the whole time. She told herself the agent, or whatever Brandi was, could obviously take care of herself when necessary. It was Heidi she still worried about. The female seemed to attract trouble just by breathing.

Matt stepped back and opened the door. "Come inside. Your feet must be freezing."

Ariel looked down at her toes. "I don't even feel them anymore. I've been naked and cold for two days."

She followed Matt back into the warmth of his office. She noticed he pushed the second guy—the leering one—back out into the street before closing and locking the door.

"We don't get a lot of visitors, especially not from other werewolf packs."

Ariel went to stand near a stove. "We only became wolves two days ago. We don't know how it works yet. I think Reed intends to teach us, but we had to survive first."

"*Two days ago?*" Matt said in surprise, digging through a large tub in the corner of the room. It was a clothing exchange his beta had started. He found a pair of heavy wool socks and a set of coveralls he thought might fit her. "From your smell, I assume you were full human before then. How are you handling the change so far?"

Ariel shrugged. "Good—except for needing sex something fierce. You wouldn't be single and interested in a quickie, would you? The fire between my legs is burning non-stop. I really need to douse it as soon as I can. I don't think a vibrator would do the trick."

The coveralls nearly fell out his hands. "You're asking me to try and mate with you? Here? Now?"

"What does *mate* mean? I just want you to—you know—have sex with me until I scream and get off. I need you to put out the fire completely—if that's possible."

He walked forward. "Not the most romantic offer I've ever had from a strange, beautiful female, but it has been awhile for me. I could probably accommodate you—as one alpha helping another.

Come into my office, Dr. Jones. We need more privacy to discuss your needs."

Ariel had leaned against the wall to put on the wool socks, which helped her cold toes a lot. Now she looked at the coveralls and frowned. They were the ugliest article of clothing she'd ever seen. She almost preferred her shredded lab coat to the awful looking garment, but not wearing it would be rude when the man was trying to help her.

She followed him back to a room similar in size to the front one. This one had a nice desk whose top was nearly clear. She imagined herself on it with him on top of her. Oh yes, that would do nicely… and so would he.

"Can we do it on your desk?" Ariel asked. "You need to wear a condom and promise not to kiss me. Those are the only two rules I have about it."

Matt shook his head and snorted at her audacity. "Come closer. I need to smell you and see if my wolf is interested. If he's not, there's no use in either of us getting our hopes up. He gets pickier as I age, so I've learned to do a sniff test before I allow myself or the female to get too excited."

Nervous about his revelation, Ariel still did as he asked and walked closer. She instinctively liked the man, even though she also feared him a little. It was an arousing combination. Her wolf squirmed restlessly. Ariel decided her wolf had no reservations about having sex with Matthew Gray Wolf at all.

She leaned her hips on the edge of the desk, surprised to find it took no effort to park her butt on the edge. Having always been average in height, she had to have grown at least four inches. No wonder her body hurt so much. The mutation had been extensive.

Matt stepped to her, leaned in, and lowered his eyelids as he sniffed. "I smell Reed, but something else, something metallic. Under those is the female. Where is your wolf hiding?"

Ariel chuckled and caught herself. "She's not hiding. She's

clamoring to get out—trust me. I feel like she could emerge at any moment."

Hearing her declaration, Matt moved even closer. Bracing his hands on either side of her body, he bent the attractive female backwards on his desk. It was the most excited he could remember being about having sex in years.

He was close to her mouth now. It looked delicious and he wanted a taste—wanted it badly. He wasn't going to let her stop him from having one, but it was probably better not to announce it.

"I guess you smell good enough. If I can't kiss your mouth, what can I kiss? I can't be with a female without marking her a little. It's just how I am. Call it an alpha thing."

Ariel's heart pounded. Her upper body was almost horizontal under his much larger one. The fire between her legs burned hotter than ever, but the rational part of her started having second thoughts. Sex with a stranger was always a bad idea. And this man had no reason to honor the limitations she'd set. What was she going to do if he refused to wear protection? She should have gone for the quiet man out front. He would have probably done anything she asked.

"You know, now that I think about it, I haven't showered in two days. Maybe we should shelve this until I clean up a bit. Sex between us is probably a bad idea anyway. I've had a lot of those recently—like the one that brought me to Alaska in the first place. Will you back off and let me up please?"

She let go of holding her shredded coat together to push at his shoulders. The pieces fell to the sides, exposing her front. Matt smiled at what she'd revealed which just happened to be two of the most perfect breasts he'd ever seen in his life.

"Now I see the perfect thing to kiss. I accept your offer. I will put out your fire."

Matt's mouth moving down her neck to hover near one breast brought a whimper out of her. A fever of biblical proportions spiked in her body. Her nanos started break-dancing when she started panting. "Condom. Please use a condom. Trust me. I'm not worth the risk to you or your wolf."

Matt wrestled his wallet out of his back pocket and handed it to her just before latching on to one nipple and sucking hard. He unfastened his pants and let the weight of his belt take them and his underwear to the floor at the same time.

Ariel's hands shook as she unfolded the well-worn brown leather and pulled a foil wrapper from inside. She felt him switch his attention to the other breast, growling against her when she flinched. His tongue laving her stomach moments later had her trying to lift her knees. But she couldn't let him go there—no matter how much she wanted him to.

"Let me do what I want," he demanded, sensing how much she wanted it too.

Ariel shook her head. "I can't. It's too much of a risk. You're just going to have to take my word for it."

His hands pressing her hips into the desk were insistent, but he stopped licking her stomach and laid his head just above her pubic bone. "I smell the wolf now. She smells divine."

"Thank you," Ariel said in awe, handing the condom back to him. "Please put this on and relieve me of this torture."

Matt was surprised to find his hands shaking as he sheathed himself with the protection he only used with human women. He hadn't been seriously interested in the new alpha when they had first started, but after smelling her growing arousal he was the hardest he could ever remember being. It was obvious she was not going to allow him to taste her, not in any real sense. Yet their coupling could not be all on her terms. It just wasn't something he could allow.

Lifting both her legs, Matt slid her up his desk. Then crawling on it himself, he straddled her body. Her look of surprise was priceless and he loved the challenge in her eyes.

"I can't let you dictate everything. Tell me your actual name before we do this. I know it is not just *Dr. Jones.*"

"It's Ariel. My name is Ariel. I graduated with a 3.8 GPA from Johns-Hopkins. I was married briefly, but left him after a year because he said I was boring. After that, I came to Alaska for stupid reasons. Next month I'll turn thirty-four."

"Umm… *Ariel.* I like the sound of your name." Matt growled softly as he put one knee between her legs. She surprised him by lifting and shoving the other one there for him as well.

"Anxious, sweetheart?" he asked in a husky whisper.

"You have no idea how much," Ariel whispered back. "And I can't let you keep torturing me. You seem plenty ready and I'm dying here."

Grabbing his hips, Ariel used them to drag his sheathed erection into her. Her body bowed as she held him in place and writhed on him. The first wave of fire quenching rolled through every cell. She vaguely felt Matt fighting her efforts to hold him still, but she couldn't let him go until the wave had ebbed. Finally, her rapid panting settled into mild breathlessness, and she realized the fire had finally died down to something less than an inferno.

"Are you okay? I'm sorry I did that, Matt. I couldn't help myself."

His name was torn from her lips again when he pulled out and thrust back in hard, sheathing himself completely. It was so damn relieving, Ariel felt like crying. Her back arched to meet Matt's nearly violent thrusts.

When that wasn't enough for her, she wrapped her legs around his legs and let him move both their bodies. For the most part, she kept her eyes closed. It let her focus on the ease he was bringing her.

"Ariel—look at me," Matt whispered.

His command broke her concentration and she opened her eyes to stare into his. His blue gaze glowed with tension as he slowed his pace, but thankfully he didn't stop moving.

"Is this helping enough?" he demanded, keeping his strokes deep and possessive.

Her head nod against his desk prompted him to press down and hold her in place as she had held him. What had started as a lark had changed into something very different the moment he'd felt the intense fire inside her. The female beneath him was no simple werewolf. He'd been with plenty of those. Whatever the demanding female was becoming, he was suddenly very glad she'd asked him for relief with her burning time. The idea of anyone else putting out her raging fire didn't sit well with him now. Neither did knowing with certainty that the alpha would have sought it from someone else if he'd refused her request.

Surprisingly grateful he'd made the spontaneous decision to be with her, he plunged hard and held still as he thought about his unusually strong reaction to her. "I will pleasure you again—as many times as you need. Don't go to anyone else in my pack for relief. Promise me," he ordered.

Ariel lifted hands and framed his face. It seemed strange to her that someone so commanding needed reassurance that he was enough for her. "Despite getting you onto your desk in the first half hour I knew you, I'm really not one of those women who routinely preys on men for sex. You have no idea how much what you're doing helps. Already, the fire is dimming. I feel like I can make rational decisions again. I hope you have a couple of guys willing to do this for the two women with me."

"My pack is mostly male. Many will be willing. If you and I are going to do this only once though, then I want to do it right," Matt said, selfishly not wanting it to end yet.

He lifted Ariel's thighs until her legs slid around his waist. The angle was the deepest he could go. She felt yielding and glorious— hotter inside than any female he'd ever known. He thrust hard a few times until he heard her whimper in pleasure. He lifted her hips with his hands and held her suspended for the next few plunges. She went nova in his arms when he hit all the right spots for her. His elation required celebrating before he lost his usefulness.

Leaning forward, he thrust hard again and sent her over the edge completely. He took her mouth savagely in the middle of her climax absorbing her screams as he tasted her release. Her arms wrapped around him tightly. She kissed him back like he was the only man in the world for her. It was a thought he relished, even if he didn't like relishing it for someone who was still a stranger.

Moments later he found relief himself, fierce like a rutting young cub. That peak was immediately followed by a sincere hope that he'd given her enough.

When they'd both calmed completely, he slipped out of Ariel's now lax body and crawled off the desk. The condom had strained under what they'd put it through, but it seemed to have held up. Working it off as neatly as possible, he tossed it into the trash can under his desk.

When Ariel remained still and unmoving, he smiled in smug satisfaction and wished they were in his king-sized bed at home. Following an urge stronger than his common sense, he scooped Ariel off his desk and sat down in his large office chair with her cocooned in his lap. He wasn't a cuddler after sex, but for some reason, he wanted to bond with the fierce female alpha just a little more than he had.

He bit back a growl when Ariel turned her face into his neck and snuffled happily. His wolf whimpered in satisfaction and he had a hell of a time holding the expression of his possessiveness in. Though still in shock at his wolf's reaction, Matt hugged her a little tighter.

"Thank you," Ariel said finally. "I feel much better."

Matt nodded, his chin touching her forehead. "You're welcome."

"Since you kissed me, I'm going to have to get a blood sample tomorrow and see if you picked up any nanos through my saliva. I don't know what they'll do to you if you did. I warned you not to kiss me, though I'm not sure all the things your tongue did in my mouth fit the description of the term."

Matt ignored her teasing to focus on what she'd shared. "Nanos? Like little robot things mad scientists inject into your body to heal you? I thought they were science fiction."

"They once were. Now they are science fact and just as real as werewolves are. Funny how someone trying to kill me wiped my disbelief about werewolves completely away even before I turned into one."

Pushing away from his chest, Ariel took a deep breath and slid off his lap. Being comforted by Matt was nice, but Reed was still in trouble. And she needed to check on Brandi and Heidi. The urge to take care of them was too strong to fight. Walking to where the ugly coveralls lay on the floor, she shrugged off the ruined lab coat. She heard Matt hiss when her bare backside came into view.

"Once was not enough for me, Alpha Ariel."

She wiggled the restrictive clothing up over her rear-end, zipping it before turning around. "You're just as nice as Reed said you were. And if I need sex again, I'll definitely let you know—and *only* you—because I promised. But right now, I'd like to go see if Reed is going to make it. I'm worried sick."

Matt nodded and stood. With evidence of his renewed desire jutting in her direction from under his flannel shirt, he stiffly walked to the end of his desk. He turned his ass to her as he stepped into the pile of clothes he had fastidiously dropped there earlier. Her grunt of frustration made him grin. Yeah, Alpha Ariel might not be admitting it at the moment, but once hadn't been enough for her either.

"Are you going to tell me your real story now that I've put out your fire?" he asked. "It seems a fair trade."

He turned to face her and let her watch him tuck his straining erection away before zipping his jeans. His mouth twitched as Ariel's gaze darkened with lust again. He wasn't surprised when she shook her head and said "not yet".

He'd never let great sex change his mind about important things either. No alpha would. His respect for her nearly doubled, as did his determination to get inside her again.

"We'll find something better for you to wear later. What did you do? Break out of a hospital? I saw the other women had on lab coats too. I'm guessing they were the only clothing you could put your hands on when you ran away."

"You would be guessing right about the only clothing available," Ariel said. "I'll tell you the rest some other time, preferably after I've talked to Reed. It's his story to tell as much as mine."

Matt walked to her and yanked her into his arms for a hug, just to make sure she would let him. Ariel fought for an instant by grabbing his arms to push, but finally relaxed and let him soothe her. It was a small skirmish over power, but he was happy when she hugged him back.

"I want you to consider me a friend, no matter what happens— or doesn't happen—between us in the future. Reed was right to send you to me. I just can't believe he's still around here. Some grandson of his is now alpha in his pack. They're up north and keep to themselves, out in nowhere land. His last mate died a few years ago and afterward Reed took off. When he passed through here, I recognized he was an old alpha and made him welcome. He told me he was tired of all the responsibility. That's why he left his pack."

Ariel nodded as she pulled from Matt's arms. "That's exactly what he called me—his responsibility. I asked if he was my father now or something. I think he laughed, but I couldn't tell. He huffed like a dog panting."

"Sounds like Reed," Matt said. "We are the closest pack, so his decision was wise, especially if he is dying. I'm glad he sent you to me. I'm glad to help—and for the record—the sex was outstanding."

Ariel chuckled. "Thanks. I haven't been with anyone since my ex-husband. You were pretty good too."

"Pretty good?" Matt repeated, sputtering at the low praise. "An alpha is never just pretty good. Try for a better description."

"Yeah, it sounds like your ego really needs it." Ariel laughed genuinely as they hit the cold air.

Matt motioned to a giant SUV. "It's not far, but you don't need to walk in your socks."

Ariel looked at her feet once she was inside the vehicle. Matt turned it on and blasted her feet with heat. She raised her head and smiled at him in gratitude.

"Two days ago, I was at least four inches shorter and my feet were much smaller. I don't even know if I'm done changing yet. You'll never believe what keeps running through my mind."

"The urge to kill when things don't go your way?" Matt suggested.

Ariel turned an interested gaze to him and nodded. "Yes. Exactly."

"Alpha problem number one. What just happened between us can be problem number two for a young alpha trying to keep desires in check. If you're a genuine were now, you're in for a few more of those sort of problems. Not all of them are this intense."

"Great," Ariel said, smacking the back of her head against the leather headrest. "Maybe it's the great sex talking, but I'm glad we ended up here. Reed said you would turn out to be a friend."

Matt looked at the female he still desired. "With benefits," he said solemnly. "I want you to be a friend with benefits. Your presence as my consort will temporarily keep the other females from thinking I'm ready to mate. I'm only seventy-five. My father lived to be four hundred and thirty. The last thing I need right now is permanent responsibility for a female and a bunch of pups."

Getting a laugh out of her as she shook her head made him smile. "What's so funny?"

"The last thing I want is another relationship. And I have no idea how long I'll live. When the nanos start to die off, changing into a wolf may kill me or become permanent. If that happens, I'll probably get nabbed by Alaskan hunters. I want to go back to Anchorage in a bit and see if the creepy place I worked is really shut down for good. Escaping means nothing if they start up their work all over again."

Matt nodded, more anxious than ever to hear her story. "When it's time for you to check, I'll take you. You might need to wait a week or so. Things happen really slowly up here."

5

INSIDE THE MEDICAL FACILITY, ARIEL FOUND BRANDI AND HEIDI sipping coffee in some sort of waiting area. Someone had found uniform pants for both of them. They looked like Crane and his asswipe assistant, but she wasn't going there, no matter how much she wanted to order the women to take off the clothes. Knowing they had obeyed her every utterance nearly without question so far, she was going to have to bite her tongue really hard.

"As soon as Reed is out of danger, we are all getting normal clothes. Matt offered and I accepted."

"We look like Crazy Crane dressed like this, don't we?" Brandi demanded. "I see it in your eyes."

Ariel put a hand on Brandi's arm and lied. "Not even on the worst day. How's Reed doing?"

"Dying," Heidi said flatly. "My heart is aching for him. They got the collar off, then cut him open and took the bullets out, but he's not healing. Something about the blood loss being too much. He's slipped into a coma."

Ariel dropped her hand. "Wait here."

Matt started after her. "You're not going back there without me."

Ariel halted and swung. Her gaze avoided Matt's and sought Brandi's instead. "Sex restores your thinking to normal. Find someone willing to have sex with you and ease the ache. Matt took care of my problem. I can't tell you how much better I feel."

His second stepped forward immediately and looked at Ariel. "I want to service your beta. If you want, I can service both females."

"No. No. No," Heidi declared, glaring at him. "I've shared all I intend to in my life. The crawling thing inside me wants to rip your throat out for even suggesting it. I want my own volunteer for this—whatever *this* is."

"Gareth, you won't be able to handle more than one of them. Trust me," Matt declared.

Ariel tilted her head at his comment. From what she recalled, Matt had recuperated within a few minutes and probably could have taken care of all three of them. White lies were obviously another trait they had in common. Maybe it was yet another 'alpha thing'.

Matt picked up his phone and sent a text. The response was immediate. "The Calder triplets are coming by shortly. Let her choose one of them. Come get me if they start to quarrel about her choice."

Matt turned to Heidi. "The men are not identical. In fact, they are very different. But they are all decent and will not take real advantage of you. They can be terrible teases and are not the most sensitive of males. They were raised in an all male household."

Heidi nodded and hung her head. "Thank you... Matt."

"Gareth, I leave you watching over these two while I go with Ariel. Take care of them."

"Isn't taking care of people what I typically get the most lectures about?" Gareth replied.

As he stood, Gareth inched his way closer to the new beta who bristled at his nearness. He turned to her. "If you don't like me, you can pick from the men coming as well. I will be disappointed, but I want your needs to be met. If you fear me, just admit it. I promise I will not think less of you."

Brandi drew herself up to full height. "Listen buddy. I'm not afraid of you. I can kill you with my bare hands—in *human form*. Luckily for you, I already got my need to kill out of my system today. It's just been awhile since I did anything with a man in a bedroom. But you'll do."

Gareth nodded. "I thought I smelled a pure arousal. Then you can be on top until you feel comfortable enough to switch places. I can perform in any position for as long as needed."

Brandi lifted her hands to make finger quotes. "Yeah, I bet you *'let'* all your women be on top. That's just a polite way of saying you're lazy, dude."

Ariel rolled her eyes. "Stop bickering so much. And don't get attached to the males who help you. Just let them take care of your needs and thank them for helping. I'm good with Matt shadowing me to see Reed. I want you both completely functional as soon as possible."

She pushed open the swinging doors to the medical area with Matt on her heels.

Brandi studied Gareth after Ariel left. "I assume we're waiting until Heidi's men get here, because I am not leaving her alone. She's like a helpless deer in most situations."

Gareth nodded. Seconds later, the front door opened and three men entered. Brandi turned to see Heidi wince as she looked at them. She was small for a female and they were giants, all of them. Any one of the men could break her in half or do much worse.

They all three skidded to a stop, staring at the two of them. One leered at her and Brandi narrowed her gaze. "Want to see me kill a man, Gareth? We can consider it foreplay."

Gareth sighed, ignored Brandi's threat, and lifted his hand to point at the frightened Heidi. "*She* is the one in need of your services."

"Hi," Heidi said, as all eyes turned to her. All three men walked in her direction, but she noticed one of them hung back.

"Tell me your name, sweetness. I want to hear the sound of it on your lips," the nearest one whispered.

"Heidi," she whispered back, clearing her throat when the answer came out a squeak.

"Back off, Junior. She's Heidi. I'm Brandi. And our alpha, Ariel, is going to kick your ass if you don't show some respect to us. Can't you see you're frightening her? Put yourself at a respectable distance and talk nice."

"Heidi, Brandi, and Ariel? Sounds like a sexy bunch of strippers. I've never seen werewolf strippers before. Are you going to perform a little show before we get busy, honey?" the second one grinned as he asked.

Heidi felt the growl growing in her midsection before it left her mouth. The two standing closest to her both smiled at her small show of aggression. She looked for the one who hadn't said anything. He frowned at the floor, about as uninterested in being chosen as a man could be. Fortunately for her, overcoming penile reluctance was something she had mastered long ago.

"Okay. I choose you," Heidi declared firmly, pointing at the solemn man. She heard him viciously swear and felt bad for making him so unhappy. "Sorry. If you really hate the idea as much as you seem to, I guess I can pick one of your brothers."

Swearing again, Ryan stalked to her. His two brothers snickered, but stepped aside. "I haven't been with a female since my mate died. I haven't been able to. I don't know why Matt made me come."

"All I'm asking for is simple sex to help me deal with the effects of my changes. But if you want to keep grieving for your dead wife, I'll pick one of your stupid hyena brothers. Just know I'd still pick you over them to try this with, even if we can't do what I need. Their attitudes are a complete turn off. I doubt they're going to be able to handle me anyway. I have a strong sex drive."

Heidi watched him rub his forehead as he swore a third time. The man was practically sweating. He must want to do this with her a little. Plus, he seemed equally distressed by her willingness to let him off the hook.

"My name is Ryan. Let me smell you and see if this is even remotely possible," he demanded.

Heidi saw his brothers snicker at Ryan's request and cover their mouths trying to hold in their laughter as he took a few steps closer to her. They were razzing him about not being able to do anything anymore under their breaths until he turned a fierce gaze on both of them.

"Leave us alone. You heard the woman. She doesn't want either of you. Your disrespect is no basis for making a female desire you. You two will never learn," Ryan barked.

Heidi's eyebrows rose when his brothers lifted their hands in surrender and moved away.

"Stand still and let me do this," Ryan ordered. Inching carefully closer to the nervous female, he leaned in and put his nose against her neck. She smelled exotic—different—like a werewolf and yet something else too.

When she quivered and whimpered at his sniffing, things stirred below his waist. He wished he dared take a lick and taste her. His loud sigh barely covered her groan of arousal. Next thing he knew, he was fighting not to growl and tell his brothers to get the hell away. His need to protect the woman suddenly kicked in as hard as the rusty clutch did in his pickup when he stomped on it. The whimpering new werewolf was the first female to even make him twitch in three damn years.

"Fine. Tell Matt I'll do this. Or at least, I'll try," he said, his gaze going to Gareth's instead of Heidi's. When he heard her whimper of relief, his jeans tightened. He had a lot of time to make up for what he'd missed—surely he could satisfy her during some of it.

"I think we'll get Celeste to give us a couple rooms at her bed and breakfast. She'll make sure we aren't disturbed," Gareth said calmly, not all surprised by the turn of events. Most mated males grieved long and hard, but eventually got over it. Ryan had grieved more than enough already. Temporary relief was how you got going again. He should know. He'd lost two mates over the last couple hundred years.

Brandi snorted. "Great. It's not bad enough that I'm a wolf. No —now I'm checking into a sleazy hotel for a couple hours of boinking. This day just keeps getting better and better. The only good thing I can say is that it beats being dead."

"Are you always so negative about everything?" Gareth asked, studying the frowning female who had held his interest since the moment he'd seen her.

"Yes. It's called being a realist," Brandi declared, shaking her head over Gareth's complaining. Sex should be lots of fun with Mr. Always Calm. Gareth probably didn't have an original move in his sexual arsenal. She imagined that a woman probably had to tell him what to do every step of the way.

But the idea of getting rid of the fire between her legs overrode Brandi's disappointment in the two remaining choices being the hyena brothers who were still snickering about Heidi choosing Ryan. And really—did it matter whose hose she used to put out her fire? Not really. Heidi had already made the best choice of all the males in the room. She supposed she'd take Gareth over either of the remaining hyena brothers.

Brandi heaved out a sigh. "I'm sorry. I don't mean to sound ungrateful. I just want to get this over with."

Gareth rose and nodded. "Okay. Let's go then. With luck we'll be back by the time Matt and Ariel get done helping Reed. I still don't know what he plans to do with the three of you... or with Reed. I guess Matt is still thinking about the situation."

The black wolf on the table was still and unmoving. Ariel swallowed hard. She couldn't let Reed die. She just couldn't. His blood had created her. Perhaps her blood could save him. It seemed a viable risk to take given all they'd suffered together at Crane's hands. She didn't want to deal with this nightmare alone. She needed the creature on the table to help her survive what had happened to her.

She looked at the medic, a native woman with a kind face. "Can you hook up a direct transfusion? I'm one of Reed's... family members... and his alpha in training. My blood stands the best chance of helping him."

"He has lost more than we can take from you, Alpha," the healer said softly.

Ariel shook her head. "Doesn't matter. I have to try. Take what you safely can. My blood is special. I should build it back quickly and it should build quickly in him. After you're done though, you will not be allowed to take my blood or Reed's again. You're better off not knowing why."

Ariel turned her sincerest gaze to Matt.

"If you trust me at all, see that the transfusion equipment is destroyed after we do this. Incinerate them completely if you can. I'm telling you this in case anything happens to me."

"What could possibly happen to you?" Matt demanded.

Ariel shrugged. "I don't have any idea about the long term effects of what was done to Reed, me, or the other women. My wolf turning was not natural. There's no time to go into the whole story, but what I've become is the result of a science experiment. Now do as I say and protect your pack, Matt. I don't want to die knowing I've harmed you or anyone connected to you."

Ariel watched the native woman walk around Reed's bed and stop in front of her. "I see the Great Alpha's life in your determined eyes, which look so much like his. I will do as you ask. There is no need to charge Matt with watching me. My brother knows my word is good."

"Brother?" Ariel said in surprise.

"We have different mothers, but similar hearts," the healer said.

Ariel sighed. "Okay. Let's do this then." She turned to Matt. "It's too cold to sit without clothes. Can you split this sleeve for me? I'd do it myself, but it's too awkward a reach, and I don't want to get naked."

Matt waited until Ariel had climbed up onto the gurney Eva had wheeled close to Reed's bed. "Eva, shouldn't Ariel shift to her wolf to make her stronger?"

Eva studied the floor for long moments. Finally, she shook her head. "No. Something valuable will be lost if she shifts. We will try the transfusion with her in human form."

Matt stepped to the side and ripped the sleeve of the coveralls up to her shoulder. He flinched when Ariel saw the size of needle Eva brought to insert into her arm. She looked away while it was being done.

"Damn. That was worse than the injections I got just before I was turned," Ariel said. "I'm going to hate needles for the rest of my life now."

Matt grabbed her free hand. "Me too. Try thinking of something you like. That always helps me. Maybe you could think of a nice hot fire and how much fun it would be for us to put it out."

Ariel's snicker made him feel marginally less helpless in the face of her pain.

Eva opened Ariel's fingers and put a hand pump into them. "Squeeze this to get it going. The pump will take over after the blood begins to flow."

Matt saw Ariel's jaw harden in determination as she did what Eva told her to do. He tightened his grip. "You are one of the most unselfish, determined people I've ever met."

Ariel snorted, her fingers squeezing the pump. "Now I know why all those women are chasing you. You're just an incredibly nice guy in werewolf's clothing."

Matt gripped her hand tighter. "That was a terrible joke. And I am not always nice. You just bring out the nice in me."

"Well, we are friends-with-benefits now," Ariel joked, hearing the pump finally kick in and take over. "Listen Matt. Seriously. If anything happens to me, take care of Brandi and Heidi. Okay?"

Matt nodded. "I will, but nothing is going to happen to you, Ariel. I'm the alpha of this pack. I forbid it."

"Crazy Crane—the guy who did this to me—was an evil SOB. Anything is possible. And last time I checked, you weren't God, though you did make me see heaven today," Ariel said, feeling herself getting sleepy.

From far away, she heard Matt calling her name, but sleep beckoned too strongly.

6

ARIEL WOKE IN THE DARK. SHE WAS WARM, DRESSED IN SOFT FLANNEL, and being held by a pair of strong arms. She sniffed, relaxing when she smelled a now familiar, sexy male. She whimpered when he rolled against her and nuzzled her throat.

"I want another taste of you so bad. You have no idea what a torture it has been letting you sleep. Eva threatened my life if I didn't take proper care of you and let you rest."

"Glad you listened to your sister. Can I have some water? And maybe a little space until my mind clears?" Ariel asked.

Sighing, Matt raised up over Ariel and reached out to touch the lamp on her side of the bed. The resulting brightness had them both hiding their eyes. "Sorry. I keep meaning to get a lower wattage bulb for the lamp. I never have overnight guests, so I keep forgetting."

Ariel stared up at his chest and let her eyes trail down the front of him. "You have to be lying. Do you torture all your overnight guests this way just to come across as some caring guy?"

"Don't be rude. I never let a female stay here with me. I go to her place," Matt said firmly, plopping a glass with straw on her stomach. "Eva said to drink this awful smelling stuff. It's a native remedy—a blood builder. Smells awful, but she's usually right about what medicine does."

Ariel slowly slid backwards until she sat up in the bed. She took the glass, sniffed, and then frowned. She took a sip and was thankful it only tasted half as foul as it smelled.

"How's Reed?" she asked, making a face with every sip.

Matt scooted up in the bed and looked into her concerned gaze. He wondered what it would be like to have her be so worried about him. "Eva thinks Reed's recovering, even though he can't shift yet. She said it was you who saved him. The spirits were already calling him home."

Ariel sighed. "Is he mad at me for saving him? He seemed like he'd been through a lot."

Matt shrugged. "You'll have to ask him yourself tomorrow. He's up and moving. Eva took Reed home with her. Her children treat him like a big dog and hug him to death."

"He is not a dog. Reed is *canis lupis*," Ariel declared, lifting the horrible drink to her mouth again and drinking a big gulp. "Been there—took that class. Think I got an 'A' when I shifted on his command."

"Your wolf is quite large for a female, even an alpha. I find that interesting... and sexy as hell," Matt said.

"You forgot magnificent," she teased, tipping the glass and draining the contents. "The guy I killed called me that. Here—it's gone. Can I have some water now?"

Matt leaned and snatched a bottle from his nightstand, handing it over.

"Thanks. And you said you weren't prepared for guests. I think you were teasing me." Ariel sighed as the water tumbled down her throat. "Wow, that's good. Thank you."

"I haven't been prepared before, but there's a whole box of condoms in the drawer of my nightstand now. I don't suppose the fire has come back yet, has it?"

Matt sounded so forlorn, Ariel laughed and choked on her

water. "No. I think the loss of blood may have dimmed the fire to a few flickering cinders."

"Oh. Well, okay. I just wanted to be sure," he said.

Ariel snorted. "You know, I figured an alpha would have just thrown me down on the bed, demanded I please him, and taken what he wanted."

"Would you like me to do that to you?" Matt asked, grinning at her twinkling eyes.

"Only if I asked you to. Otherwise, I'd probably rip your throat out. I did that to a guy who just slapped me on the ass. Call me spoiled, but I like sex to be my idea."

Matt sighed in resignation. "Then I guess I will wait for the fire to blaze again and hope I get another invitation. Do you mind that I brought you to my home? Your beta is with Gareth—at least for now. I'm not sure what happened with them, but she's sleeping in the spare bedroom in his house. He refused to let her be alone at the bed and breakfast."

"What about Heidi?" Ariel asked.

"Heidi is with Ryan, still where they started their fire extinguishing. He said her fire is nearly impossible to put out, but that he wasn't leaving until it was done. He said if she would just let him kiss her, he felt it would be much more effective."

"I really, really don't want to know why I care about any of this. But I do. I want them as functional as possible. Text him. Tell him to tell her I said to let him kiss her. She'll obey me. And then the man can get some rest. Tomorrow, I'll test you and Ryan both and see if nanos travel out through saliva. And I'll need to test Gareth too, if Brandi slipped up with him, though I doubt that happened."

Matt laughed as he reached for the phone on his nightstand and began typing. "So do you want something to eat?"

Ariel smiled. "No. What I want is to be held again while I sleep. That may not be good friends-with-benefits etiquette, but you asked."

Matt reached out and pulled her to his side with one arm. He was surprised as hell when her head slid down his chest and into his lap. Before his fantasies could race ahead, she quivered and shuddered out several little stressful breaths. His wolf whimpered in sympathy and wanted to ease her worry. His hand went to pet her hair before he could stop himself. Ariel was an interesting blend of vulnerability and strength. But the only two males she ever showed her vulnerability to so far were Reed and him.

"Everything is going to be okay, Ariel. You did good in saving Reed," he said.

"Thank you, Matt—for everything. I'm sorry I'm too tired to pay you back for all your help."

Rolling her face, Ariel kissed his erection through his clothes. When his wolf whimpered in happiness, it made Matt want to laugh. When Ariel had fallen back asleep, he lifted her to the pillow beside him. He watched her sleeping for a little while, then reached over and touched the too-bright lamp until it went off.

He put the empty water bottle back on his nightstand and tucked himself around her body again. Doing as Ariel asked, he held her while she slept, feeling oddly content to be needed.

In the morning, Matt woke to no female in his bed and lost his mind. Jumping up, he ran down his stairs, skidding to a stop as he found Ariel in the kitchen talking with an unexpected visitor.

"Mother Gray Wolf? What are you doing here?"

Ariel's smiling face turned his way. Her smile faded as her gaze fell straight to his straining crotch.

Matt looked down and saw himself tenting. He swore then realized how disrespectful it was. "Sorry. Let me get dressed. I'll be right back," he said, stomping back up the stairs.

Ariel stared for a while at the place where her... what the hell was she supposed to call him? Her coitus buddy? Her werewolf friend with benefits? Her fellow alpha—when she found out what an alpha was? Boyfriend was too inane to even be added to the mix, even if they had already had marathon sex once and slept together after a crisis.

She was feeling very mellow toward Matt this morning. He had held her all night just like she'd asked him to. No human man had ever shown her such consideration. She turned back when Nanuka spoke.

"I knew his mother. Matthew is more like her than he is his father. He rules with precision and logic, but can be very physical when he needs to be. He likes his peace and quiet. His pack honors that for the most part. The young ones have to be taught lessons sometimes."

"Was he always as nice as he is now?" Ariel asked.

Nanuka Gray Wolf shrugged, but smiled at the wistfulness in the young alpha's voice.

"Matthew was always nice to me. His father and I mated one year after Matthew's real mother died. It was considered disrespectful by some, but Matthew whipped anyone who criticized me or his father. Because of his acceptance of me, I supported his campaign to be the Gray Wolf alpha. Most alphas are born to the role, but not all alphas can rule well. Matthew is exceptional. My natural child with his father simply adores him. I'm sure you met Eva at the medical center."

"Yes, I did. Eva is amazing too. There's a lot to like about Matt," Ariel said, nodding as she spoke. "I will always be grateful to him for helping us, and to Eva for helping save Reed."

"Ah... you speak of the Great Black Wolf Alpha. Is it true he turned you and your friends into werewolves only a few days ago?"

Ariel snorted. "Not willingly... and not the way everyone seems to think. I can't discuss what happened until I speak with Reed first. As I told Matt, it's as much his story to tell as mine."

"You're very loyal to a man who has changed your life so much," Nanuka declared.

Ariel snorted and shook her head. "Reed didn't change my life. Reed saved it. The men—the humans—who changed my life are both dead."

Nanuka narrowed her eyes and nodded at the unspoken pride in her tone. "They were your first blood?"

"Yes—and I have no regrets. They deserved to die. Reed was locked in a cage and dying. Brandi tried to stop them, which is how she ended up trapped. Heidi's story is very different, but changing wasn't a choice for any of us. Don't ask me to tell you more, Nanuka. Matt deserves to hear first."

Nanuka bowed her head. "Forgive me, Ariel. I can see your alpha side rises up when provoked. You're so pleasant to talk to, I forgot to be properly respectful."

Matt cleared his throat to announce his entry. He knew well that Nanuka had heard him eavesdropping. He hoped she wouldn't rat him out. It took all the effort he possessed not to walk over and chastise Ariel for getting out of his bed without letting him know she was leaving it.

His gaze bounced between the women.

"Why so testy this morning, Matthew? I thought you preferred waking up alone. In fact, the whole village thinks the same thing. Your father sent me here and Ariel heard me prowling in the kitchen. She came to protect your home while you slept. She tells me you two are... good friends."

Matt gave his stepmother—or stepwerewolf whatever —his back.

Ariel covered her mouth when Nanuka winked at her and watched Matt wordlessly get a cup out of the cupboard. He said nothing in reply to her speech until he'd poured a cup of black coffee. When Matt brought the pot over and poured her a refill without asking, Ariel bit her lip to keep from laughing at his puny show of control over her. Oddly, she found it charming rather than annoying after he'd held her all night, but she could see the charm might wear thin fast if he did such things all the time.

"You should have woken me if you heard a noise you didn't recognize."

Ariel snorted at the comment and lifted her coffee for a sip. "I was already up using the downstairs bathroom so I wouldn't wake you. I figured out it was a friend, or you'd have had blood and guts all over the kitchen floor by now. It's not like I attacked her on sight, Matt. I introduced myself and she introduced herself. It was all very civilized. Just like the way you fold your clothing before you toss them into the dirty clothes hamper."

Matt narrowed his gaze. "Did you just insult me?"

"No. I called you civilized—definitely not the same thing as an insult," Ariel declared, the laugh breaking free.

Before she could blink, calm Matt was gone and a fiercer one had hold of her head. He leaned her back and attacked her mouth ruthlessly while she fought for breath. He gentled only before he raised his head.

"Still think I'm civilized?" When she blinked in surprise, Matt made himself let go and walk back to his coffee.

He wanted to order Nanuka to leave and order Ariel back to his bed.

Neither were good ideas. And one would never work. The young alpha female would die trying to kill him before she let him have that kind of control over her. Ariel probably only restrained herself now because Nanuka was present.

Searching her gaze for signs of anger, all he saw was irritated knowledge. Now he was sure she was being polite for his sake.

Damn it. He had screwed up.

Setting down his coffee, Matt gripped the counter and took three deep, calming breaths. "I'm sorry, Ariel. I shouldn't have done that. You do not owe me any control over your actions."

"Damn right, I don't."

Ariel felt more than saw Nanuka's head swinging in her

direction in surprise. She calmly lifted her coffee cup and took another drink. It pleased her to find she wasn't shaking. Should she have been pissed over his show of power? Probably. But she wasn't in that sort of mood this morning. She looked his way and rolled her eyes where he could see.

"Matt, we're friends. Get over yourself. I'm sorry if I hurt your feelings with my teasing about your OCD habits. It's just hard not to make fun of someone who's such a neat freak."

His blazing gaze raised to hers. "We are more than friends. We're..." He stopped cold.

What the hell had he been going to say? They weren't more than friends. They were barely friends.

"I think I'll leave you two alphas alone to work this out."

Nanuka slid from her seat and walked around the counter to hug a now glaring Ariel. Matt's declaration had been a bit premature.

"It was very nice to meet you, Ariel. While you're staying here, I'll make sure I call before stopping by. Blood and guts make a nasty mess on wood floors. I should know. I've cleaned up my fair share in my life. Matthew, I'll tell your father you said hello and are doing fine. He heard Reed was back and wondered what it meant. He sent me by to check on you."

The door closing with a quiet snick echoed everywhere in a house as solemn as Matt normally was.

Ariel chuckled. "No wonder you don't bring women here. I wouldn't either. Nanuka neglected to tell you how hard she'd pumped me for information before you showed up. She'd asked me the 'so how did you meet Matt' question in about ten different ways. I had to growl to shut her up. She's isn't an alpha, is she?"

Matt burst out laughing. He'd expected a fierce fight. He'd expected a demand for a better apology. Maybe he and Ariel were really friends. At least she had a decent sense of humor. He silently gave her more points.

"No. Nanuka is not an alpha. She's a busybody, even if a loving one. She was my father's consort after my mother died. Later, he made her his mate. My mother wasn't an alpha either. Alphas rarely mate other alphas. There's too much clashing over control. But the males in my family always choose strong women to stand with them. Alphas almost never choose doormats. Such pairings do not work."

"Sounds like natural-born werewolves don't have much of a sense of humor, if they can't share a bit of control now and again," Ariel said, draining her cup. "I'm starved. Nanuka offered to cook, but I didn't want her to get too cozy."

"Why?" Matt asked, suspicious still because Ariel hadn't once blasted him with anger over kissing her.

Ariel sighed. "I feel the fire coming back. I think Eva's potion worked a little too well at getting my blood pumping normally again."

Matt gripped the counter tighter. He had to feed her first. It was the right thing to do. She hadn't eaten since she'd found him.

"Cold cereal and fruit, or hot food?" he asked, the words barely leaving his dry throat.

"The fastest thing you can put in front of me, so cereal is fine. If you have any raw bacon, I'll take that too. Don't bother to cook it. It will take too long and the smell would torture me."

"How about smokehouse cured ham?" Matt asked.

"I'd let you kiss me again any way you want to for any kind of ham," Ariel declared, closing her eyes and shivering at the thought. "I can't believe I woke up starved, cold, and naked just yesterday morning. This morning is ten times better."

Matt carried cereal, bowls, and spoons to her. He got out the milk and the whole plate of ham he'd sliced off the bone himself. Her sigh was his undoing. He felt like the worst of asses and he owed her a sincere apology.

"I'm sorry I kissed you that way in front of Nanuka. She'll tell my father and he'll be over here checking you out next."

Ariel shrugged as she lifted a slice of ham, rolled it between two fingers, and chomped into the meat happily. Food had never tasted so good. "I'm not worried about explaining myself to your father. This ham is wonderful."

"It looks it," Matt said, choking on the words as he listened to her humming as she ate.

Ariel saw his eyes on her food. "You're not expecting me to share my ham, are you?"

Matt walked around the table. "It would be an exercise in self-control for you to share your food with me, especially when the urge is so strong not to do so."

Ariel swallowed and had to fight not to push him away. "This is another one of those pesky alpha problems you warned me about, isn't it?"

Matt ran a hand down her hair and nodded. "Yes. Give me a little taste, Alpha Ariel. There's plenty more. You won't go hungry in my house. I promise."

Ariel felt the wolf inside her whimper in rebellion. "You're scaring my wolf, Matt."

"She's just worried about starving. I would never let that happen to her. Now give me a bite of what you have left and you can have a whole fresh piece all your own."

Ariel had to shake the fury from her gaze as she lifted her hand to his mouth. "If you bite me instead of the ham, you're going to have the fight you expected over kissing me earlier. Make sure you behave, Matt. I'm not joking."

Laughing, he bit off a small bite of the food she offered and chewed. "Nice work." Reaching out to the platter, he rolled a thin slice of the ham as he'd seen her do. He offered it to her to eat.

"If you bite me, I'm tossing you over my shoulder and carting you upstairs to show you my real alpha side. The aggressive kiss earlier was just the edge of it. There's a lot more where that came from."

He held the ham to her mouth. Snickering, Ariel bit off a chunk. Matt smiled and ate the rest as she ate the rest of hers.

"Hunger can be used as a weakness against a werewolf. Reed has probably gone several weeks without food before. He's learned to hold his hunger at bay, but it's not an easy thing to do for a werewolf, especially for an alpha."

At the memory of Reed, her food lost all its flavor. "I don't even really know Reed and yet I can't stand the thought of what he's suffered. I don't even feel this way about my real family who probably thinks I'm dead."

"You can always reappear and tell your family some version of the truth," Matt said softly, lifting the forgotten food in her hand to her mouth. "Eat your ham. Eva will feed Reed, whether in human or wolf form. He will never go hungry in my pack. You can release that concern."

Ariel battled back tears. She hadn't cried a drop since the last fight she'd had with her ex-husband. Bet he wouldn't find her so boring anymore.

She sighed when arms came around her—strong supportive arms. "I'm sorry for crying on you. My emotions are catching up with me. I haven't cried about anything in a long time."

Matt hugged tighter, then finally had to let go before he changed his mind about letting her eat. "Eat your cereal and ham. Afterwards, we'll go find Reed and check on your pack. Quentin is watching the office for me until we get this sorted out. Gareth is protecting your beta and watching over Heidi."

Ariel sniffed, her tears drying. "Quentin is the leering guy you pushed out the door?"

Matt chuckled. "You don't miss much, do you? Did you say you used to be a cop or something?"

"No. That's the woman you keep calling my beta. Brandi was the cop... or something... she hasn't really said. I was... guess still am... a scientist. And I haven't forgotten anything about that side of me."

Matt lifted a brow as he took the chair across from hers. "A scientist? What kind of scientist?"

"Bio-Molecular Genetics. My specialty is DNA mapping. My claim to fame in the scientific community is that I discovered some unique strands in certain people's DNA and postulated their purpose. What most people don't know is I did all my research on myself because I couldn't get funding to use test subjects. Turns out, I had the very strand I was investigating."

"Why does this story make me so nervous?" Matt asked, crunching cereal.

Ariel hung her head. "Because the scientist I worked for at Feldspar Research figured out the strands I identified were people potentially capable of being genetically converted to werewolves. His problem was that an artificial transpecies mutated change might potentially kill his human subjects the first time it happened. But he found a way to make sure they healed quickly."

Matt stopped crunching and swallowed. "That's the job of those nanos you keep worrying about."

Ariel nodded. "You're sharp." She hoped Reed wasn't going to be mad she had told, but she trusted Matt.

"The guy sounds like one of those mad scientist types in the movies. What happened to him?"

"Ever heard about a man's work biting him on the ass when he least expects it?"

Matt laughed at her not so clever wordplay. "Yes. Did you bite the mad scientist on his ass?"

"More like on the back of his neck… and then I chomped down hard until he was dead. I killed the Egor dude who was helping him too."

Matt went calmly back to eating before answering. "Good. That saves Reed the trouble of doing it himself later. Wait until you see Reed in his human form. You're going to be surprised. I'll give you a hint—he's a native and a lot bigger than me. He keeps telling me my wolf is bigger than his, but I don't see it."

Ariel smiled and reached out tentatively for another piece of ham. "Can we try our food thing again later? My wolf is still mad me for letting you have a bite. I have the strangest urge to grab the entire plate of ham and run someplace with it."

"We'll calm her down later. She needs to learn to give in gracefully... and to share with those being nice to her," Matt said firmly, grinning when Ariel laughed. "What? I can be very nice— when I want to be."

7

Matt swung his SUV into the lane leading to Eva's house. His sister had gone in to work at the clinic, but reported Reed had chosen to stay at her house. When he and Ariel climbed out, he motioned her around to the back with him where Eva's deck faced a large wooded area.

"Reed must be off exploring, but he will have smelled us by now. Have a seat. We might be in for a bit of a wait if he's busy doing something."

Ariel nodded and smiled, liking the way the hard ground gave under her new hiking boots. "I'm not in a hurry. And I don't think I ever really said thanks for buying me new clothes. It's great to have shoes again. It's hard to believe the things you take for granted until you don't have them anymore."

As she chose a chair to sit, Matt looked at her long sweater, longer t-shirt, and brand new jeans. While not as attractive as she deserved, the female at least looked comfortable with herself, and not nearly as wild-eyed as she had in her ripped up lab coat.

He kept the conversation light until he heard what sounded like a bear running through the woods. Ariel stopped mid-sentence, her attention going to the sound as well. Then she smiled. It wasn't just a small smile either. It was a smile that took over her face. She was out of the chair and running by the time the big wolf hit the tree line. Ariel's laughter carried back to him, each sound she made echoing in his chest and through his heart.

Matt shook his head when Reed galloped to her full out. While most werewolves would have shit themselves in fear of the giant Black Wolf Alpha, the female who didn't know about such things rushed joyously to greet him. She laughed as Reed circled around her and rubbed against her legs—legs which had been twined around his while they'd slept last night.

If he hadn't known her story with Reed, he'd have been jealous as hell of the other male wolf. What the fuck was going on with him? He'd never been jealous of a female in his life.

And hell—he still didn't know enough about the laughing female to tell if she was even worth such caring. Sleeping with her once did not have to lead to any sort of commitment. Neither did having great sex with her, no matter how badly he wanted to be with her again.

Sighing over his confused feelings, which were probably being caused by the throbbing between his legs every time he looked at the laughing female still playing with Reed's wolf, Matt leaned back in the lawn chair and closed his eyes.

The two alphas dancing around each other in his sister's yard didn't need him to make their formal introductions.

"Reed. You look amazing. Your coat is so shiny and black. You look so healthy now. Are you able to shift back to a human yet?"

Ariel's face wrinkled as Reed growled low and backed up. Then suddenly where the wolf had been a moment before, a man now stood, a nearly seven feet tall native man with black hair to his waist. And he was dressed in clothes similar to what Matt wore. Wait... *clothes*?

"Hey. How come you get to keep your clothes on when you shift?" she demanded.

Reed laughed as he walked back towards her. "Hello to you as well, Dr. Ariel Jones."

Ariel giggled, covered her mouth, and looked up and up to meet his steady gaze. "I'm sorry. If you're someone's grandfather, I can't wait to see your sons and grandsons. Have you seen yourself?"

"Not in a while. Come here," Reed ordered, opening his arms.

Ariel dropped her hands and started forward, fighting the urge to whimper. "You're not going to do anything strange, are you?"

Reed laughed again, a big booming laugh. "Yes. I am going to hug you very tightly and say thank you for saving my life."

Laughing at her trepidation, Ariel let herself be drawn against his chest. Reed smelled like home—only no home she'd ever known before. He smelled like love and kindness and welcome. She thought of him yesterday, nearly lifeless on Eva's medical table. He could have died without her ever getting to do this. The knowledge had her sniffling.

"I made Eva do a direct blood transfusion. I don't know what will happen to you long-term, but I wasn't ready for you to die."

"I wasn't ready to die either," Reed said logically, pushing her away to look at her face. "You seem better too. How are you adapting to being a werewolf?"

Ariel shrugged. "Matt has been nice... and just as helpful as you said he'd be."

"That is not what I asked you," Reed said, smiling about her first comments being about Matt. "How is *Ariel Jones* doing? How are the other two women? I have no mind link with them. I can only tell they are good souls."

Ariel stepped away a little, but took his outstretched hand when he offered it. "Brandi and Heidi are doing as well as I am. We're all just trying to figure out what to do. Thanks to Crazy Crane, the world thinks we're all dead. None of us are in a hurry to change the situation yet. We seem to need time to figure out what to do about what we are now."

She felt Reed's arm tighten around her in a reassuring hug.

"I'm sorry, Ariel. Do you miss your families? You could go back to them and tell a story they would believe. There are many werewolves living among humans these days, but they get lonely for others of our kind. They take long, extended vacations and visit their pack."

"I don't think any of us have had time to think much about the future. Surviving has taken all our energy. Today's the first day I've even had actual clothes to wear. Matt bought them for me."

"Well, it was the least he could do after sleeping with you," Reed declared, shrugging.

"You can tell we slept together?" Ariel demanded, her face flushing.

Reed laughed. "Every werewolf with any decent sense of smell can tell. But I'm sure it only matters to the females who Matt has been saying no to for a long time."

"Oh—okay. I guess I can't complain then. Why does everything I say make you smile?"

"You remind me of my last mate. She wasn't an alpha though. She was just a happy person trying to lead a happy life. She went to help a family member one cold day and never returned. We found her frozen body two days later. There were no signs of struggle, but I did not deal well with her death."

"I was married once, but it didn't take. He said I was boring. Maybe I was. Science is not the most exciting career—normally. Being made into a werewolf is something I never expected to happen to me."

"Of course not," Reed said, nodding. "Human turnings are not done any longer—and yet I cannot undo what has happened. You three are now part of me, no matter how the Great Spirits brought us together. In a few days, we'll talk about what our connection means and decide on the best course of action to take going forward."

Ariel nodded. "Brandi and Heidi are going to be shocked at how good-looking you are."

"Good-looking? I like that. Do I have gray hair?" Reed asked.

Ariel frowned and shook her head. "No. Why?"

"I did before yesterday," Reed said. "Dr. Jones, I think your blood did some amazing things to me."

"I need to test us… and Matt. Damn it… and Ryan Calder, who helped Heidi. I don't know about Gareth who spent time with Brandi. You see, Crane shot the three of us with a couple billion nanos each. They help us bear the shift change to our wolves. What I don't know is if the nanos stay constrained in our bodies in the middle of… uh… *certain activities*."

Ariel slowed her speech as Reed lifted one eyebrow.

"Like blood transfusions?" he offered.

Ariel cleared her throat. "And other kinds of fluid exchanges. We kind of had to address a pressing physical problem yesterday."

"Ah yes… *the burning*. It comes hard with the first few shifts. So Matt helped you with your burning?"

Ariel nodded. "You know this is exactly as bad as talking to my father about sex, don't you?"

Reed's laugh burst out again. He saw the Gray Wolf Alpha rise from his seat and start their way. He felt the boy's jealousy across the yard. "Quickly—tell me the truth. Was Matthew able to put out your fire?"

Ariel sighed as she watched Matt walk to them. "Well, he did, but it's back again today."

Reed chuckled and rubbed his nose. "It's been so long since I felt the flames, but I remember how bad it was. There is no shame in seeking ease when you need it, child. I'm sure Matt will set you up with a place you can check on the outcomes of your fire joinings. I think my lack of gray hair and the vigor I feel sort of answer the blood transfusion question. However, you may still check anything you wish."

Ariel nodded and looked at Matt when he reached her side. "Do you think Eva will let me use the healing house as my lab for a little bit?"

"You can ask her if you like," Matt offered. He turned to the male he had thought he knew. "Reed, you're looking very different."

Reed grinned and slapped his young friend on the back. "Yes. Ariel and I are going to try and figure out why. Thanks for taking care of my girls for me."

"Reed, by girls... do you mean something like... *daughters*?" Matt demanded, crossing his arms.

Reed sputtered when Ariel punched Matt's arm. His laughter over the younger male's jealousy echoed through the woods and scattered all the birds from their nests. It was the best he'd felt in years.

———

"Why is Brandi smiling at Reed?" Gareth demanded. "The female doesn't smile. Ever. No matter what you do for her. Even in bliss she frowns."

Matt lifted his gaze and looked across the waiting area to where Reed sat chatting with a smiling Brandi, and a giggling Heidi, who looked like she wanted to crawl into his lap.

Beside their seats, Ryan Calder paced like a mad wolf, saying nothing. "You okay, Ryan?"

"I'm fine," he said, tight lipped and glaring at the Black Wolf Alpha.

Matt went back to flipping the pages of his magazine. "You don't have to stay, Ryan. Gareth and I can watch things. You can go back to work until she needs you again."

"No. I'm not leaving," Ryan declared. "Not while *he's* here."

"If you're talking about Reed, he's their primary, and you're worrying about nothing. The females are like his children. He doesn't desire any of them."

"They aren't really related to him," Ryan said in a fierce whisper.

"They are related by blood. To our kind, such a bond is binding. If you see Heidi through her burning and find you want to keep her after, you will likely have to get Reed's approval to do so. Ariel's her alpha, but Reed is their true leader for now."

Ryan growled and ran a hand over his face. "Don't pay any attention to me. I don't know what I want, except back inside Heidi again."

"Now you understand why I have always stayed away from females during their burnings. They're far too addictive. Reason and logic are lost to lust," Matt said sharply. Beside him Gareth grunted his support.

"Heidi makes me alive again, but does not take our bonding seriously. She expects nothing more than to be serviced and left alone. How do you know where you stand with such a female?"

"You don't," Gareth answered flatly. He studied the steady smile of the most unusual female he'd ever met. "But they were ordered by their alpha not to get attached to us. Perhaps you need to be more appreciative of a female who shares herself without requiring anything but pleasure in return. There are not many of those in the world, my friend."

Matt's senses went on high alert when he felt Ariel return. She drew everyone's attention as she came out of the back of the facility. Wearing one of their stolen doctor's coats over the clothes he'd bought for her, Ariel looked every inch the scientist she had claimed to be.

"Good news. The only kind of fluid exchange we have to worry about is blood. So no one has to worry about kissing... or other similar activities. Just don't bite each other. No blood exchanges allowed."

Total silence from everyone made her raise an eyebrow, until Reed's laughter rang out. Ariel looked over at him. "Glad you still find everything I say so damn funny, but I bet that changes soon. You and I have to have a different sort of talk."

Reed nodded. "I am properly chastised by your severity, Dr. Jones."

Snorting at Reed's flippant remark, Ariel turned her attention to Matt. "Can the three of us go back out to Eva's place to talk? She said it was okay with her. The kids are in school and her husband is at work. Then I thought you and I might go back to your house and have our own private discussion."

"Are you still able to think clearly?" Matt asked.

Ariel narrowed her eyes. "Would I have suggested doing things in that particular order if it wasn't the case? If I remember correctly, I was the one talking you onto the desk in your office, not the other way around, Matthew. I told you I would ask for what I needed and I am asking, but I think the fire can wait a while. Talking to Reed is more important at the moment."

"Well, I can't wait any longer," Brandi declared, happily interrupting their argument. "I need a fix now. Reed said the worst should be over in a week or so. I'm comfortable with Gareth, so if you don't need anything from us, he and I will just be heading back to his place to take care of business."

Gareth rose slowly from his seat and smiled at Brandi's demand. "I guess that's close enough to what I said I would do for you."

Brandi narrowed her eyes. "Look—don't do me any favors, buddy. You helped me, but Reed said my body won't care about the male. Ryan can call one of his brothers as far as I'm concerned —well, maybe not the jackass one who made the stripper remark. Bottom line here—I'm good with whatever you decide. I wouldn't want to inconvenience you."

Gareth narrowed his eyes in return. He opened his mouth, but Matt intervened.

"Don't call Ryan's brothers. Call Mark Lafayette. He's seasoned and won't mind helping Brandi. He keeps to himself too much anyway. He'd probably like some enthusiastic female company. And Brandi's definitely his type."

"No. She's not... I mean I don't... " Gareth glared at Brandi for making him swallow his pride. "Meeting your needs is not an inconvenience. I'm just not great with words. Don't go with someone else. It's not necessary."

Brandi shrugged her shoulders. "Whatever. I just wanted you to know I'm not taking this personally. Hell, I never thought I'd be an 'any man will do' type of woman, but I don't want to be anyone's charity case either."

"You're not a charity case, so stop saying it. I'm going out to warm up the truck. Come out when you're ready," Gareth said, gritting his teeth. Sparing Matt one last hard look for the hell he'd started with the offer to call Mark, he headed out of the building into the cold.

Brandi crossed her arms as she watched Gareth go. "Thankfully, he's not like that in bed. He actually drops the *I'm-too-badass-to-care* act there. That's the only reason I'm going with him. Ariel, are you really as good as you seem?"

Ariel nodded. "Yes. So stop worrying. Tomorrow, see if Gareth will show you around. It would be helpful for us to know where we've landed." She smiled when Brandi nodded, waved to everyone, and left.

Ariel turned then to Ryan and Heidi. "You two still good to hang together?"

Heidi looked at Ryan. "Ryan's been great. I'm good with him. If it's alright with everyone, I think I would like to see if Eva will let me help out here for a few hours. Ryan needs to check in with his work anyway. They keep calling him on his phone. I promise I will stay out of trouble. For some reason, I want... " She stopped and sighed.

"Don't hold it in, just say it," Ariel demanded. "Nothing can be stranger than turning into a wolf."

Heidi nodded. "Okay. I think I belong here... like in this building. The urge is not explainable, but it's very strong."

Ariel looked at Reed, who was studying Heidi. "What's your take on Heidi's urges, Mr... what's your last name, Reed?"

"Black Wolf," Reed supplied. "My grandmother was a powerful Eyak Shaman. It is possible Heidi has inherited some of her healing talent. Each werewolf in a pack brings a gift which manifests shortly after their first shift. Except for alphas. Alphas are formed differently. I was quite surprised to find someone so cerebral like you had such a large amount of alpha in her."

"Great. Damning praise from another werewolf named Wolf," Ariel said, grinning when she earned a chuckle for her teasing.

"My name is Gray Wolf. Do you think that's ironic too?" Matt asked.

Ariel turned her grin in Matt's direction. "I think I'd rather answer your question after you've put out my fire."

The vibrations of Matt's chuckle travelled through her. His body talked to hers with great ease. It was going to be hard to say goodbye to the man when it came time to go on to whatever the next step was in her journey.

"Gray Wolf is my pack name. Black Wolf is Reed's pack," Matt explained.

"Oh. I thought you were the Wasilla pack."

Matt shrugged. "That's slang. The pack is officially named for the founding alpha's family."

Ariel sighed. "Is there some sort of textbook I could read about all this? Maybe a copy of *Werewolves for Dummies* or something? Like Reed said, I'm cerebral."

"We keep our history in the oral tradition. It safeguards us from humans getting too interested. Let me walk Heidi back and talk with Eva for a few moments. We'll leave when I return."

"Can I accompany Heidi as well?" Ryan asked, a muscle in his jaw tightening when his alpha put a hand on Heidi's arm.

Matt looked at him. "You can, but she is safe with me."

"I never said she wasn't, Matt. I just want a chance to say goodbye if Heidi gets to stay," Ryan lied, crossing his arms.

Matt laughed and shook his head. "Maybe I should have issued the same warning to you and Gareth that Ariel issued to her females."

"Well, it's too late now," Ryan said sharply.

Matt laughed again and motioned for the jealous male to come along.

Ariel looked at Reed when they were alone. "Are all werewolves so possessive of the females they're having sex with?"

Reed smiled. "Yes. And it works both ways when the match is one leading to a mating. Ryan is pretty committed to Heidi already, though I'm not sure she returns the same level of interest. As for the other pair, Gareth doesn't want to be involved, but he wouldn't have intervened in Matt's offer if he didn't care for Brandi. I spent several months here when I first passed through. Gareth doesn't keep company with females beyond a quick tussle. He's lost too much and is determined not to care so much again. I share that trait with him."

Ariel shook her head. "So are you saying it's just going to be me and Brandi trying to figure out what to do with the rest of our lives? Is that what you're trying to tell me?"

"You will always have a home in my pack, but not until I make sure my deceitful grandson has been eliminated. There is another who should be alpha, but he didn't even compete for it. The younger generation has no sense of duty."

"How old are your grandsons?"

"The current alpha is around Matt's age, but with only half the maturity and wisdom. The other is younger, but only by twenty years."

"Well with all those nanos running around inside you now, you might be nearer Matt in body age based on werewolf DNA. You seem to be getting younger—just one of the many things you and I need to talk about. There's a click-off in the nanos to make sure they stop working or they'd burn out trying to keep us super young. I don't know what it is though. Nanos were never my specialty, but watching just one of them under a microscope was illuminating."

"Were you harmed by our blood exchange?"

"Not that I can tell. My size has altered so much in human form that I can't measure the difference in myself. I'm both taller and bigger. Taller, I like. Bigger, I could have lived without. Brandi and Heidi said everything for them is just a lot perkier than before."

Reed laughed and draped an arm around her neck. "Are all scientists so matter-of-fact?"

"Usually, but Brandi said I'm a different person from the one who asked Crane so many questions when he was getting ready to turn us."

"I believe Brandi is correct. Does discovering your alpha side bother you?" Reed asked.

Ariel sighed. "If I told you the truth, you'd laugh even more."

"Let's see, shall we?" he demanded.

"The truth is that I could shift to my wolf and never shift back. Life in wolf form is very simple. Shifting back to human is what depresses me."

Reed pulled her into his arms for a hug. "I don't find it funny at all." He let her go when Matt pushed through the door and glared. Reed smiled and wondered if the Gray Wolf alpha had any idea that his feelings were showing on his face.

8

Ariel swung her long legs out to span down two full steps of the deck stairs. She was pleased they were so long now. Each day she felt stronger despite what she'd learned. She didn't turn as she tried to explain things to Reed.

"Nanos are really molecular assemblers. Unlike what science fiction portrays, they do not create new things from nothing. It's more like they reposition tiny particles of existing building blocks for optimal reaction in repair processes. This means if your body wants to use them to fix and replicate molecules, it can. But nanos can only work with what is already there. They do not really create."

She looked at the very fit, very handsome male beside her. "In you, new nanos are being born all the time. In each of the three blood draws I took from you, I saw more and more of them. Since you're feeling vigorous instead of tired, only some of the nanos must be dedicated to the propagation task. Your body seems to have embraced the opportunity to reverse the aging process. My guess is the molecular machines will replicate their number to some pre-programmed stop point to avoid ecophagy, and then everything will go quietly into maintenance mode. Over time, some will die off, but most won't for a good long while, short of a nuclear reactor going off around you."

"Ecophagy?"

"Yes. Sorry for the big word, but I met the original scientist. He doesn't like the term *gray goo* even though he coined it. Ecophagy is a theory that says if the nano machines inside us ever get too carried away with their programmed work they would turn our insides to *gray goo* in an effort to repair us and replicate themselves."

"Doesn't sound very promising. What is happening on the inside of you since the transfusion?" Reed asked, searching her gaze for truth. "I feel your trepidation, Ariel. You must always speak your truth to me, no matter your reservations. Am I going to become gray goo? Are you?"

Ariel picked at a piece of lint on her sweater wishing she had a real answer. "I don't know what's happening. The same level of growth I'm seeing in your blood is not occurring in my blood samples, though there does seem to be a little bit of propagation going on. Or at least, I wasn't able to track much growth in the three samples Eva took from me today. Of course, half of two billion nanos, or whatever number is left in me after the transfusion, will still assist me during shifts. The feisty little suckers were able to make up the difference in my blood loss, so they're obviously still functioning. We could live hundreds of years and die when the nanos wear out trying to fix us. On the other hand, one major illness could end everything. All I have is a bunch of theories."

Reed looked off at the woods. "And yet you gave up some of that life you believe is limited to save me. I now owe you two life debts, Dr. Jones."

"No you don't—well, maybe one. If you hadn't told me what to do in the lab, I would have let Crazy Crane get hold of me and we wouldn't even be having this conversation. Since I wasn't ready to die, I'll take my half of whatever Crane forced into my body and be grateful," Ariel said. Then she saw the depth of Reed's concern reflected in his gaze. "Look—if it ends one day—it ends. I can't change what happened to us. But I don't have a crystal ball either."

Reed leaned his arms across his knees. "Have you shifted since the transfusion?"

"No. I'm not shifting again until you tell me how to do it with my clothes on. Despite the last few days, I assure you I am not an exhibitionist. Matt gives every male who comes near me the stink eye as it is. Helping with my burning has made him nuts, I think. His possessiveness is annoying, but he's been so nice otherwise, I haven't said anything to him yet."

Reed shook his head sadly. "I'm sorry to once again be of absolutely no help to you. I use my mind to keep my clothes hidden with my human form, but I can't tell you how it works. Some werewolves can do it. Others can't. I find it keeps things entertaining. Seeing werewolves reacting to their naked human forms is very funny."

"Damn it. I was afraid you were going to say something like that. Accepting disappearing and reappearing clothes is as crazy as believing in string theory," Ariel complained, kicking the bottom step with her boot.

"I don't know about your theories. Would it help if I said werewolves don't judge nudity the way humans do? No one would ever criticize your human form, regardless of its condition. They might comment on your wolf's size, but only because she's very large even for an alpha bitch... I mean *female*," Reed corrected, grinning at Ariel's offended glared.

"Don't make me kick your ass. I hate the 'b' word with a passion."

Reed chuckled. "Before I am reduced to gray goo, I need to fix some things in my pack. Are you going to be okay if I leave you alone with Matthew Gray Wolf until I get them done?"

"What kind of things?" Ariel demanded, her gut clenching.

"The idea of you being somewhere I can't see you is alarming on just about every level. My attachment to you borders on neurotic."

Reed scooted closer and put an arm around her to hug. "I'm sorry. You're not being neurotic. You're learning to live with the wolf side I gave you, so it's natural you'd look to me for guidance. I didn't mean it to work out this way, Ariel Jones. Maybe I have become your father. I will return to you when my pack is back to normal. Maybe Brandi can give me information that will shorten my investigations."

"What kind of information?"

"Let's talk to Brandi together so I don't have to tell another long story right now. Let's give ourselves the afternoon to absorb all you've learned already. Spend some time relaxing with Matt. He's running through the woods to burn off his energy so he won't attack you once you're alone again."

Ariel felt power in the ground and looked up to see a giant silver and gray wolf emerge from the woods. "Are alphas always so… amazing?"

"Yes. Now go out to meet him. It will make your friend-with-benefits happy," Reed encouraged, teasing her about her connection.

Sighing, Ariel slid down the other two steps and stood to her full height, which was even taller in the boots. She walked toward the wolf who was equal in size, if not bigger, than Reed. A bit of fear skidded through her unchecked as she got closer. It was an emotion she never felt at all with Reed. Images of Matt climbing up on his desk to cover her body with his flitted through her mind non-stop. The wolf stopped two feet in front of her to sniff the air.

"Yes, I'm having dirty thoughts about us, only in them we're both human. There's no fooling your wolf nose, is there?"

Matt hung his head and looked back at Reed.

"What are you worried about? Reed's the one who sent me out to you. And you're just as big as he is as a wolf—maybe bigger. He was right about your size being equal to his."

Nose down, Matt walked forward and nudged her hand until it went to his head to stroke. Ariel laughed softly, and ran her hand over his crown and down his sleek neck. His whimper of pleasure was soft, but she heard it. The sound had her dropping to her knees to embrace him. It was all she could do to hold his giant wolf form in her arms. When he licked the side of her face, she giggled.

"Your wolf's just a big old puppy dog, isn't he?"

It only took a tiny push from Matt's large form to put her flat on her back and staring up at a set of snarling teeth. Instead of shivering in fear, she had to fight another giggle.

"Now shift back to human form and make all my fantasies come true," Ariel ordered, laughing at his wolf's shocked reaction.

Whimpering and shaking his head, Matt backed up and away from her. His shift to human form had her swearing.

"I will give you the sexual favor of your choice if you will tell me right now how to shift with my clothes on," Ariel said.

Matt chuckled as he reached down a hand. "I wish I could tell you just to see if you'd keep your word about the favor, but I swear I don't know. One day it just happened. I've been able to do it since. I was probably around your age when I figured it out."

"A declaration of what you can do is not the same as an explanation of how it is done. No special sex for you today," Ariel declared.

Matt laughed as he pulled Ariel up to stand and it felt good when he saw Reed smiling at them. It was like gaining approval of his unwilling courtship. He also imagined the Black Wolf Alpha was hearing every word they said to each other as well.

"Come home with me and I'll feed you again. I called Nanuka and asked her to shop for food. I made sure she bought more ham."

As if on cue, her stomach rumbled at the thought of meat. "You sure are saying all the right things. I'm starved... and for more than just food this time, Matthew Gray Wolf."

Smiling, Matt grabbed her hand and tugged her with him up the yard.

"We're going home," he told the Black Wolf Alpha when they were level with the deck.

"Good," Reed said, grinning. "About time."

"I want to be involved in any discussion involving the women. One of them may be joining my pack soon," Matt declared.

Ariel snorted. "Don't go getting any ideas about us."

Matt looked sideways. "I was talking about Heidi. Ryan called me several times asking how to get her to admit she likes him."

Ariel rolled her eyes and swore. "Sorry I presumed."

Matt smiled at Reed when Ariel refused to look at him.

Reed smiled back. "I have no problem with you knowing my truth, Matt."

Matt had to let go when Ariel rushed to Reed and hugged him tightly. He looked off to keep from glaring over it.

Ariel smacked his arm hard as she stomped back to him. "Reed's like my father. Get over that shit before I look for someone who can better handle how screwed-up my life is."

Matt grunted and smacked her ass as he flew passed her in a full-out run.

"Hey. I killed a man for doing that, Matthew Gray Wolf. Don't make me sick my wolf on you."

Behind her, she heard Reed laughing as she rubbed her butt.

9

"You've kept me waiting so long, I don't know what to do first. I'm like a starving man at a feast."

Ariel groaned at his sexy declaration and raised as far as she could until her mouth latched onto his. Matt had hold of her wrists so she couldn't drag him down to her. She probably should have been offended at being restrained, but she could tell he was doing it more for his benefit than hers. It made her wonder what Matt was holding back from her.

She spun out of their kiss until his mouth followed hers back to the pillow her head landed on. He was tense in her arms, corded muscles solidly pressed against her. All his strength seemed dedicated to slowing down what she wanted to happen as soon as it could. When he broke away from her kiss at last, she was gasping for breath.

"Matt—I don't think I can keep playing the part of the obedient bed partner if you decide to torture me."

He released her wrists and let his mouth trace down her neck, his tongue licking the last third of the way. "Fine. Keep your wrists up for as long as you can. No taking over this time," he ordered.

Ariel nodded, her stomach rippling as Matt's tongue licked a line between her breasts and down. A groan was ripped from her when he travelled lower and lifted her hips in both his very large hands. One spectacular lick into her had her arching upward. The second sent her over the edge she'd been hanging on. A few more languorous licks left her nearly comatose as she crested through the violent release he gave her. She quivered with even more anticipation when Matt let go and climbed back up the bed to straddle her body. His bed was so much better than being on his desk.

"Your burning is every bit as delicious as it smells. Are you sure about not using a condom this time?"

"It's your call."

"Conception heat in a female werewolf is different from regular lust. I haven't experienced it, but I've heard a lot about it. I don't think that's what happening with you."

"I don't think my nanos are ever going to let an egg be fertilized. That wouldn't be Crazy Crane's style to let conception happen naturally. As for today, Reed said I needed everything you have to offer to really reduce the burning's urges. He was being polite, but I assume he meant my body needs to absorb the hormones contained in your ejaculate."

"Stop. Gag, that sounds so awful. No more science words during sex with me," he ordered, listening to her laugh at his protest.

He shook like it was his first time with a female as he eased the full naked length of his erection inside her. Ariel moved beneath him to accommodate his size, just like she had before. The intense heat of her pulsing channel made him gasp for breath, fighting to last more than an untried boy. Her burning made demands on his body, but because it was Ariel, he didn't mind meeting every single one of them. She would never deliberately take advantage of the edge it gave her physically. Her mind was too logical to care about normal female manipulation.

As he began to move, her body matched each slow thrust he

made. It was the most luxurious fucking he'd ever indulged in with any female. She moved sensuously in his arms, following his lead, and did so without ever realizing her actions were a form of obedience. It was just natural... and easy... and everything he'd always wished for with other females and never found with them.

Delirious with the satisfaction Ariel provided, he kissed her over and over. He kissed her through the whimpering groans of her climax rebuilding because of his thrusts. When she crested a second time, he let himself find release inside her as they both rode the last wave of climax together.

"You are the most incredible female I've ever known," he whispered, smiling when she patted his face in reply instead of speaking.

Moments later her body grew lax under his, her arms dropping away from holding him, but he couldn't make himself leave her. So he stayed where he was, semi-erect within her, kissing her face and brushing her hair back as she spun down from lust and headed into a peaceful sleep.

When he felt himself finally getting drowsy too, Matt rolled them both to their sides. He started to speak, but noticed Ariel was already out cold in his arms. Her absolute trust in him to take care of her filled some hole in his gut he hadn't even known needed filling.

Damn the young alpha for being so perfect.

He truly never intended to like her so much, and worse, Ariel wasn't even trying to get him to. Her falling asleep with no thought of protecting herself made him feel at least as important to her as Reed was turning out to be. The thought that he might one day come to matter more to her than her creator was very appealing. Not that he had a problem with the ancient one. He actually had a lot of respect for the way Reed had stood by the women and been there to make sure the males in his pack were treating them well.

Matt laid his head next to Ariel's on the pillow. He was worried about what she and Reed had discussed while he'd been in the woods. Whatever it was, she wouldn't have to face it alone.

Gareth watched Brandi gathering her clothes knowing she intended to head to the spare bedroom he had provided her. Ironically, the only reason he'd offered the other room was because he knew Brandi didn't want to spend the whole evening in his bed, much less the whole night.

"Are you sure you got enough satisfaction to put out your fire?" he asked, offended by her snicker at his concerned question.

Brandi shrugged as she draped her clothing over her arm. "Yes. Reed was right. Not using a condom was way better and the effects were immediate."

"And did the oral gratification help as well?" Gareth asked.

Brandi laughed, unable to help herself as she picked up her boots and socks. After sex with Gareth, she was always too hot to have anything touch her skin. It was the only time being naked ever felt truly good to her.

"Your tongue technique is excellent. I guess that's a big plus for all werewolves, huh?"

Brandi heard Gareth growl low at her teasing as she headed to the door. The grumbling from her nearly silent lover had her hesitating. Man, she sucked at the after part. She always had.

"What do you want from me, Gareth? You want some ego stroking. Fine. Your dick is a pleasure tool and your tongue a gift to all women. There. Does that cover everything? Tell me what you want to hear and I'll say it. I've already thanked you. Now I need to get some sleep."

"Brandi—stop. I want you to come back to my bed, look me in the eye, and share your damn feelings with me."

Brandi barked out a laugh and shook her head. "That's not what you want. You just want me to make myself into an emotional doormat so you can pat yourself on the back for the good deed you're doing taking care of me. Well, tough shit, buster. I'm not an emotional doormat. I'm exactly what you see."

She started out the door, but changed her mind and turned back.

"And don't bullshit me about your *feelings*. There was a reason you picked the hard-ass soldier over the fluffy girlie-girl and the too passionate scientist. I see your emotional reticence in bed exactly for what it is, but guess what? I don't mind, Gareth. I actually like the emotional wall you put up between us. It makes all of this way easier than it would have been with some smart-ass kid like Junior Calder. I might have been tempted to kill him in his sleep for his stupid lines and that's no idle threat from me."

"You can't actually believe I'm that cold. I have feelings. Why do you think I don't have feelings?" Gareth asked, truly offended.

Brandi glanced back over her shoulder and snorted as she took the first step out the door. "Maybe you do have feelings hidden somewhere deep inside, but your dick doesn't run on them. Judging from your silent proficiency at sex, you've probably had more emotionless fucks over the years than I have. But like I said before—I don't mind the emotional distance. You get the job done plenty well enough for me, and it was way better this time without using the condom. I'd forgotten how good unprotected sex was."

"You still didn't let me kiss you on the mouth."

"Please… dude. I hardly know you. And what I do know, I barely like. However, I do respect you. I'd also probably kill for you which means you've earned my highest form of loyalty. If you're worried about your rep as a stud in your pack, I'll say nothing to anyone except how it was great of you to help me out with the burning thing."

"You don't like me? *Why the hell don't you like me?*" Gareth demanded, his voice rising at her words.

He found it impossible not to be surprised by the news. Yes, he realized Brandi wasn't the typical female early on. That didn't mean he had to accept Brandi's coldness, her lack of need to cuddle, and her jumping from his bed the moment the deed was done enough to make her sexually satisfied.

Well, what about him? He never got enough. He never took or asked for what he most needed from their exchanges. Oh sure, he got off just fine, but regular sufficient fucking was never the same as... well *really* getting there with a partner.

It had been a long damn time, but he knew what he had been doing with the young werewolf was only a fraction of what was possible. Brandi gave him her body, but never once gave him anything of herself in the process. Being with her was as emotionally unsatisfying as using his own damn hand to relieve himself.

"I am not putting up an emotional wall. If you want to know what I want most right now, I want you to sleep with me—without having sex," Gareth said firmly.

Brandi sighed and rolled her eyes. "Oh, please. Don't do this emotional crap. Whatever voice in your head is telling you shit about how it's supposed to be, tell it to shut the fuck up. *This* is how it is. You and me—getting it done—and going our separate ways afterward. This is how we started. This is how we'll finish. Any time you want to get out of this obligation, just call Junior. But he's always wearing a condom. I'd hate to think of all the oozing ya-yas that braggart has been in."

"No. I will not be calling anyone to take my place with you," Gareth said.

"Good. I don't really want you to. You're an okay guy and I really am grateful. Maybe one day I can return the favor and do something so selfless for you."

"You can return the favor today. Come back here and sleep with me," he demanded, his tone growing sharper.

"No can do, Gareth. But I'm glad we cleared the air and had this talk. It's better to stay honest with each other. I'll see you in the morning. Night," Brandi said quickly, fleeing the room before the ego-bruised beta came after her.

Gareth's surprising neediness was one more unwanted complication. She was full up on all she could handle.

"Heidi, come back up here. There was no need to return the oral favor. Now I'm up again and you need to crash. My dick's going to be dragging the dirt tomorrow as it is."

Giggling, she climbed back up Ryan's body and into his lap. He was leaning against the headboard in the perfect position. Putting one arm on each side of his head, she pressed her lips to his until he groaned. Then diving into his mouth, she reached a hand between them to help impale herself.

His hands came out to help and drove her hips down hard on his erection. Stars burst behind her eyes as he filled her completely. His corresponding kiss was full of desire—real, honest, *give-it-to-me-now* desire. Since her conversion to a werewolf, she could never do it well enough, or often enough, to slake the burning within her —until tonight.

The absence of a condom had made a world of difference. Relief made her as giddy as desire to do it again made her wet. She rocked happily on Ryan's hardness inside her while he groaned in her ear. Guilt had her slowing.

"I'm sorry for making you do this again. I couldn't help myself. Just this one last time and then I swear I'll leave you alone."

Ryan chuckled at her apology just before he felt her tighten around him. "I don't want you to leave me alone. I just want us to sleep for a few hours so I can do this with more energy. Climb off for a minute. This position is not going to do it for either of us this time."

"Climb off? Seriously?"

Laughing, Ryan lifted her body off his protesting one and to the side of the bed. "Yes. Now get on your knees. We're finishing this werewolf style."

"No thank you. I prefer to see who's doing it to me. I don't like it that way," Heidi said, biting her lip.

"You will with me—I promise," Ryan swore. He ducked quickly behind her and lifted her hands to the edge of the headboard. "Grip the headboard hard, honey. Now spread your knees and let me in. Hmm... that's perfect."

Heidi closed her eyes and sniffed. It was Ryan. Her body settled into ease. When he slipped inside her body from behind, her needy channel moaned in welcome like always. As he slowly thrust, his hand came around to the front and ran through her curls over and over, barely brushing against anything interesting. As his thrusts got a little more aggressive, her heart hammered, but she tilted her pelvis until Ryan was hitting against the perfect spot. Little stars danced behind her eyelids. The man was beyond talented... and willing... so willing.

"Harder—*please*," she begged in a whisper.

"I think you mean deeper, baby," Ryan whispered back, shifting his upper body over the back of her until each thrust embedded him inside her as far as he could go. Her gasp of pleasure made him dizzy. He wanted to send her over the edge. He wanted to make the damn trip with her. He wanted to do it a hundred times more—maybe forever.

"Okay, let's try harder too," he said hoarsely.

He folded one of his hands over one of hers. Then, with accuracy he reached around the front of her and between her legs, cupping everything in his palm. He could feel himself thrusting against his own hand, which always met some base need in him, but it was the scream of climax wrenched from her that thrilled him most.

"Ryan—oh God—aaaahhhhh... "

Closing his eyes at the pleasure of the female in his arms, he buried his face in her neck in deep satisfaction. Marking her was so tempting. Her fragrant skin now smelled like him. He'd filled her so many times with his essence, he knew other males were envious of his enthusiastic lover. But the ancient Black Wolf Alpha would kill him if Matt didn't do so first.

"Beg me again," Ryan ordered, pretending she already belonged to him.

"Please don't stop. I want everything. I want to feel you."

At her entreaty, Ryan pushed hard and deep and stayed there a moment, until he felt her legs tremble in reaction. "Oh, baby. Just give it all up to me. This time is going to be the best ever. I promise you. When two people want each other so much, the lovemaking can't help but be outstanding."

He got a head nod in response as her body finally shattered in complete release. His growl of pride over her obedience to his words was a tipping point inside him. Heidi called out as her hands slid bonelessly down the headboard losing their grip.

"Ssshhh... I have you. Just let me have you... " he whispered.

He had to grab Heidi with both arms wrapped around her to hold her in place. Her surrender was so total, he sniffled into her hair. He thrust slowly and smoothly a few times more to find his own release as she hung limp in his arms.

Then he carefully turned them both until they fell sideways onto one of the bed pillows. He kept them connected, even after Heidi began snoring.

"Finally," Ryan declared, snickering as he chased her into sleep. He couldn't bring himself to disconnect from her after what they'd shared, so he didn't. Sleeping inside her wasn't quite as good as marking her as his, but it was the closest he could come without risking everyone's wrath, including Heidi's.

Gareth couldn't figure out why it even bothered him, but it had taken him hours to stop being mad over the things Brandi had said. He had just finally dozed off when her scream woke him. He was on his feet and running before he was totally awake.

Entering the room where she slept, he found Brandi backed against the headboard and curled into a defensive ball. Seeing the sharp-tongued, brave female reduced to that condition made him want to kill things and people and whatever was hurting her. Her eyes were glassy, seeing only what haunted her mind.

Gareth inched cautiously toward the bed, moving slowly and carefully. When he got to the side of it, he whispered her name gently, only to have Brandi launch herself at him in full attack mode. More years of fighting than he wanted to remember had him snatching her body from the air and body slamming it to the mattress of his guest bed.

Her frightened gaze peered up at him in stunned surprise. "You didn't have to shoot him six times."

Gareth felt confusion wrinkle his face. "Shoot who? I didn't shoot anyone—at least not yet."

Brandi twisted against the hands which held her. "No. Let me go. I'm not going to watch you hurt him. I have to stop you."

"Brandi! Wake the hell up! You're having a dream," Gareth yelled.

He flinched as another, and a louder, scream came out of her mouth when Brandi left the dream state, but at least her eyes cleared. Then it scared him when she went completely limp in his arms and starting sniffing back tears.

Not stopping to think about what he was doing, Gareth knelt by the bed and gathered her up in his arms as best he could. "It's okay. It wasn't real. It was just a bad dream," he insisted.

Brandi rubbed a hand across her eyes. "No. It was more than a dream. It was some sort of –I don't know—vision or something. Crazy Crane, the guy who had us all trapped, had help capturing Reed. The guy who shot Reed looked like Reed's clone. He's the one who put the silver bullets in him. He's related to Reed—I just know it. He looked just like him."

"I see," Gareth said, but he didn't really.

Brandi groaned at his attempt to placate her. She hated the pity in Gareth's voice. "Forget it. I'm a nutcase. I'm sorry I woke you when I called out. Go back to bed."

"No. I'm not sorry you woke me. It gave me the excuse I'd been lying awake in my room trying to think of for hours. Now move over. No—skip the request. I'm not taking no for an answer this time. *Move the hell over because we are sleeping together.*"

He stood, reached down, and scooped Brandi up until there was room for him in the small guest bed with her. He'd have preferred to go back to the bigger one in his room, but instinct warned him she was a lot less likely to go along with such a plan.

Once he was in bed with her, he turned and laid Brandi down on a pillow. Then he scooped the covers from under her and flipped them deftly over her body to try to offset any physical shock. Lying down next to her, he looked into her troubled gaze as he tucked the covers around her.

"Whatever the fuck you're going through, we'll deal with it in the morning—together. After breakfast," he ordered.

"Okay."

Nodding her head, Brandi looked away from him. He didn't like it. Gareth reached out and rested a hand on her waist. "No more bad dreams tonight. I forbid it. Now let's both get some sleep."

"Okay. I am truly sorry I woke you," Brandi said again.

Feeling furious over her quiet obedience instead of elated like he should be, Gareth's hot mouth on hers swallowed the rest of her lame apology. He gave her no choice but to respond. Even after he broke the kiss, he pulled her against him. He was reeling from the sensual impact.

Kissing her in anger was wrong, but if he'd known how good she tasted, he would have done it the first time he slid inside her. "I know. I broke your no kissing rule, but you scared me to death when you screamed. I needed the reassurance you were out of the spirit world and back with me."

"You don't have to worry about me, Gareth. I've had bad dreams plenty of times. It's going to take a lot more than that to spook me," Brandi whispered, her mouth covering his gently in thanks.

Gareth quivered with relief after she kissed him. The thing he'd feared most from the first moment he'd laid eyes on her was already happening. After Brandi pushed gently away, he insistently gathered her closer and held her while she fell back into a restless sleep.

Hearing the nightmares chase her once more, he frowned and wondered what werewolf magic was visiting her. There hadn't been a visionary born in the Gray Wolf pack in a couple centuries. He'd been a whelp of less than twenty years when the last one died.

10

MATT FROWNED AT HIS CROWDED KITCHEN. HE USUALLY USED THE lodge when he entertained so he'd had no motivation to expand his home. Today Ariel, Reed, Brandi and Heidi sat around his four-seat table. It left no room for him or the two men he didn't have the heart to order to leave. So the three of them leaned against the counters and listened.

"My great-uncle, Nicolai, was excommunicated from his pack in Russia. Before he found our pack, he travelled over many miles of the Bering Strait and Greenland, staying in wolf form most of the time so he wouldn't freeze to death. He liked the Black Wolf pack though, which is why he ended up mating and staying with us. He was what werewolves call a visionary, which is a fancy way of saying he had a lot of dreams that seem to mean something. They were not always pleasant. His previous pack used to blame him for causing the things he warned them about. They were not very enlightened about intuition. My grandfather was. He and Nicolai became good friends, as well as family."

Brandi nodded and stared at a spot on the table. "So what I saw could be something that really happened, or is going to happen?"

Reed nodded. "Yes. I hate to burden you with more than you've already endured, but yes. It could be either of those."

"If someone is trying to make sure you get dead, it's a safe bet he's going to be unhappy to find you not only alive, but thriving. He's also not going to be too thrilled with us either. I'm betting he knows Crane had you—and us," Brandi declared.

Reed crossed his arms. "That is a good point. Okay. My gene pool is very strong. In over three hundred years, I've taken several mates. Children have blessed all my unions. My children are good, but in my grandchildren, I have not been so lucky. My grandson, Hanuk, carries my closest likeness. He is the current alpha in my pack. Another grandson, Travis, also favors me greatly. If anyone is trying to kill me, it is likely Hanuk. He is a lazy fighter, so he settles disputes by having dissidents torn to shreds in public displays."

Brandi snorted. "It's going to be his turn one day. Men who rule by intimidation draw others of like kind to compete with them. Destiny becomes a question of which asshole kills the other one first. I know what I'm talking about because my job used to be hanging around to collect the winner of those bad guy fights."

"No wonder you can't sleep," Gareth declared.

"I sleep fine when I'm alone," Brandi declared back.

"No you don't. You wrestle nightmares all night long. I know because I have watched you try to sleep," Gareth corrected.

Brandi glared at him for telling a truth very few people knew about her.

Ariel looked at Reed. "So you gave up being the Black Wolf pack alpha and Hanuk took your place. Why would he want you out of the picture entirely if you're already gone? Seems like he has everything he wants already."

Reed shrugged. "Perhaps he wants me dead because he is not well liked. If I were to return and question him, other alphas might rise up and compete for his place. Alone—he is not capable of running the pack. He surrounds himself with wolves who have weak minds and strong bloodlust, then he manipulates them to enforce his will."

"Isn't leaving someone like Hanuk in power like condemning your pack to a slow destruction of their society?"

Reed sighed at the question, and then nodded at its validity. "Yes. This is true. Travis should be running the pack, but he doesn't seem to want the responsibility. In his wolf form, he is almost as big as me, but he lacks the desire an alpha needs to rule."

Ariel crossed her arms and said the obvious. "If your children don't want the position, and your grandchildren can't handle it, maybe it's time for an alpha to be chosen outside your family tree, Reed."

"The thought saddens me greatly, but has much merit," Reed declared.

Ariel drummed fingers on the table. "I think it's time we check in town and see what happened at Feldspar. Brandi, I think this is a job best suited for you. Matt and I were going to do it, but maybe Gareth can go with you. I think it's best we have a local with us when we travel and you probably want to disguise yourself somehow. Keep an eye out for men who look like Reed wandering around."

"I'd like to go back to the healing house and work," Heidi said. "If that's okay with everyone."

Ariel reached over and patted her arm. "Sure. Just stay with Eva and don't wander around on your own. Contact Ryan or me if you need to go somewhere. Some of Matt's people are still not happy we're here. I see them watching us wherever we go."

"They will not harm you while you are under my protection," Matt said firmly.

Ariel turned to him. "You may believe that, but Heidi is not a fighter. I'm not willing to risk her. She doesn't have Brandi's skills or my urge to kill things. She will have an escort if one of us isn't here."

"Remember our lesson about trust?" Matt asked.

Ariel snorted, listening to her gut instead of her private parts. "I trust you, Reed, Gareth, and Ryan. Beyond that, no one in your pack has my trust."

Matt didn't like her argument, but it was valid, so he nodded.

"I hate your hair. The color is far too dark for you," Gareth said, wheeling his pickup down the road leaving Anchorage.

"Who asked you for your opinion? Besides, this was the only temporary color your general store had in stock. It's supposed to wash out in twenty-six washings. That's better than something permanent," Brandi said back, titling down the mirror to check her black locks. It looked great to her. She didn't recognize herself. With sunglasses on and the black jacket she'd found in the bin in Matt's office, she disappeared totally.

Her gaze went to the main entrance, which was roped off now. A 'For Sale' sign was hanging off the rope with a number to call. "Drive by this entrance and veer left at the fork. I know another way into the building site."

Snorting, Gareth glanced at the lock on the rope which could have held a passenger ship securely at any dock. The twisted rope was larger in circumference than his leg. He followed Brandi's instructions until they came to a dirt road that wove through the woods behind their destination.

"Turn here? Are you sure?"

Getting a chastising look for his question, Gareth sighed and eased off the roadway onto the dirt path. They drove slowly for about ten minutes until they emerged into what looked like a bombsite from an old World War II movie. Only rubble remained. The outline of the building foundation was all that was left.

When he pulled up and stopped, Brandi jumped from the truck and stalked to the edge of where the building once stood. Whipping off her sunglasses, her eyes took in everything all at once. He wondered what her mind was doing with the information. She walked around the site partway and then came back to him.

"Do you have a phone that takes pictures?" she asked.

Walking to meet her, Gareth pulled his phone from his pocket and keyed in the security code to unlock it before handing it over. Brandi pulled up the camera app and took shot after shot, even though he could see nothing of value in getting photos of cinders and ash. The ground couldn't have been more level if a wrecking crew had hauled all the debris away.

"It stinks of chemicals here. What do you see?" Gareth asked.

"Nothing. That's the problem," Brandi replied. "There's not a glass beaker, a metal cage bar, or any evidence at all of what was going on here. Someone's cleaned this place up already. There should have been a lot more debris left, even if the building exploded and burned."

Gareth nodded. "Think that company is done here?"

Brandi shrugged. "The 'For Sale' sign gives that impression. Maybe Matt can get someone to call and check to see what they're asking for the land and lot. Here—I wanted pictures to show Ariel and Reed. Maybe we can get them off the camera later."

"I'll call for the sale price, when we're safely away from here," Gareth replied, taking the phone back when she handed it over.

"I'm going to walk up into the woods a bit, see if I can remember anything more about the day I got abducted. My ID and personal carry weapon were confiscated by the men that took me down. They either went up in smoke when the building did or were used to fake my death more convincingly. I'd like to know which. That's going to be tricky to find out, unless I decide to become alive again."

Gareth frowned and wondered how heavy her internal burdens were about what had happened to her. "How much does all this shit bother you?"

Brandi laughed at his question as she turned her face to him.

"Gareth—as surreal as this seems, it's not the first time someone has tried to fake my death. Last time was in Zimbabwe. Maybe one day we'll get drunk together and I'll tell you about it."

"Werewolves process alcohol too fast to get drunk, unless you drink like a keg. Then you're too busying urinating to enjoy the buzz. It's a no win situation. I gave it up."

Brandi grinned at his complaining. "Hang back and keep a watch out while I take a walk with my gut. Make sure you have a good story made up in case someone shows up to investigate why we're here."

Not waiting for his answer, Brandi headed to the woods. Something strong was driving her there. She veered left, then right, then following some instinct she couldn't name she walked to a grove of trees growing close together. Near the base of one of them were some shiny silver shell casings. One burned her palm when she picked it up. It was like the chain around Reed's wolf.

Closing her fingers around the shell casing, she felt her eyelids closing. An image of a younger version of Reed shooting a long-range rifle appeared immediately and very clearly in her mind. She opened her eyes, swore, and dropped the casing before it burned through her palm. She pulled off her jacket, gathered all the casings into it, and used it to carry them back to Gareth.

"I found several leftover silver shell casings by some trees. I think Reed got taken down just a couple days before I did. From what I recall, I was tracking Reed because he was a giant wolf who kept coming around Feldspar without digging through the trash for food or attacking any of the people coming and going each day. I knew someone was capturing the wolves, but they had never been able to catch Reed up until then. The guy who shot him is the reason it finally worked out the way it did."

Gareth ejected the coin tray from the truck dash and held it out for Brandi to empty the shells into it from her coat. "That's a lot more than six casings here."

She had counted nine casings, but said nothing about the

number. The only ones which mattered were the six that almost killed Reed. "Guy must have been a lousy shot. Or he took down more than one wolf. I would have thought Reed would have said something if there had been other werewolves trapped with him."

Gareth nodded and set the casings in the back floorboard, a good distance away from both of them. They had residue from the silver bullets on them because Brandi shook her hand as she shrugged back into her black jacket. He wasn't sure that was a good idea either.

"You need to see Eva about that hand... and we may need to replace your coat," he said, a muscle ticking in his jaw at the thought of Brandi in pain and not admitting it.

Brandi looked at her hand, barked out a laugh, and then showed it to him. "Nope. Look—already healing. Got to admit I'm growing to love those little robots they put inside me."

"Hearing about your creation only makes me want to kill those who did this to you. I'm trying my best not to think about what you have going on inside you."

Brandi slid her sunglasses back on and smiled. "Too late. Ariel killed both the bastards by herself... and loved every minute of it from what I could tell. I only wish it had been me."

Gareth shook his head as they climbed back into his truck. Brandi was certainly not like any woman he'd ever known.

"Damn it. You said they don't actually disappear completely. So where the hell do my clothes go?"

Reed held out the blanket for Ariel to walk into it. Her frustration made him want to laugh, but her cold shivers held him back. "They don't usually go far. They could be on the ground nearby or the last place they were before you put them on."

"Great," Ariel said, stomping to Matt's house. "Let me run in and check Matt's bedroom. The man is a neat freak and I can't get it out of my mind. I had laid them over the back of a chair last night. He refolded them and put them on some fancy dresser he has in there."

Reed crossed his arms and nodded, even though Ariel didn't see him. She was gone less than two minutes and reappeared loosely wearing her clothes, with the blanket tucked under one arm. He noticed she hadn't bothered lacing the boots back or buttoned things up more than partially. She was obviously expecting more failures. It was all he could do to hold back his laughter as he thought of how angry she was going to be if she found she just couldn't do it.

"Tell me again what it feels like when it happens correctly," Ariel demanded. "Give me all the details you can. I have to envision it to figure it out."

Reed took a deep breath and ordered himself not to laugh as he went through it for the millionth time. "I picture my human form dressed in my clothes and order it to stay dressed when I shift. It requires I completely know every piece I am wearing at the time it happens. For the most part, I wear the same kind of clothing every day. It's helps me remember without working at it so hard."

Ariel nodded. "I'm glad now I was never one of those scientists who thought she knew everything. Plenty of string theorists have postulated matter as being some sort of reality agreement your mind makes with the world. Maybe this is the same thing. I just have to believe my mind can order my clothes to stay on my human form. I have to let go of the idea when I change back that I'm going to always be naked when it happens."

"Try shifting into an upright position too. It's like doing a rolling somersault and landing on your feet," Reed advised. If you do manage to keep your clothes, you don't want them getting dirty on the ground."

Ariel snorted as she handed Reed the blanket again. It was too cold out to stand around naked if it didn't work. "I'd just be happy to keep them on my body no matter where I ended up." She walked a few feet away from her teacher. "Does shifting ever stop hurting, Reed?"

Reed shook his head. "I don't think so. It hasn't for me in over three hundred years. But I always think it's worth it."

Ariel rolled her eyes. "You are just chock full of unhelpful advice today."

"Not liking my advice does not mean it's unhelpful," Reed corrected.

Ariel snorted. She closed her eyes, pictured herself with her clothes, assembling her outfit piece by piece right down to her boots. "Okay. I'm ready. I can do this."

She shifted into her wolf. The female she had been disappeared, as did all she was wearing. She prowled around a little, enjoying her wolf form as she always did. She had loved it from the beginning.

Her head raised as she sniffed a familiar scent. Two seconds later she saw Matt walk around the house to where they had been practicing near the woods. She called out in welcome, surprised once again at hearing herself howl so loudly. Matt's laughter carried to her.

She swung back to Reed, who was grinning. *What's so funny?*

Reed smiled. *You. Your perfect innocence. Your enjoyment of your wolf. Your pleasure in the male who satisfies your cravings. The unquestioning way you have embraced your circumstances is very much like the way I deal with the unexpected. Many born werewolves don't handle life as gracefully as you and your friends have.*

Well, Grace is my middle name, Ariel sent, hearing him laugh. *I'm not joking, Reed. My name is Ariel Grace Jones.*

Reed nodded and tried—mostly without success—to stop laughing about her name being Grace.

Ariel huffed a breath, noting the steam rising from her nostrils as she did. *Okay. Let's do this. No more naked shifting.*

She ordered herself to shift back to a female. She did do the somersault move and managed to land on two feet instead of hands and knees. Feeling herself standing upright, she let out a whoop of happiness.

And then she looked down.

"Oh, fuck this shit. What the hell did I do wrong now?" she demanded. She was naked except for her unlaced boots.

Reed held out the blanket, his shoulders shaking. The moment she took it to wrap around her, he staggered away laughing his ass off.

Ariel lifted her chin as she tucked the blanket around her shivering body. "At least I kept some of my clothes. It's only a matter of time until I keep the rest of them. I'm a positive thinker. I will get this done. Laugh all you want, but you'll see."

She marched to the back door where a grinning Matt was rubbing his nose and pretending not to care she was nude under the blanket.

"I have to go get dressed again. Apparently, my clothes keep showing up folded on your fancy dresser. At least I kept my boots this time."

She stopped and glared as she passed by him.

"I can see you're dying to comment. What's on your mind?"

"Congratulations on keeping your boots," Matt said, trying unsuccessfully not to laugh as he said it.

Shaking her head and rolling her eyes, Ariel moved passed him and into the house. Behind her, she heard Matt giving into his amusement at her expense. Knowing no one thought she would ever manage it only made her more determined.

"How about this one?" Eva asked, waiting until Heidi walked around the man on the examining table. She shook her head. "Try touching his arm or leg. Physical contact is usually needed. That's why doctors touch their patients, even though some have forgotten to use all their senses."

"Is it okay if I touch you?" Heidi asked the older man. At his silent nod, she placed a hand on his arm. Her other hand went to his side. "Something right around here isn't right. It's cracked or broken."

Eva looked at the man. "What happened, Howard?"

Heidi swallowed hard as she watched his chin nod in her direction.

"I fell when I went to feed the sled dogs. My side has burned ever since in the place she said."

"You probably fractured a rib. Have you tried shifting to fix it?" Eva asked.

Howard shook his head. "No. I don't have any tolerance for my wolf these days. He's always nagging me to do things I don't want to do."

"Better listen to him before he hurts you again," Eva advised. "I'll wrap your ribs for today, but if you shift a couple of times, you'll heal faster. Settle things with your wolf, Howard."

Howard grumbled, but nodded. Eva wrapped the bandages tightly around his midsection and then stepped back. When he was gone, Eva turned to a stunned Heidi.

"Why are you acting so shocked? You have a special gift."

"Thank you. Would his wolf really hurt him?" Heidi asked.

Eva shrugged. "Even humans develop mental issues if they live in denial. The same is true for shifters who don't honor their animal side. Sometimes your animal side knows better than the human what is needed."

Heidi nodded as they walked to see their next patient. Not being super comfortable with the fact she had a wolf side now, she preferred not to think about it any more than she had to.

Ariel came back to the yard fully dressed with her boots completely laced this time. She stomped past a grinning Matt and back out to Reed, who was pondering the trees. Ariel stopped near him to gaze up into his serene face.

"You can come inside. I'm done for the day. I'm tired of dressing myself over and over. Are you always this calm about everything that happens?"

"I've been alive a long time and tend to prioritize a little differently than someone younger. At this stage of my existence, I find it's best to conserve my energy whenever possible—though that was more necessary before you saved my life."

Ariel snorted. "You never get angry and I'm always angry. I can't say I wasn't always like this a little bit, but I can say that I never let it out so much before I met my wolf."

"I don't like being angry. The emotion makes me irrational. If I had let anger rule me when I was captured, I would not have been alive to help you when you were turned. Edgar had already died the week before."

"Edgar?"

Reed nodded. "Another werewolf. Crane captured many. Most died quickly and it was a blessing for them. Edgar and I were traveling companions. He was from a Canadian pack. We met one day when we were hunting. It suited us both to hang out together. Then one day, a pack of hunters on snowmobiles came through where we were. Edgar was captured and I escaped. I went after him and that's when I found Feldspar Research. Edgar was one of several wolves they experimented on trying to learn all they could about our kind. I don't know what they concluded. They cut him open, studied his insides, and then threw his remains out in the trash. I did get very angry that day."

Ariel ran a hand through her hair, which had grown into a mane of thick blonde in less than a week. Her thin locks were no more.

"From what I read in Crane's notes, none of the wolves they captured talked. So all they knew was some kind of molecular activity occurred during a transpecies shift from one form to another. They could never pinpoint the origin within the human form or the timing for the animal form. When a captured wolf died, they dissected it looking for abnormalities, like mutated DNA, which might provide clues. From what I read, they concluded the animal form was as normal as any regular wolf. Transpecies shifting remained a scientific mystery. The best I can determine is with us, Crane either got lucky, or someone specifically told him how to do it. Nothing in his data revealed anything close to what happened when we were converted. He hadn't even documented the process he used on us in his notes."

"His level of secrecy is even more troublesome. It means he was probably afraid of the one in power over him," Reed said.

"Possibly. Crane talked to us about being military weapons in our wolf forms. I think he was planning to sell us... or at least the process to make us. But then he also mentioned needing to show proof that the process had worked."

Reed rubbed his jaw. "There are many unanswered questions about Feldspar and my grandson. What would Hanuk gain from helping Crane, other than to make me look like I was being irresponsible in converting humans so needlessly? Discrediting me may have been his plan, but helping werewolves be created doesn't seem to serve any purpose for him or the pack. Werewolves have a long legacy of organic propagation. Mating with a human is discouraged and a cause for discrimination when it happens. Our history says that most humans cannot survive the change when bitten. If this had not been true, the human species might have disappeared during the middle ages when humans and werewolves weren't co-existing so peacefully."

"If your grandson did assist in our conversions somehow, it seems like a lot to go through just to keep a position he already holds. What would stop other humans from coming after him and his people for the same kind of experiments?"

Reed shook his head, not really wanting to theorize about the reasons. Such mind games always seemed like a waste of energy to him, but it was Ariel's method of understanding the world.

"For some, a war between werewolves and humans would be a welcome break from what they view as the monotony of pack life. Lazy males make war. Fighting is commonplace, and it takes less effort to earn glory."

"What are you going to do about all this, Reed?"

He turned and looked down into her face. "I consider the three of you to be gifts from the Great Spirit. You have reminded me of my value to my pack and to the world. I have to go back and try to unseat Hanuk. There is no other choice."

Ariel nodded. "I want to go with you. Brandi and I could be useful in your task. I don't know about Heidi."

"Heidi is becoming a healer. Healers are always welcome in every pack. They are considered the highest of blessings. I would gladly take you all with me. First though, we will contact Travis and get him to come escort us. Perhaps on the way, I can show him the wisdom of becoming the alpha."

"What would a hot tempered, alpha scientist be considered to your pack?"

Reed laughed. "I don't know. No pack has ever seen a werewolf like you. You look good in nothing but your boots. That's always a plus—at least for the males."

"Wonderful. You really know how to make an intelligent woman feel appreciated, Reed."

Reed snickered and dropped an arm around her shoulders as they walked back to Matt.

11

She was in Matt's backyard practicing alone when her wolf picked up the scent of a stranger. It reminded her faintly of Reed, but contained something more. Looking at the house where Matt was hiding out and pretending not to watch her, she whimpered before trotting into the woods. She wouldn't go far—just far enough to get a look at whoever was headed their way.

Picking her steps carefully, her paws were nearly silent as she trotted. Maybe she hadn't perfected a fully clothed shift yet, but her wolf definitely knew how to move confidently through the world.

Her ears picked up a series of soft footfalls. They grew louder as she stood by a tree and waited for the person to appear. Sniffing the air, Ariel discovered she could tell a few things from his scent, like he was male *and* a werewolf. She wasn't quite sure about the source of her knowledge of the second part, but she trusted it just the same.

When he first appeared in her line of sight, she saw eerily familiar, silky black hair hanging to his waist. Then she forgot he was Reed's clone when she saw the gun over one shoulder, held there by a wide leather sling. Her low growl of warning had the man's head snapping up and the gun coming automatically to his shoulder. It irritated her how rapidly Reed's clone made ready to use his gun to shoot her.

She waited until he was level with her, then lunged sideways from her hiding place, knocking the gun from his hands as she landed on him. He seemed totally startled at first, but then threw up his hands as she stood over him snarling.

Boy, she wanted a bite. She wanted a bite bad. She also wanted to make sure he never brought a gun back to any area where she was living.

"I'm sorry if I frightened you. I'm not going to shoot. I use the gun for killing game when I travel. It makes it easier to blend in with humans. I'm Reed's grandson—well, one of them."

When he tried to rise, Ariel used her front paws and her size to push him back down. Her considerable weight in her wolf form was greater than his weight in human form. Unsure whether to believe him or not, she pushed her nose into his neck to check for adrenaline spiking, growling the whole time as she sniffed and checked him out.

His outright laughter over her actions stunned her into backing off and staring at him.

"You must be Reed's new alpha. He told me about you when he called. Hi. I'm Travis Black Wolf."

Huffing at hearing his name, Ariel turned and headed back to the house. So this was the other grandson. She wasn't impressed.

On the way back, she picked up the man's gun and carried it in her teeth, growling to make sure he didn't try to take it from her. She heard him laughing more at her actions, but she didn't care. She wasn't taking any chances of getting shot in the back.

When they cleared the tree line and walked back into the yard, Matt and Reed were just coming out of the house, no doubt to check on her. She trotted over and laid the gun at Matt's feet. Matt stooped down and smiled into her gaze, putting an arm around her for a hug.

"I don't blame you for not letting him keep his gun. Play it safe and don't be sorry—that's a good rule to follow."

Ariel whimpered at his support and nudged Matt's hand, wanting to be petted for her good behavior. Now she understood why he had done that to her.

"Is the golden wolf your mate?" Travis asked.

Matt stood and shook his head. "No. But we are the kind of friends no one should get in the middle of right now. We have an agreement between us."

Travis snorted. "She's good at sneaking up on prey. I didn't smell or hear her until I was on the ground."

Reed chuckled. "Ariel is surprisingly talented for a newly turned werewolf." He turned to look at her. "Why don't you shift and I'll introduce you to my grandson?"

Because Reed knew she'd be nearly nude when she shifted, Ariel gave him a look she reserved for the giant piles of crap she made while in her wolf form. It was disgusting to know that much poop could come out of her wolf body.

Rising, she kept her back to the men as she shifted into something with hands to open doors.

The cool breeze on her bare ass told her what had not happened. So did Reed's laughter echoing behind her as she stomped into the house wearing nothing but her boots.

Travis reluctantly pulled his attention away from the amazing backside that had disappeared into the Wasilla Alpha's house. He smiled at the older version of himself. "You're looking well, Grandfather. Very well in fact."

Reed nodded. "Yes. I owe it to Ariel. She saved my life… twice."

Travis rubbed his chin as he followed the two men indoors. "From her smell, I can tell Ariel came from you. Is it really true you turned three women into werewolves? Rumors about it have been coming up everywhere. They say you have gone mad in your old age and started biting people."

"It is true my blood was used to change the three women, but I didn't bite them. None of us were willing participants in what happened. It was done scientifically. Ariel can explain better than I can."

Travis nodded. "Hanuk is the one spreading the rumors. Many believe him, even though he rules their judgments with fear."

"Hanuk is most likely the reason I was captured by those who experimented on us. One of the women turned is becoming a healer. The other is a visionary. The visionary has seen someone shooting me six times with silver bullets. I nearly lost my life because of it."

"Well, you look much better now than when you left the pack. What happened to the gray in your hair?"

"I'm not sure, but I feel like a wolf in his prime," Reed declared.

Travis nodded. His head whipped around as the tall blonde strode into the kitchen fully clothed. She was just as magnificent in human form. "Still mad at me about the gun?" he asked.

Ariel shrugged, unwilling to admit how much the younger version of Reed irritated her. It was the same kind of nervous Matt made her feel and she didn't like it. The last thing she needed was another alpha male wanting a piece of her. She stepped forward and held out her hand to get the introduction over with. "Dr. Ariel Jones."

"Travis Black Wolf," Travis replied, holding her hand until he'd earned another glare from her. She was a prickly thing. He almost choked on his coffee though when the Gray Wolf Alpha stepped to her side and put an arm around her shoulders.

"Are you sure you two are just friends?" Travis asked.

"Friends-with-benefits, not that it's any of your business," Ariel said sharply.

"So are you having your trial time? If so, why not just say as much?" Travis asked.

Reed laughed and coughed into his hand. "Ariel has only been a werewolf for a short while. Matt is helping her endure her burning."

Travis felt his eyebrows go up. "I see. Lucky Matt that she chose him."

Ariel narrowed her gaze on the kid who kept making innuendos. "This isn't high school. I'm sleeping with Matt because I want to, not because I must. Don't ever doubt he's my choice."

Travis shrugged his shoulders and grinned. "Did I wrong you in another life, Ariel Jones? Or do you just not have a sense of humor? I swear I was not trying to offend you."

"Then stop talking about me like I'm not in the room," Ariel said, crossing her arms.

Travis laughed again at her fierce statement. "I see you haven't learned not to issue challenges to other alphas."

"Oh, it wasn't a challenge. It was merely a statement of fact. Just because I like your grandfather, doesn't mean you get instant trust. You walked here with a gun slung over your shoulder. I've learned the hard way not to trust anyone with one of those. I don't trust them around Reed either. But I do trust Brandi's vision about who shot Reed."

Travis nodded, sobered by her tone. "My apologies if I seemed too flip about your concerns."

His apology made her uncomfortable, but Ariel couldn't have said why. "It's okay. Forget about it. I'm having a bad day. Maybe I need to stop talking."

Ariel pulled away from Matt's hug to get herself a cup of coffee. She needed to quit overreacting. Travis was the good grandson, not the bad one. Reed had said so. Needling Travis wasn't going to conjure up Hanuk in his place. She frowned when she saw Reed hide his smile over their truce behind his hand.

"Hanuk will not be forced out of power easily. His death may even be necessary. Are you prepared to challenge him for alpha and end his life, Grandfather?"

Before Reed could answer, Ariel spoke up. "Reed shouldn't have to kill his own kin. I'm more than happy enough to do his fighting for him. I want to find out what he knows about Feldspar Research. What did he have to gain by aiding Reed's capture?"

Ariel frowned when Travis looked away. She didn't like the way he was smiling at her.

Travis eventually brought his gaze back to her. "So you would kill for Reed, Ariel Jones?"

Ariel snorted. "I already have once, so I don't see myself having any problems doing it a second time."

"Ariel is the reason we escaped our prison," Reed explained. "She killed our captors and broke us out."

"That sounds like something a Black Wolf Alpha would do. If Ariel has such strong bloodlust, then she's a natural alpha," Travis declared.

"I don't know what any of that means," Ariel said.

"You will in time," Travis declared. "So when do we leave for the pack, Grandfather?"

Reed stared at a spot on the table. "We'll wait on Brandi and Heidi and see if they want to go along. Then we'll decide what needs to be done about Hanuk."

Matt looked between the men. "Reed will need to produce all three women to prove he speaks truth, but they are still too new to how things work. It would not look right if I came with you, but I am unwilling for the women to go without their temporary consorts. One of the males is my second. He is a couple centuries wise. Gareth and Ryan will not get involved in your pack politics, but they will make sure the females come back to us safely."

"Matt, I can tell you are upset, but I have to go with Reed. What if Hanuk has some crazy scheme or is in contact with the money behind Feldspar? I can't let more of us be created. Everything in me says that's not what nature intended to happen."

Matt ignored the strange way Travis was staring at them as he cupped Ariel's jaw in one hand. "I don't want you go, but I'm not going to waste my breath begging a natural alpha not to do her duty. You must do what you feel is important and necessary, even if it means you end up running the Black Wolf pack when it's done."

Ariel shook her head against Matt's hand. "I don't think I'm cut out for the kind of ongoing leadership such a role requires, but I am determined to solve the puzzle of my creation. I can't move forward or figure out what to do with the rest of my life until I know who was helping Crazy Crane. My instincts are still saying it was a werewolf."

Brandi ran a hand through her hair and stared back at the deck where all the males were standing and talking. "This shit is crazy. Reed smiles at me and I want to crawl into his lap for a hug. All I want to do with his clone is kick his ass and make him leave. Are you sure this is the good grandson? I'm not getting a good vibe off him."

Heidi frowned. "I'm having the same reaction, which is strange, because he's extremely good-looking. I usually don't react so negatively to men who look that good."

"He knows how good he looks and I'm sure he uses it every chance he gets. That doesn't make him the bad grandson. It just makes him... *young*," Ariel decided, stating the obvious in disgust. "You two still haven't answered the question I dragged you out into the freezing cold to discuss. Are you willing to tag along with us to Reed's pack or do you want to hang back here? I'm okay either way."

"What does Matt say about it?" Heidi asked.

Ariel sighed. "Matt says Reed's credibility will be higher if he produces all three of us. He knows I have to go no matter what.

After Reed kicks Hanuk's ass off the Black Wolf Alpha throne, I want a chance to interrogate him about what he knows about Feldspar."

"What are we going to do if we're traveling and need a fix of our guys?" Heidi asked.

Ariel chuckled. "Already taken care of. Matt's sending Gareth and Ryan with us if you two go. I'm the only one with a problem. Matt can't go at all. Apparently, that would be bad pack politics."

Brandi snorted. "I don't need Gareth to go. I'll be fine."

"Maybe I could borrow him then," Ariel said, laughing when Brandi's eyes flashed. "I was kidding and you can't get by without him yet. You may still not like it, but Gareth is necessary for you, Brandi. Unless you want to do the tango with Travis or someone like him."

"Eww… don't even joke about that," Heidi whispered.

Brandi snorted. "I don't think so, Ariel. It would feel like incest or something else equally as gross. I'll keep Gareth for now."

"So are you two coming along?" Ariel asked.

Two heads solemnly nodding were finally her answer.

12

THEY STOOD OUTSIDE MATT'S OFFICE TALKING AND LOADING THE TWO vehicles they were going to take. Ariel headed to drop her bag of clothes into the back seat.

"Matt's loaning me his pickup. I'm driving Reed and Gareth's driving the four of you. Reed says it's a four hour drive up there from Wasilla."

She threw the bag into the truck and slammed the door. At the back of the truck, she saw six females staring non-stop at her. She walked their way and all but the prettiest one backed up. Her hair was midnight black, straighter and longer than even Reed's. Her face was quite beautiful if you could overlook her wild-eyed, angry stare.

"You are an unnatural alpha. You don't belong here. Matt deserves someone better than you warming his bed, " she said.

Ariel glared at the dark-haired, dark-eyed beauty giving her the evil eye. "Isn't it Matt's decision about who warms his bed? He's twice my age and your pack alpha. I figure that means he knows his own mind."

"Matt cannot be blamed for giving in to a typical male

weakness for a female. You have deceived his senses. He does not see beyond your magic."

Ariel huffed, more indignant about the female's word choices than her threats. *"Magic? What the hell are you talking about? Get a grip on yourself. This is not Salem, Massachusetts and I'm not a freaking witch."*

"No one knows what you are. You reek of strangeness, even though you are a werewolf. Leave with the Black Wolf Alpha—the ancient one who created you. You do not belong here with us."

Ariel glared defiantly. The woman was merely pretending to be clueless. Hadn't she seen her loading her stuff in the truck to leave? She was minutes from heading out with Reed, but didn't want to confess it.

"Look—I don't have anymore time to waste arguing with you. If you have a problem with what Matt told me, or our relationship, you need to take it up with him. Now I think you need to get out of my face before I lose my urge to be polite. My wolf is getting upset."

"Your wolf must never be freed again. Receive my gift so the world can be done with you."

It didn't occur to her to back up when the woman stepped close. But she did flinch when the woman blew black dust into her face. She coughed when she got a mouthful, and then inhaled to try and get a breath. But she couldn't. It was like someone had pulled the breath right out of her. Without breath, the world turned dark in moments. Ariel sunk to the ground, glaring at the woman's smile.

"Ariel." Brandi yelled her name as she watched Ariel's body hit the ground with a thud.

She turned to Heidi. *"Go. Get Matt. Run, Heidi. Now."*

Heidi spared one tortured look at the fallen Ariel before bolting.

Brandi jumped in front of Ariel before she'd even realized she'd run to guard her. The five who had stood with the confronting woman took off running in fear. But the woman stood looking at Ariel's fallen body with a pleased smirk lighting her face and gaze.

"What the fuck did you do to her?" Brandi demanded.

"I did what was necessary to end this."

Turning back to Ariel, Brandi stooped and checked her pulse. "Her heart is still beating, but her breathing is shallow," she said aloud, needing to hear the words to believe them.

"There is nothing to be done. Death will eventually find her. I bound her unnatural wolf in her body. She will now forget who she is and what she is. Normally, this sort of punishment was only done to those who had committed pack treason. It was my idea to use it on the abomination."

Before the woman could blink, Brandi was beside her, her talented thumbs pressed against the woman's throat cutting off her air. "Don't even think about it. I'll kill you before you manage to shift," she warned.

The woman didn't struggle against her grip, but Brandi didn't think she was quite right in her mind at the moment. The woman's eyes were wild-eyed and dancing. She needed to make sure the woman understood how serious she was.

"Before I was turned into a werewolf, I used to kill people for a living. I did it as a human—often with my bare hands. Killing someone like you won't bother me a bit, lady. Now I'm going to ask you again and you're going to give me specifics—what the hell was in the dust you blew at Ariel?"

"Stop choking me. It was wolfsbane, mountain ash, and mistletoe. It doesn't matter if you know what was done. It's far too late to stop what is happening to her."

Brandi loosened her hold, but just enough to grab the woman

by the hair. She drug her forward with it just as Matt and Gareth came running outside. She threw the woman at Matt's feet, pleased when she screamed in pain as she hit the dirt.

Seeing Ariel's body on the ground, Matt's growl shook nearby building windows as he lifted the groveling woman up by the front of her clothes. His anger brought people running outside to see what was happening.

"I don't know why I ever thought you might be worthy of mating anyone in my pack. Your heart is black with envy and you hate what you don't understand. I have been patient in hopes you would change, Cheryl. My patience has now ended."

"What wrong have I done to you, Matthew Gray Wolf? She is an unnatural creation of the ancient one. The blonde alpha is not worthy to be your mate," the woman protested.

"She is my choice for whatever I wish. If Ariel dies, you and your friends will follow her quickly—I promise you that," Matt said fiercely, his gaze going to where Heidi was working on Ariel. "Gareth, lock Cheryl up. I want a guard on her until the other five turn themselves in for what they helped her do. Everyone involved is going to be punished—openly—so the pack knows I will not tolerate this kind of interference in my choices. There will be an official pack meeting about it as soon as the others are found."

Imitating Brandi, Gareth grabbed the woman by the hair of her head and made her call out again.

"Wait," Brandi said. She peeled off her coat and then her shirt. Grabbing the woman's arm, she wiped the remainder of the black dust from her hands off on the shirt. Maybe Eva or Heidi could use it to find out what the shit really was. "I don't know why the stuff she used on Ariel isn't taking her down too. It's all over her hands. You'd think it would have the same effect."

"Cheryl's training is in herbal remedies. She's probably shielded her skin with some kind of protection," Matt said, moving forward to where Ariel was lying.

Brandi followed Matt to where he knelt. She held her shirt out to Heidi. "This is a sample of what she used. It looks like coal dust. She said it was a mixture of wolfsbane, mountain ash, and mistletoe."

Matt's vicious swearing over what he heard had him rising and pacing away. His anger was making his whole body shake.

Heidi glanced Matt's way once, then back at Brandi. "I think Matt is about it to lose it, but I can't afford to get emotional. Now don't judge me for what I'm going to do. I'm following my instincts… I think."

She morphed into her wolf, and pushed Ariel to her back. She put two paws on Ariel's shoulders and lifted her chin to howl. The eerie sound she made was piercing and seemed to vibrate forever. Everyone in human form grabbed their ears and bent forward from the pain.

Heidi looked down at Ariel and growled, pawing at the front of her. Then she hopped twice, letting the full force of her wolf land on Ariel's chest. Suddenly, Ariel seized and coughed up what looked like a ton of black smoke. Heidi backed off just in time for Ariel to turn her head and start retching up the rest.

Brandi looked at Heidi. "Nice howl you got going on there, party girl. I don't even sound like that when I'm hitting the high notes with Gareth. Maybe I should have chosen Ryan. The man obviously has some serious mojo in his juju."

Heidi snarled at the offensive comments, but still leaned against Brandi's leg in relief. They watched Ariel come around after the vile concoction got ejected from her system.

Brandi rubbed Heidi's head and laughed when Ariel sat up and swore viciously.

"What the hell did the stupid ass she-wolf blow on me? Next time I see her, I'm going to kick her butt to hell and back. Then I'm going to carry her beat up wolf body around town in my teeth just to embarrass her in front of everyone she knows."

Matt looked at Brandi and Heidi in disbelief, then walked

forward to drop to his knees besides Ariel. "Do you know who you are? What you are?"

Ariel shook her head and glared at Matt. "What do you mean? I have a bad headache from whatever the hell just happened, but I don't think the fall gave me a concussion."

Matt snatched Ariel up in his arms and held tight. His relief about her being alive had no words. He knew many full-bloods who had been killed by the mixture Ariel had just coughed up. "I thought you were gone. It scared me to realize it could actually happen."

"Yes, well, I might have been gone with Reed, if your old girlfriend hadn't gotten her panties in a wad about the two of us. Now I don't think I can drive until this headache passes. The trip is going to have a wait a day. In case you didn't get to hear the argument, some of the females in your pack think I'm not purebred enough to be your current friend-with-benefits. By the way, how do you say 'go to hell' in werewolf? The deceitful she-wolf didn't seem to respond to any of my human threats."

Matt looked at the black powder covering both their shirts now. He peeled his off, then peeled off Ariel's. The powder covered clothing was no longer safe to wear and would have to be burned. And the ground where it happened would have to be cleansed.

"My head is spinning like crazy. Why are we getting naked? After today, I'm all about making our relationship public, but I don't think I have it in me to do you in the middle of the street in broad daylight. Plus, I just threw up. I'd really like to go somewhere and brush my teeth."

Chuckling, Matt lifted a weak Ariel in his arms and stood with her clutched to his chest. He couldn't imagine what he would have suffered if she had died. Those few minutes of fear still had his insides quaking.

"When you come back from visiting the Black Wolf pack, we're going to have a little talk about you moving in with me as my full time friend-with-benefits… or something."

"Because I'm better in bed than the she-wolf?" Ariel asked.

Matt laughed. "That's not the reason I want you in my life, but it is a perk. I've decided I like you more than any female I've ever known. I'd like you to live with me and keep me company. I've never felt that way about anyone before you."

Ariel laughed. "Two weeks ago I was a dowdy divorced scientist who thought her love life was over. Now the hottest guy I've ever met wants me to live with him. This werewolf thing might be okay after all. And I like you too, Matt."

"Brandi? Tell Reed the trip has to be postponed. Explain what happened. I'm going to get Eva to check her."

"We'll take care of everything else. You just take care of Ariel," Brandi replied.

"Count on it," Matt vowed, carrying Ariel to the passenger side of his truck.

Eva was waiting at the house when they got there and held the door open to let him carry Ariel inside. She had the microscope and the blood-drawing kit laid out on his kitchen table.

"Ariel still has some of the dust on her. We need to shower it off first," Matt explained, as he continued walking Ariel slowly up the stairs.

In his tiled walk-in shower, he stripped the clothes from both of them and tossed them into a pile to be burned. Ariel didn't fight him when he washed her completely, including her growing mane of hair. He shampooed it several times and then poured a healthy dose of conditioner into it.

"I can't remember the last time I was this relaxed. It's a bit like being drunk. I feel like I could sleep for hours and hours," Ariel said.

"No sleep yet, babe. We have a little bit of work to do first," Matt said. "Eva is waiting downstairs to help."

Ariel nodded. "Okay. But don't be taking my complete obedience tonight the wrong way."

"I'm not challenging you—I'm just taking care of you," Matt whispered, toweling her off and kissing little trails down her clean face and throat.

Every flutter of her pulse sent alarm skittering through his cells again. He couldn't seem to forget how close he'd come to losing her. "Dr. Jones the scientist needs to let Eva the healer make sure she's doing as well as we think she is. I know how important it is for you to know all the facts."

Ariel patted Matt's jaw. "Listen to you. You're being all scientific. That's so cute. Okay, I'll behave while Eva looks at me."

"Good. Now before I start kissing you in ways I'm not going to want to stop doing, let's wrap you up in the butt-ugly robe Mother Gray Wolf gave you."

"Nanuka gave me a robe?"

"Yes. It's hideous," Matt declared. "I didn't tell you because it's ugly and far too big."

"I think it was very thoughtful of her to give me a robe," Ariel declared, holding out her arms.

Sighing, Matt wrapped the miles of fluffy, furry, white fabric around Ariel's supple body. He crossed the massive front flaps and tied the belt to hold it closed.

Ariel looked down at herself. "Even as out of it as I am, I can see why you didn't mention it now. This is a real libido killer, isn't it?"

"Not really," Matt said, grinning at her concern. "I just hate covering up the best parts of you. I'd rather see you wearing my old pajamas or sweats."

"I think I'd rather be wearing them too, but I have to admit the robe is keeping me warm."

Holding his hand for support, Ariel padded down the stairs a step behind Matt.

Eva was washing her hands at the kitchen sink in preparation to work on her. Ariel slid into a chair at the table, fighting the dizziness that just wouldn't go away.

"I don't know how she's even so alert," Eva said, her mouth tight with unhappiness over what had happened. "Tell me again how she was… saved."

"Heidi released her wolf and bounced on Ariel's chest. She coughed out a black cloud of the stuff, and then threw up the rest. She's been lucid every since she stopped retching."

"How long was the mixture in her system?" Eva asked.

Matt shook his head. "I don't know. When Brandi told me what it was, and I saw her lying in the street, I just assumed the worst, Eva. She was nearly lifeless."

Eva nodded. "These women are all special. A normal werewolf would not have survived such an attack. There are good reasons your great-grandfather outlawed the wolfsbane punishment. Its effects are irreversible."

She efficiently drew a half-vial of blood, then tapped a sleepy Ariel on the cheek. "Dr. Jones, we need you to be a scientist for a few minutes. You need to look at your blood under the microscope and tell us if you are doing okay. Once you do this small thing, I promise we'll let you sleep this off."

Pulling her sluggish body upright in the chair, Ariel pulled her microscope closer. They hadn't thought to bring more clean smear slides. She took the one from the microscope and handed it to Eva. "Wash this off with just cold water. Then clean it with alcohol."

While she waited, she felt Matt's hands slip down inside the wide collar of her giant robe. They went to work gently kneading the tension from her shoulders. "I might have to seriously consider your live-in girlfriend offer. You're going to make someone a great boyfriend one day."

Eva handed back the now clean slide, her gaze moving between her brother and Ariel as she lifted a brow. "I didn't know you two had advanced to labeling yet. Mother didn't tell me that information."

Ariel giggled. "Oh, that's right. Nanuka is your real mother," she said, patting Matt's hand to get him to stop rubbing so she could work.

She borrowed the alcohol swab, smeared the slide, then added a drop of her blood. Peering at it under the microscope, she had to adjust the magnification several times to make sure she was seeing correctly.

"Something has hit my little nano guys pretty hard. Some seem confused and disoriented. Others are scrambling fast like someone slipped them cocaine. I'll need to keep an eye out for mutations. What was in the black dust again?"

Eva looked at Matt, who nodded it was okay to tell her.

"Wolfsbane, mountain ash, and mistletoe. All are extremely poisonous to werewolves. Mistletoe causes paralysis, but the other two can kill. Madness comes first and you lose your sense of self. Then death follows closely behind the amnesia."

Ariel pushed away from the microscope. "Even when I watched Brandi and Heidi being injected at the lab, some instinct told me none of us were going to die. I knew Crane wanted us alive. Today is the first time I've had to confront the fact that there are people in the world who will kill me if they get the chance. Today wasn't even about anything important. Your old girlfriend just thought I had taken her man."

"Old girlfriend?" Eva asked, her gaze going to her brother.

"She's referring to Cheryl," Matt said, his tone severe.

Eva snorted. "She was never your girlfriend. You never even slept with her for a trial."

Matt shrugged. "Of course I didn't. What would I want with someone who feeds on drama? The pack's real problems are enough for me."

Ariel held up a hand. "Wait a minute. Are you telling me the woman who tried to kill me today has no idea how good you are in bed?"

Matt crossed his arms, trying not to smile at Ariel's compliment. "No. She does not. But once upon a time I was working my way through all eligible females in my pack, hoping I could find one I could tolerate for a more permanent bond. I stopped trying out females twenty years ago. Now I just look for women with calm minds who can make pleasant conversation."

Ariel snorted. "If that were true, you'd never put up with me. You demand to be respected, but secretly you just want to be liked for you. There's nothing wrong with holding out for a woman who gives you exactly what you want, Matt. You're a good man and you deserve to be wanted for yourself."

"A matter we agree on completely," Matt declared. He looked at Eva. "Are we done for tonight? I would like to take my nano wolf to bed and make her happy before she sleeps."

Ariel snickered and shook her head in shock. "Wow Matt... that wasn't even innuendo. You're really rude to all your family members, aren't you? You need to work on your manners before your family starts to hate me as much as your old girlfriends do."

"Never going to happen," Eva said, patting Ariel's shoulder as she walked by. "Be careful with her, Matt. Ariel is not as strong tonight as her teasing words make her seem."

"I know," Matt said softly, smiling at his sister's concern. "Thank you for coming, Eva."

Matt walked his sister to the door and hugged her goodbye. Eva's giggle into his shoulder had him pulling away and looking at her curiously.

"What?" he asked.

"Your *nano wolf*?" Eva repeated, the term sounding funny still.

Matt sighed. "I called Ariel that only because it doesn't matter to me what label anyone puts on her—or me—or us. The only important reality is what I felt when I saw her nearly lifeless on the ground. Everything I thought I knew about my life changed in an instant. Ariel is the female I want in my bed—permanently."

"Then I am happy for you, brother. It is not easy to find the right mate. Do the parents know?" Eva asked in a whisper.

"Nanuka probably thinks she does, because she has seen us together," Matt snorted, whispering back. "But I did not know myself until today."

Eva held her beloved brother's face in her hands and whispered a blessing in her mother's native tongue. She reached up and kissed his cheek before saying goodnight.

Matt walked Ariel up the stairs, pausing in the hallway to untie the belt of the giant robe and let it fall to the floor. He kissed her deeply, his tongue tasting the rising desire in her.

Growling at her response, he lifted her into his arms and carried her the rest of the way to his bed.

"You always make me feel so yummy. Being drugged just heightens the effect. Are we really having sex tonight while I'm high on whatever it was I ingested?" Ariel asked.

"Yes, but I will be gentle. We are having the kind of sex which will make us both feel glad to be alive," Matt said, spreading her thighs with his hands and burying his face between them. He shook at her moan. Her arching against his tongue had him nipping the tender skin he was torturing.

Then he suddenly couldn't stand not being in her. He crawled up her body and eased himself inside, stroking gently but firmly as she climaxed around him. He never tired of pleasuring her.

"Ariel, you are never allowed to die," he ordered, only to hear the woman beneath him laugh.

"Matthew, we all die sometime. I don't think even an alpha can stop it from happening eventually," she answered, stroking his shoulders.

"Well, today was not your time… and tomorrow will not be your time either. You will go with Reed and come back to me in one piece. My pack will never harm you again. There is no room for argument here. I am ordering you to live."

"I must be really out of it. Your bossiness sounds sexy as hell to me right now," she whispered.

Ariel laughed as he whispered his intentions to meld them together permanently in her ear, but it was still a truth borne out by the way Matt's body dominated hers. There was no fire burning in her at the moment other than the one Matt built with his endless kissing and possessive stroking. She felt a desperate edge to his every surge inside her which had never ceased since he'd climbed on top of her. She sleepily decided it was nice someone so amazing might miss her so much if she died.

"After I broke up with my ex, I wondered if the chance for this kind of relationship had passed me by. Sometimes when I'm with you, I still wonder if I'm going to wake up and find none of this has even happened. Other times I think it was almost worth the pain of becoming a werewolf just to have this chance."

"The words I want to say back to your declaration would probably scare you, Dr. Jones. How about you just give yourself to me and be mine completely tonight? I need you more than air right now. And I need to prove to myself you really are alive."

At her nod, his lips slid possessively against hers. His tongue kept rhythm as he softly pounded her surrendered flesh with proof of his great need. When Ariel gripped him in orgasm again, her straining thighs triggered his willing response to flood her receptive body with part of himself. He wanted to be bound to her in every way he could. The fierceness of the need for once didn't surprise him, but the ideas it gave him probably should have.

While the woman beneath him languished in climax, calling his name in her lingering bliss, he did what he had vowed to himself never to do to a female without permission. Holding Ariel on the edge of her pleasure, he put his mouth to her sweet neck and raked his teeth down until they sharpened instinctively and slashed the tender skin just above her collar bone.

It was not a mating bite, not in the truest sense. He was careful not to draw more than a few droplets of blood, which he licked away to seal the small wound. But the rakings were a mark of possession. If the nanos she worried about removed his bite tomorrow, he would just do it again until they finally accepted his right to mark her as his.

Now if Ariel Jones ever died, the world would know someone would mourn her. They would know *he* would. And next time a competitive female questioned her relationship to him, Ariel could show her his mark. His pack would know on sight what it meant.

When she whimpered in protest, he ran his lips over the rapidly healing scars, fighting all the other rising urges in his body. Ariel needed to sleep. He needed to let her.

"Matt? Did you really just bite me? Wow, my head hurts bad. I think I really need to sleep now. We're going to talk about this in the morning."

Her sharp tap on his cheek had him reflexively growling at her chastisement, then he ended up chuckling at all the reactions Ariel caused in him that he could never seem to control. One day— when she was healed completely—he was going to turn his emotions loose on Ariel Jones and not stop until his sexy cerebral scientist conceded to feeling equally possessive about him.

"I love you," Matt whispered aloud, knowing his declaration went unheard by Ariel's deeply sleeping form.

He rolled off her body reluctantly, but stayed close enough to hold her while she slept, which he knew emotionally meant a lot to her. His reward for meeting her unspoken need was Ariel snuggling deeper into his arms and humming in contentment. The jaded male he'd become in seventy-five years was figuring out what his wolf had known from the first moment he'd laid eyes on the naked Dr. Ariel Jones and handed her back her shredded lab coat.

Sighing at the dilemma he hadn't seen coming, Matt realized he had no choice but to accept that he'd finally found the only female he'd ever considered mating.

13

"THANK YOU FOR DRIVING. I CAN DO IT, BUT MY MIND WANDERS TOO much. I am not safe behind the wheel today, but I feel guilty since you are still recuperating from your latest ordeal."

Ariel nodded without smiling. "It's okay, Reed. I don't mind driving. I usually find it relaxing. That's not exactly the case today, but I'm doing alright."

Reed turned his face to give her his full attention. "I could tell something was wrong. You've been silent and fuming for two hours now. When are you going to vent your complaints and just get them out of your system?"

"I'm just pissed at Matt," Ariel declared, snorting at all the emotions she released by saying it aloud. "And I'm not used to being this emotional."

"Most women like talking about it. Are you not used to talking about what you feel?" Reed asked, already knowing the answer, but it would be good for her to vent.

"No, I guess I'm not. Being pissed is worse than just be angry. Pissed creates a state of mind where I want to run this truck of Matt's off the nearest cliff to prove to the jerk that he can't control my life. I'm mad because he marked me last night without my permission. He bit me on my collarbone while I slept after we... well after things. It was like a damn dream happening. I knew he was all worried about me dying and—okay—I did let him have his way with me to make us both feel better. But the nanos didn't even try to fix the bite—not that they haven't had more important work to do in the last twenty-four hours. The place he put it is going to show to the world no matter what shirt I wear. And it looks like a cat scratch. I hate cats."

She glared when Reed burst out laughing. "You know—you've been laughing at me since the day we met, Reed. If I didn't get all mushy inside every time I looked at you, I'd kick your laughing ass. This is not funny. I've been all about turning into a wolf since I found out I could. That's the honest truth and it surprises the hell out of me. But what if Matt's people get the wrong idea about our relationship? After that woman tried to kill me, Matt didn't need to give me the werewolf version of a damn hickey."

Reed shrugged. "Alphas rarely ask permission to do anything. They just tend to do what they think is right."

Ariel snorted. "If that were true, I'd have knocked Matt's teeth out of his head this morning. I didn't because I owe him for all he's done to help me, but nothing gave him the right to turn me into one more piece of Gray Wolf property. I'm not his property. Anything could happen to me and probably will. Our situation is not normal and I'm not a normal werewolf. He needs to get over himself. He doesn't rule the world—or at least not my world."

Reed nodded and worked to school his expression into something sober. "Matt says he loves you. He wanted to know how I felt about it. I told him your approval was all that mattered."

Ariel snorted again. "Matt doesn't love me. He just loves that I give him sex without wanting anything in return. Any male would love a female who did that. We agreed to mutually take care of each other *without* emotional strings. We agreed to be friends. The benefits of that friendship did not extend to permanent werewolf hickeys."

Reed couldn't prevent the chuckle that escaped. "I think you are friends. Friends can be great lovers. Why can't you believe Matt loves you?"

"*Why?* Because we've known each other less than two weeks. And we're not really of the same species. Matt is always telling me how much I still smell like a human. I find that ironic because my wolf side now seems more real to me than anything else I know about myself. One side of my mind pursues logic like it always has, but the other part of me wants to kill and drag dead things around in my mouth. If Matt wanted to spend his life dealing with a mentally unstable female, he should have slept with the crazy woman who tried to kill me."

"Bah… Matt felt nothing for the girl who harmed you. Well, he wanted to kill her, but I'm glad he showed mercy in her case. Killing outright usually starts more problems than it solves."

"Matt is just confused. Great sex is not the same thing as love. I've had great sex before—okay, maybe not Matthew Gray Wolf-great sex—but I know the difference between the two things. I'm just a novelty to him. If Matt's ready for a real relationship, he needs someone of his own kind."

Reed laughed. "Ariel, what you are saying is irrational. You are his own kind, no matter how you became a werewolf."

Ariel shook her head. "You know I'm not a real werewolf. Hell, I don't know what kind of weird anomaly I am. I survived something that usually kills werewolves. And look what I've done to you, Reed. You were dying and I experimented on you just like Crane did."

Reed looked sideways and growled. It was the first time Ariel had ever made him angry. "You saved my life. Never speak of it differently. I don't want to get upset at you over your negative attitude about what you are."

Ariel battled back the butterflies Reed's anger caused inside her. Finally, she nodded and sighed. "Okay. We'll go with saying I saved you. And I'm sorry you're getting the brunt of my irritation with Matt. I saw his mark in the bathroom mirror this morning and all he did was laugh while I indignantly shrieked about it. I should have just kicked his ass right there and then so I could have put the anger behind me."

Huffing and shaking his head, Reed looked out the window at the passing landscape he knew so well. He was going home—to the only home he'd ever known.

"I agree it wasn't fair of Matthew to mark you without your permission. However, I can also see he might consider your body letting the mark linger as a sort of *higher* permission than your words might give. He knows your body can erase nearly any sign of harm."

"Would you ever mark a woman without asking her first?" Ariel demanded.

Reed laughed. "I did it all three times I mated. I was raised to be assertive with females and didn't really give them a choice. I was their alpha. But I did try to win them over before I completely mated them. It worked for me because I was careful in who I chose to mate."

Ariel frowned and stared at the road. "But that's not fair, Reed. They deserved to have a say in the matter."

Reed laughed at her careful words. "Did you witness my relationships? How do you know it wasn't fair? I concede none of my matings were quite as civilized as any human courtship. To the best of my recall though, none of my mates ever complained that what I did was unfair. Perhaps it was because I made it worth their while in every way I could. And I loved them with everything in me. I was always, always faithful. Being mated was a source of great joy for me."

"I think we should stop talking about this while I can still remember why I like you so much. Otherwise, I'm going to start throwing around words like *sexist* and *caveman*," Ariel declared.

"Human terms and human rules," Reed stated flatly, shrugging at her glare. "I am an alpha—so are you. One day, I think you will understand how a sense of gut rightness can rule your decisions and banish all your mind's rational doubts. I see your wolf is trying hard to teach you this lesson."

"Now that's where I have to disagree with you, Reed. My wolf was just as mad about the mark this morning as I was. It was my human side which kept calm about it. I can't let myself care about another man who thinks he can control me. Those days are over."

It was shocking when hundreds of miles of road bordered by untouched land finally parted to reveal signs of civilization on each side of it. Reed's village was remote, but very picturesque. Houses were painted bright colors, neatly maintained, and all had well landscaped yards with a variety of foliage. It was an Alaskan suburbia in the middle of nowhere. They pulled over at a general store slash welcome center, which could have easily been located in Wasilla.

Several men walked out of the store as they climbed out of the truck. Ariel couldn't take her eyes off the one who looked like yet another replica of Reed. She looked at the man seated beside her. His genes were obviously determined to survive and to replicate him as many times as they could.

She slammed her door closed and walked around to the front of the truck to stand at Reed's side.

"Greetings Hanuk," Reed said, addressing his grandson.

"Have you come back for a visit, grandfather?" Hanuk asked.

Reed nodded. "Yes... and to dispel some rumors. This is Dr. Ariel Jones. A human science organization she worked for captured me. Thanks to Ariel, we all managed to escape. However, her employers used me to turn her and two other women into werewolves."

Hanuk smiled. "Science? We heard you bit them and turned them."

Reed raised an eyebrow. "Who would spread such rumors about me?"

Hanuk shrugged. "Travis—for one. But the same rumor is believed throughout the pack."

"Travis? Is that right?" Reed asked, walking closer. "Travis told me you were the one spreading the rumors."

Ariel narrowed her gaze when Hanuk laughed at the accusation. She glanced at Reed, who was staring stoically at his grandson, not laughing or smiling. When Hanuk stopped laughing, he shrugged.

"Like many others, I have been discussing the rumors... and wondering if they were true. As current alpha, I was concerned what your lack of mental stability might mean to us, especially since you seemed to have formed some sort of unusual alliance with the Gray Wolf Alpha."

Reed smiled. "Matthew Gray Wolf's healer saved my life. That is my alliance with him and his pack. He also took care of my scientifically made family when I was unable to see to their needs. Being newly converted, the women are passing through their burning time. Two of the Gray Wolf pack have accompanied Ariel's charges to assist them. I expect you to make all the Gray Wolf members feel welcome and to show them respect while they are here. They will not interfere with Black Wolf matters."

Hanuk snorted. "Your expectations for the pack are no longer my concern, nor are your promises something I can take for granted. Yet for the sake of maintaining peace, I will make the Gray Wolf members welcome."

Ariel felt Hanuk's stare switch to her before he spoke.

"Who is acting as your consort during your burning time, Ariel Jones?"

Ariel crossed her arms. "I'm not in the habit of answering personal questions from strangers."

Hanuk laughed. "Come now. We're not strangers. We're *family*. Unless you plan to go off and start your own pack, you belong here with us."

"Reed says the two women are my pack. Since that feels right to me, I'm working on figuring it out," Ariel declared.

Hanuk mirrored her crossed arms and made his companions laugh at his disrespect of her. Ariel had a sudden urge to attack him and take him down, but pushed it back. The man was rude, but also something worse than just arrogant. He was playing with them. Every instinct she had said so. Still... it wasn't her place to correct the situation. It was Reed's.

While she waited, she bit her tongue, settling for a stoic glare at Reed's nearly identical—but evil—twin. Behind her, she heard Crane's jeep roll into a stop. Moments later, the rest of their group poured out. She felt Brandi's alertness and Heidi's mistrust without even turning around. Gareth appeared to stand on the other side of Reed.

It mildly surprised her when Travis walked by everyone and went directly to Hanuk. Ariel watched Hanuk nod, his mouth twisting into a snarl.

"Yet another wanderer finally returns to the pack," Hanuk said, his tone ironic.

Travis nodded in reply. "Yes. I am home... and I'm willing to keep my part of our agreement."

"What agreement is between you?" Reed asked, surprised to see the cousins conversing so intimately.

Ariel's stomach fell as she watched Travis smile. It never reached his eyes.

"Hanuk and I have been sharing the role of Black Wolf Alpha the whole time you've been gone, Grandfather. We look similar, and smell similar, which is not surprising considering we share the same unfaithful male for a father. The pack has never questioned the switch. He serves a year and I serve the next. We use his name —and avoid pack females who might betray us."

"For what purpose would you deceive the Black Wolf pack in this way?" Reed asked.

Ariel saw Travis step closer to Hanuk who glared at Reed. A fight seemed imminent.

"For the same reason you and our parents kept your deceit from everyone. We like having control, so listen well, *Old Man*. If you challenge us for the alpha position, you'll be challenging both of us and the alliances we have made among the pack's people. Your ancient ways have no place here now. But if you have come to try—we will gladly let you have your death."

Ariel lifted an eyebrow when Reed seemed to grow several inches taller. He glared at his second generation offspring. The original was a bigger man than either of the clones. There was no doubt about it and she had no doubt he could best them. But it had to be eating at Reed to see his grandsons aligned against him. He had been so sure Travis was a good man.

"I want to talk to your parents. I'm sorry, Travis. But I do not believe your story about your parentage."

Travis shrugged. "Your belief makes no difference to what is the truth. It's not our fault if you were never told."

Hanuk smiled. "Go in peace and visit who you want. It will change nothing. You can stay three days and then I want you all gone unless you intend to challenge me. Otherwise... I will have you removed."

Ariel winced as Reed turned without replying. He told all them to get back into the vehicles.

Before Ariel climbed into the truck, Brandi stepped up beside her and leaned in to whisper. "Now that I've seen them both, I'm pretty sure it was Travis who shot Reed, not Hanuk. But I don't know why he would do it. He seemed to like his grandfather."

Ariel searched each man's nearly identical face. What were they getting from their ruse? Were they getting money from the pack? Or just power?

Her instincts held her on an edge of hyper alertness while her wolf paced back and forth, restless and worried about what was going on.

1 4

THEY WERE INSTALLED FOR THE NIGHT IN A SERIES OF SCARCELY furnished cabins near the edge of the village. She and Reed ended up taking the one with two beds, giving the ones with single beds to the couples.

When Reed disappeared to visit his children, Ariel went out to walk. She ended up by a stream cascading energetically over a lot of big rocks. It reminded her of a white water rafting trip she'd taken once in Colorado. That had been before she married.

Putting everything into her studies, she'd never had time for making genuine friends. When she'd gone on the white water rafting trip, it was with all strangers. After they'd fished her out of the river three times, they'd been pretty tired of her. Some had verbally expressed their frustration with her incompetence.

Feeling ostracized had been a normal occurrence in her life, which is why she was surprised by her happiness to see Brandi and Heidi walking toward her. If having a pack meant having people in your life who just accepted you without questioning your weirdness, then maybe it wasn't such a bad deal. It might be worth the sense of responsibility she felt and all the concern she had about whether or not the two women coming toward her were happy.

"Hey. I was just heading back to the cabin. Figured you two would be taking care of your personal business, not traipsing out here after me," Ariel joked.

Brandi snorted. "Gareth is fast. Business resolved for us long ago. I left him sleeping it off."

"Same here," Heidi said. "Ryan is nervous. I faked it so he'd go to sleep. I'm too worried to enjoy myself."

"Why? Are you all as worried about Reed as I am?" Ariel asked, looking between them to see both heads nodding.

She sighed when they were in sight of the cabins again and headed to a covered shelter with several picnic tables under it. When she sat, they each took seats across from her. It had been this way since their conversion. On the gurneys, they'd been complete strangers. As werewolves, they were a solid team of three.

For the first time since her conversion, Ariel felt emotion rising in a wave which threatened to bring on a flood of tears. Other than being extremely lonely, she couldn't describe what her life had been like before she knew these women.

"Reed refers to our connection to each other as having a *pack mentality*. While my scientific mind struggles with his explanation, I do feel like I've known you two all my life," Ariel confessed.

Brandi nodded. "You're not the only one who thinks this is weird, Ariel. I have this constant sense of your... I don't know... personality or something reaching out to me all the time. It's almost like you're a family member... I guess... or at least what I've always imagined having a family would be like. I never really had much of a family."

Ariel sighed. "I've never been one of those people who butt into other people's personal business, but I don't seem to be able to stop the urges where the two of you are concerned. Have you given any thought to what you want to do when we get back to Wasilla?"

Heidi tucked her hair behind her ears. "My life before all this was not so great. My parents were killed when I was a junior in college. They left behind mostly debts so I had to drop out of school. Thinking I was going to start over fresh, I followed a guy I met to Anchorage. After he ditched me and took off to the lower forty-nine again, I was suddenly left in Alaska with no car, no money, and no way of making a living. I found a way to get by, but kind of lost track of my self-esteem in the process. It's not like I slept with all the guys I entertained, but I got paid to make them happy any way I could."

Ariel shrugged, but held Heidi's gaze. "Given what Brandi and I have done to survive the shitty part of our lives, I don't think we're going to be throwing any stones. What were you studying in college?"

"Medicine," Heidi said quietly. "I hadn't decided whether or not I wanted to be a doctor, but working with Eva has been great for me. I like helping heal people. If I get to do it for the rest of my life, then I think I'm going to be okay with being a werewolf... or whatever we are."

Ariel smiled. "Science made us, but Reed says we're definitely werewolves. According to him, conversion only works one way. All we can do now is adapt to what we've become. Denial wouldn't keep our wolves from breaking free now and again."

Brandi huffed out a breath. "Well, I'm fine with being a werewolf, even if I decide to go back to my old life, which really would be just to my old job. My parents took off when I was a kid and I was raised by my grandparents. They died within a couple years of each other while I was serving in the military. All I really have in my life is my work. Frankly, being a wolf makes me more kick-ass than I was as a plain human. I admit shifting hurts like hell, but that's the only bad thing."

"I like my wolf too," Ariel admitted. "And I have no reason to go back to my old life either. My father died when I was fifteen. My mother remarried in her late thirties and started a new family while I was in college on scholarships. She never understood why I wanted to study science, much less do lab research. After my two step-sisters were born, I became nothing more to my mother than a reminder of her past. I'm sure she's not grieving over my death. She probably rolled her eyes at the news and resumed her soccer mom life without missing a beat."

"So are you two planning to stay in the Gray Wolf pack when we get back?" Heidi asked.

Brandi shook her head. "No—I want to get to the bottom of who's behind Feldspar and turn them in to be investigated. We don't want more of us getting made. Not that I plan to reveal what I am to anyone by going back to my job. Who would believe me? I'd end up in a rubber room talking to myself. But I think I'm going to need to see you guys… now and again… to fill the hole in my gut. I don't think I could be at peace if I didn't. Whether I get it or not, I think we do have some sort of real connection."

Ariel nodded. "I'll be honest. I don't know what I want to do. My wolf is not going to let me go back to my old life. She needs… hell I don't know how to say this… more important work I suppose. God only knows what I'm going to end up doing. Maybe I'll have to go into Brandi's line of work so I can do something productive with all these violent urges I have now."

Brandi snorted and then laughed. "You might not want to do that, Ariel. I'm not productive—I'm destructive—and life sucks regularly. The whole naked and trapped on a gurney thing had happened way more often to me than you ever want to know about."

Ariel laughed. "I still admire your destructive urges in ways I can't admit in front of our sweet little healer here."

Brandi snickered over Heidi's glare. "Want to go off into the Alaskan wilderness and start our own village like Reed's family did?"

Ariel laughed aloud. "No… and hell no. I don't even want to be in Alaska, but I also don't want to leave. I can't figure out the source of my conflict. I hate the cold. And I swear I'm going to learn to shift with all my clothes on if it kills me."

They all laughed, but Ariel noticed Brandi and Heidi exchanging secretive glances. "What? Why are you two looking so guilty?"

Brandi grinned. "Well, I know you're the *alpha* among the three of us—I mean your wolf is freaking huge—but oh bloody hell, I can already shift and keep my clothes on."

"Bullshit," Ariel exclaimed. She glared at Heidi. "Let me guess —your smile means you can do it too?"

At Heidi's nod, Ariel's swore even more viciously. Her language was definitely more colorful since her conversion. Her wolf's raw emotions seemed to need a deeper verbal expression than her logical scientific decisions ever did. Politeness and formal language didn't do anything to ease the frustration at all.

"You're worrying too much about keeping them on," Brandi declared, feeling the need to be helpful. "Don't over-think it, Ariel. Just decide to do it and it will happen."

"Exactly," Heidi agreed.

Ariel laughed at their encouragement and their bobbing nods. "Well, so far all I've managed to keep on when I shift are my stupid boots."

She wanted to be offended when they laughed uncontrollably at the image, but she couldn't. Even she thought it was funny. After Reed and Matt's laughing at her many failed attempts, she was nearly immune to ridicule.

"Do you think Reed's son really did father both Travis and Hanuk?" Heidi asked.

Ariel thought about it and nodded. "Yes. I think they were telling us the truth. It kind of also explains why they look so much like Reed. The gene pool was one stream after all."

Brandi nodded. "I saw part of this situation in a vision. But Reed's mate... I'll never be able to tell him, but I don't think she wandered off. I think she was left in the cold to die by one or both of his grandsons."

Ariel drew in a breath and let it out slowly. "Reed was obviously wrong about Travis being good. I see him still dealing with that disappointment. If he has to challenge his own grandsons for the alpha role, I don't know how he'll hold up mentally. It's not the physical fight that will take him down. It will be knowing he's fighting his grandchildren. Look how he's been with us. He has invested three hundred years here as the Black Wolf Alpha. His level of caring about these people exceeds what I can even imagine someone feeling."

Their heads turned toward the cabins when Gareth stuck his head out. Ariel kept her smile hidden as Brandi sighed in frustration and stood, but she couldn't resist teasing the fierce woman. "Guess it's past your bedtime, Brandi."

Rising to head back as well, Ariel winked at a grinning Heidi as Brandi swore and stomped off toward the cabin door Gareth held open as he waited for her.

Ariel woke to Reed lying on the bed next to hers, staring at the ceiling. It was obvious he hadn't been asleep yet. Still wearing most of yesterday's clothes, she quietly got up, went to the bathroom, and returned to crawl under her covers again. It was cold in the cabin even if Reed seemed impervious to it.

"Good morning," she said, trying for conversation.

"Good morning," Reed replied, turning his head. "My son admitted to being the father of both boys, but it was not unfaithfulness in the truest sense. His older brother, a child I had with my second mate, was unable to give his mate a child. They asked for his help to keep his inability a secret within the family rather than just remaining barren. My son broke down and told his mother the day before she walked off and froze to death. Guilt kept him from confessing the same thing to me. Somehow both Travis and Hanuk found out and decided to punish everyone involved for their embarrassing parentage. When I left, they used my grief to gain control of the pack. They emotionally blackmailed their parents into maintaining their silence. I think exercising power over so many people gave them back some of the personal dignity they thought our family took away. Rather than punish just their mutual father though, they punished the pack with a heavy-handed form of justice. And apparently both of them rule the same."

Ariel waited for the silence to stretch out before answering. "What are you planning to do, Reed?" She watched him shrug his shoulders without changing positions.

"I'm not sure yet. If I challenge for the alpha position, they have already said they will band together to stop me from ever ruling again. If I don't challenge though, I leave my pack at the mercy of two vindictive children who rule with cruelty. I am glad my mate is not alive to see this happening and it is the first time I've been glad she is gone. My heart hurts from those thoughts."

"I can tell and I'm sorry you're hurting," Ariel said, watching him nod. "Why don't you sleep for a little bit? I'll check on everyone and make sure they're doing okay. We'll get together to talk about it later."

"Rest seems like an unworthy escape," Reed stated, rolling to his side.

"It's not an escape, it's a respite. Sometimes a little sleep changes how you see things," Ariel said softly.

When Reed didn't answer, Ariel crawled out of the bed and gathered the rest of her clothing. Slipping into the bathroom again, she dressed for the day and went to find everyone else.

"Gareth, what do you think?" Ariel demanded.

Not really wanting to get involved in another pack's political drama, Gareth shook his head. "What I think doesn't matter. This is a problem for the Black Wolf pack to solve. I have no say here."

Brandi smacked him on the arm. "Then how would the same politics work in the Gray Wolf pack? What would happen if Matt got challenged?"

"His challenger would die," Gareth said flatly.

Ariel snorted. "Or Matt would." Gareth's glare made her smile at the man's loyalty. Matt was lucky to have the loyal man as his second.

"Matt has defeated twenty challengers over the years. Only two of them were spared their lives. The others died in the fight. It was their choice," Gareth declared.

Ariel's gaze went to Ryan who was quietly shaking his head before moving back to Gareth. "Do the challenges have to result in participants dying?"

"Not always, but usually," Gareth admitted.

"Okay then," Ariel said sharply. "I guess I need to get my personal effects in order. You might as well know this, I'm going to challenge Reed's grandsons for the Black Wolf pack. If I win, I'll turn it over to Reed. If I lose, I'm going to take one or both of them out with me to clear the way for him. One of them shot his grandfather and is the reason I'm a werewolf just as much as Crane was. But my fight is not about revenge... it's about stopping them from hurting other people. Reed has heard story after story of how cruelly they've been running things here."

Gareth frowned. "What about Matt? You promised to return to him."

Ariel sighed and glared. "And I intend to keep that promise if I can. Matt is a friend—maybe even more than a friend—but this situation is bigger. I'm an alpha and part of the Black Wolf pack. My first loyalty is to Reed, then to Brandi and Heidi. Matt is coming in third. He admitted a male alpha doesn't want to share his female with others for any reason. I'm not the greatest choice for him."

"Perhaps... but he is more bound to you than he has shared," Gareth said softly, feeling disloyal, but also feeling the need to defend his missing friend.

Ariel shook her head. "Matt has no more hold on me than you have on Brandi, or Ryan has on Heidi. That may change in the future for the four of you, but Matt already knows how I feel. I appreciate him. I value him. But we're talking about a whole village of people who spent three hundred years under Reed's care. If I was Matt, we wouldn't be having this conversation. He would do what he thought was right. And that's what I have to do."

Gareth held up a hand. "Okay. I can admit that if you were Matt, I wouldn't question your decisions. Alpha and female are not two words I have ever had to use together."

Ariel snorted. "Well, I don't know what being alpha and female means yet either. But I can't let Reed languish between a rock and political hard spot when I have the power to possibly resolve this for him. Besides—I've been wanting another real fight since I killed Crane. This is the perfect opportunity for me to get it out of my system."

"Can we help her fight?" Brandi asked, looking at Gareth.

Gareth sighed and nodded, not wanting to see Brandi fighting, but he knew he had no choice. He would never let Matt stand alone. Brandi would never let Ariel face a challenge without her. It was just how betas operated.

"Ariel can pick two others to stand with her. My guess is only one of the grandsons will actually fight. His beta will stand with him. The third only fights if necessary. Challenges are very public and very brutal. I don't think you know what you're getting into, Ariel. And as the Gray Wolf beta, I won't be able to help you. To do so would violate the peace agreement between our packs."

"You're right. We don't know what we're getting into," Brandi agreed. "But I agree with Ariel—it makes sense for us to help Reed save face with his people. Heidi can patch us up afterwards."

Heidi sighed heavily and shook her head. "I think you all should be careful. I don't know if I have another miracle in me."

"It's okay," Ariel declared. "My wolf and I don't intend to lose."

15

By the time Reed woke up, Ariel had issued her challenge. The fight was planned for the next day. Telling Reed what she'd done hadn't gone well though. Not even bothering to lecture her about why she shouldn't have acted for him, he'd stormed off in a huff many hours ago.

Now she was alone and staring at the ceiling while she lay on her small bed wondering how much her life would change again tomorrow. Maybe she should have been worried about fighting the two males who seemed willing to do anything to hurt Reed. But she just couldn't drum up the necessary anxiety.

In her mind, she could see herself winning. And she could see her wolf enjoying the conflict.

When darkness fell over the room, she finally slipped into a restless sleep. Several hours later she woke to find a giant wolf straddling her body, growling softly at her. Unafraid of the beast, she reached up and ran a hand over his nose.

"So who ratted me out?"

Instead of shifting to answer her in human form, Matt just stretched out on her as his wolf. The whole werewolf species might be 'canis lupis' like Reed said, but from all that she had seen, wolves acted like big stubborn dogs most of the time. His actions in squashing her made her laugh. Instead of moving, he put his nose on his paws and stared into her gaze, his nose between her breasts.

"Did Gareth tell you what I did?"

Her answer was more staring without a sound. Ariel giggled at his solemn gaze glowing in the dark.

"Was it Brandi or Heidi? No, I doubt they would have said anything. Their loyalty is to me—not to you."

She watched his eyes shift from side to side in consternation. Matt looked irritated with her guesses, but he still said nothing.

"Somehow I don't see Ryan telling you. All he cares about is keeping Heidi safe. He only acknowledges me when Heidi makes him. While I find that offensive, I'm still very glad you sent him with her. He's cut my worry in half."

The wolf's eyes closed as he huffed out a breath. Sighing, Ariel ran a hand over his head. How could she reason with his wolf if the human side of him was angry too?

"I know you could take my hand off with a single snap of those sharp teeth of yours, so don't bother with the lectures about how much tougher than me you are. The way I see it, we have an unspoken agreement. I don't go all alpha angry on you, just like you don't go all alpha angry on me. That doesn't mean I can't take care of myself when I have to. Now tell me who called you. Was it Reed?"

A small whine had her sighing.

"Okay—damn it. I knew I made him mad. Look Matt, I have to do this. Reed can't risk his family's honor, not if he ends up the ruling alpha again, which I see happening."

A long tongue came out and licked across her chin. She couldn't stop another giggle from escaping. "The tongue thing would be so much more fun if you would just shift to human."

Two seconds later, a naked Matt was wrapped around her. She hugged him tight.

"I'm still mad about the mark, but it wasn't why I did this. Both Travis and Hanuk are bad guys. Reed can't challenge them because they're blackmailing the whole family about a secret. It's a complicated and completely fucked up situation. I think it's even worse than Crane capturing us all for his experiments."

"I know. Reed told me. But I snuck in here to tell you something while you were awake and could hear me for once. I fell in love with you the first time I saw you. I climbed up on my stupid desk and dove into you without a single thought of self-preservation. Every time we've been together—every time—it's just gotten better. It took me seventy-five years of my life to find a female I liked. Maybe I shouldn't have marked you the other night, but I went a little crazy when I almost lost you. I haven't wanted to claim a female before, so I'm probably not doing a very good job of making you want to be my mate."

Ariel held his face in her hands. "There must have been an apology in that pretty speech somewhere. I guess I can forgive you for marking me."

"Did you hear what I said, Ariel Jones? *I want you to be my mate*," Matt declared, boldly stating it again. "I know you haven't been a werewolf long, but finding your perfect mate can happen really fast between the right couple. No one really knows what triggers the sort of connection that just instinctively clicks in all areas."

"Matt—I like you too—but I don't know if I'm ready for another serious relationship yet."

Matt put his forehead against Ariel's. How could he explain it in a way she could really hear what he was saying?

"I was already feeling possessive of you. Then I saw you lying on the ground and thought you had died. I lost my mind. I was ready to kill everyone who had anything to do with harming you. If you don't win your fight tomorrow, I'm going to be at war with the Black Wolf pack. I won't be able to stop myself from avenging your death. Reed called me to come to you even though he knew damn well that's how it would be. He wants us to have a chance, Ariel. I want us to have a chance too. Don't you?"

"Yes. So I guess I better win tomorrow," Ariel said firmly, swallowing the lump in her throat. "If you have to avenge my death, just take out Travis and Hanuk, and maybe their betas. Promise me you'll just kill the bad people, Matt. Leave the others. They're just regular people like the ones in your pack."

Matt snorted over her plea. Her logic drove him crazy, but it also made him love her more. "Okay. I promise to only kill the bad people. How will I know which ones are bad?"

"I'll point them out to Gareth and Ryan before I die. They can tell you," Ariel joked.

Terrified by her teasing, Matt buried his face in her neck, kissing the mark on her collarbone. He regretted making her angry, but did not regret making her his in even so small a way. "I can't stay the whole night. It would look very bad if I were caught here with you."

Ariel laughed. "I know. Gareth already gave me the lecture. How good are you at quickies?"

In answer, Matt lifted his weight and rolled her over under him. He slipped the leggings she was wearing down to her knees. He lifted her hips and spread her thighs until she was open for him. His hands slipped inside the front of her undershirt to cup bare breasts in his palms. His aching erection stroked between her legs, torturing them both as he lovingly massaged.

"I don't know if I like this position, Matt. It seems impersonal not to look in your face while we do this," she whispered.

Chuckling, Matt pulled her hips back against his crotch and ran one hand around to her front until he could slip two fingers inside her. Arching over the back of her, his mouth ran up and down her neck, stopping to nip and suck as he aroused her with his probing fingers. Her moaning and rhythmically rocking back against him made him laugh.

"When I make you mine forever, I'm going to bury myself so

deep in you that your womb is going to call out for our children to be conceived. Then I'm going to sink my sharpest teeth into your shoulder just as deeply. Our shared climax is going to make us mates—real mates—the kind who stay with each other no matter what happens. So if your destiny is to be the Black Wolf alpha for a while, Dr. Jones, you better enjoy that time of power before you come back to me. I'm not going to be able to let you go so far away again."

Ariel trembled at his words and at his actions. Matt held her on the edge of her climax—and she knew he was purposely doing it.

"Matthew, you suck at quickies," she accused, not returning his romantic words at all. What could she say to answer his pledges of lifelong devotion? Nothing. She could say nothing until tomorrow was over and she'd had time to figure out what she wanted to do with the rest of her strange new existence.

Matt clamped a hand hard on one breast as he used the other to guide his erection to her opening. Plunging hard inside her in a single thrust, Ariel's legs shook with the speed of his entry.

"Now you're making me be rough with you to prove my point. I wanted to be loving... gentle... supportive. I'm trying not to show you my true alpha side yet. It would only scare you to know how demanding I will be once we are mated."

"Okay. We'll talk about it later. But right now, can we do this a little harder and faster?"

Ariel flinched in surprise when Matt pinched a butt cheek in retaliation for her request. Then she laughed as Matt held her hips and thrust like he was trying to break her. His swearing about how good she felt made her feel sexy... and wanted... and nearly invincible.

"Better?" he asked roughly.

Groaning, Ariel lowered her chest to the bed to make the angle even better for him to go deeper. Matt's increased swearing echoed in the room as he throbbed and bent further over her back. Finally, he grabbed a handful of her hair and twisted her face to his until he could clamp his mouth over hers. His plunging tongue drove her over the edge she was riding as much as his persistent thrusting. She quivered around him as he finished himself. Matt always slowed his movements as he neared his own peak. He always tried to draw out every second of being in her, obviously not wanting their lovemaking to be over. For the first time, Ariel found herself wondering if it really could always be so good between them.

When her mouth was free, she sniffled back tears from her emotional epiphany and bared her soul to him instead. "Okay. I admit it. I'm probably falling in love with you too, but damn it, this is some seriously shitty timing for me, Matt. Can we talk about this when I get back to Wasilla?"

Hearing her sweet admission of loving him at last, Matt yanked Ariel upright by her hair and twisted her face to his again. He stared into her teary gaze, still pleasantly firm inside her heat despite his climax. *His. She really was his.* He wanted to yell at her for waiting so long to tell him. His teeth sharpened. He knew his sharp canines were visible to her when he smiled.

"Too bad about the timing of our demanding relationship, Dr. Jones. No apology will be given for it. Instead, I intend to do all I can to keep you in my bed and my life. It's all I can do not to finish this today. Be grateful I have learned some patience over the years."

Even with tears running down her face over his declarations, Ariel laughed. Matt wrapped her so tightly in his arms, she had to wiggle just to be able to breathe.

"You call this being patient? I saw you flashing your wolf teeth."

"My wolf wants the same thing I do. Win your fight, give the pack back to Reed, and then come the hell home to us," he ordered roughly.

Unable to restrain his wolf completely, he nipped Ariel's shoulder because he couldn't resist. Her flinch as she tried to pull away made him instantly regretful. "I'm sorry. Truly. It's just that I'm worried for you. I don't want to leave you here alone, but I can't stay without causing more trouble than you can handle. My frustration has no outlet."

Ariel nodded as she sighed. He'd never believe that she was less concerned about the fight with Travis and Hanuk than what kind of mark he had left on her this time. Apparently, she was a vain werewolf. She didn't want to be sporting a brand like she was a cow or a sheep he owned.

"I'm a lot less worried about tomorrow than you are. Being with you makes me stronger because I always think better afterward. So I'm really glad you came to see me. I'll get Gareth to call you with an update as soon as it's all over."

Slipping reluctantly out of her at last, Matt crawled around her body on the tiny bed until he could pull her into his arms. "I understand your decision to fight—I do. I know you can't help being an alpha and following the urges it brings. Though I frequently wish like hell you weren't one, I will learn to support you in dealing with it. I wish now I'd been more focused on teaching you how to fight better, instead of getting you into bed as often as I could."

Ariel was drowsy as she lifted a hand to his face. "My wolf loves to fight. Without your uber alpha presence, she'd have me attacking people all the time. Thank you for being there to advise me about my urges… and for everything else you've done. You've been better to me than any man I've ever known."

Knowing Ariel was only moments away from sleep dragging her under, Matt rocked and held her, holding them both on their knees, repeating how much he loved her over and over.

When Ariel's full weight sagged against him, he gently redressed her before tucking the bed covers around her body to keep her warm while she slept. Never in his life had he wanted to stay with a female so badly. Caring for the unconscious, sleeping

Ariel was just as humbling now as it had been the first time he'd felt that sort of protective urge for her.

But it wasn't safe for him to stay. If his presence was discovered in the Black Wolf pack, it wouldn't help her or Reed. He placed a final kiss on her cheek, happy at least to leave her smelling of his love and lust. He hoped it would comfort her as much as it did him.

"Fight well tomorrow, Alpha Ariel. I will be waiting anxiously for your return."

Shifting back to his wolf, Matt reluctantly left to make the long, lonely run home alone.

16

THE CROWD AROUND THE LARGE PAINTED CIRCLE DIDN'T FAZE ARIEL. Her arrogant wolf preened under the focused attention while her human eyes searched the crowd to determine their mood. It looked like most of the townspeople had come to watch, but every face was frozen in a frown as they stared at her.

Followed closely by a vibrating Brandi, Ariel stepped into the circle where Travis, Hanuk, and another male she didn't recognize already waited.

"Where is your third, Ariel Jones?" Travis asked.

Ariel met his gaze steadily as she answered. "I don't have one, Travis. I can't risk Heidi. She's a healer. Skills like hers have to be protected."

"I am Ariel's third," Reed declared, stepping into the circle.

Ariel's gaze swung to Reed. Given the shocked whispers running through the crowd, she wasn't alone in her surprise. "I can handle it. You don't have to do this."

"Child, there was never any choice in the matter, but I thank you for trying to spare me."

When Hanuk laughed at their personal exchange, Ariel's

irritated gaze returned to him. "Do you have any redeeming qualities at all?"

"Yes. I can kill without a single bit of remorse. I learned it from my grandfather," Hanuk stated flatly. "It makes me a strong, worthy leader."

"Or just a mean asshole," Ariel added quietly, speaking low enough that only he could hear.

"The female alpha is mine to fight. No one touches her but me," Hanuk declared.

Brandi turned to Reed. "I can't prove what I'm about to tell you, but I'm pretty sure Travis was the one who shot you and left you on Feldspar's doorstep. Maybe that makes things a little easier for you, Reed."

"Since today I will finish what I failed to do before, I see no reason to deny it was me," Travis offered.

Reed looked at Travis. If he hadn't heard the boy say it, there would have always been doubt in his mind. "But why would you betray me, Travis? You were my choice for alpha. I offered to help you challenge Hanuk."

Travis snorted in reply. "Why would I challenge the only real family member I have? When I was most ashamed, it was my brother Hanuk who lured my talkative grandmother out into the cold to stop the spread of the information. It was my job to make sure you never returned to challenge what we were doing. Hanuk has things running the way they're supposed to in the pack. Giving you to the humans seemed an easy way to keep the blood of your death off my hands. They were carving up wolves and tossing them out in the trash nearly every day. Only they never tossed yours out. I never bothered to find out what they were really doing. How was I to know they were creating fake werewolves like them?"

Ariel stared at Travis, who was pointing at her and Brandi. She didn't know whether to be relieved he and Hanuk weren't in league with Feldspar, or appalled to know his grandsons were seriously trying to kill Reed just to keep a secret no one probably would have cared about.

"Enough talking. Let's get this farce over with. I have three other pack members to punish today," Hanuk declared.

Ariel turned back and glared. "Your punishing days are over, Hanuk."

Before her eyes Hanuk morphed from a grinning man into a large snarling black wolf. A slow smile spread from her mouth to her eyes as she calculated his size. "Well, I guess that explains why you feel the need to make people fear you, Hanuk. Can you say —*compensating*? Glad I got my genes from the giant wolf side of Reed's gene pool. Hold on a second. You're going to love this."

She let her form dissolve until she glared back at him from all fours. When he leaped at her, she leapt too, instinctively grabbing him by the scruff of his neck. Without stopping to think about the reaction, she literally slung Hanuk out of the fight circle. The crowd parted to let him land at their feet, but no one offered any encouragement to him.

Her edge in their battle didn't last long though because Hanuk jumped up immediately, insanely angry about what she'd done. Teeth snapping and eyes flashing, he charged back to where she calmly stood her ground. She let him come at her full force, her wolf quivering in anticipation of their clash. She waited until he leapt again before rising to her full height on her hind legs. Using her greater size and weight, she met his flying body with a hard push from her paws. Hanuk went flying backwards, landing and rolling several feet away. Before he could rise, she pounced on his back and locked her jaws around the back of his neck. One hard bite and he went still. But as much as she intended to keep biting until she had killed him completely, Ariel found that just couldn't do it.

Lifting her confused gaze to the others, she saw Brandi in human form standing over the beta's still human body. Arms crossed, Brandi stood watching Reed and Travis, two of the largest wolves she'd ever seen, circling and snarling. If there was ever a match that could turn out to be a draw, it was that one. But maybe not if she gave Reed a psychological edge.

Dragging the unconscious Hanuk over with her, she dropped him near where Reed and Travis were sparring. She sat down beside Hanuk's body and offered up a triumphant howl that split the air. People outside the circle grabbed their ears. Suddenly, she felt Brandi sitting next to her, also in wolf form. Her second howl had a sharper accompaniment which made the air tremble. Between the two of them, their combined howls sent all onlookers to the ground in pain.

Travis stopped circling Reed, backed up, and looked around in stunned surprise at all the kneeling people. Reed looked at Hanuk's still body and immediately morphed back into his human form. She and Brandi trotted over and took their place on either side of him. Travis whined in rebellion at their unity, barked several times, and then whined some more.

Then surprising them all, he turned and fled the circle, barking loudly to split the crowd as he ran.

Ariel stood, intending to chase him down, but Reed restrained her. "No. Let him go. He's not evil. He's just hurt and confused."

Then they realized the three of them were alone in the circle—well them and the two males who had lost the fight. Brandi swiftly changed back again to a human. Ariel huffed in frustration at Brandi's fully dressed body and leaned against Reed's leg to brood about it. She was not going to shift and embarrass herself. Reed was still staring where Travis had exited and not smiling, but his hand came out to rest lightly on her head in understanding.

Ariel turned and looked around in amazement. All the Black Wolf pack members were still on the ground, with their gazes lifted cautiously to her. Ariel whined in gratitude when Heidi walked into the circle with a small blanket, shaking it out to drape it around her wolf form. Ariel shifted and stood tall, wrapping the blanket around the middle of herself. At least it covered the important parts.

"The beta is dead. Check Hanuk. He was still alive when I dropped him," she ordered.

Heidi looked worried about the request, but took a tentative step toward the motionless black wolf. Ariel heard Brandi snort before she headed in the same direction. "I'll check him," she declared.

She turned and looked at Reed. "So what happens now?"

"You tell me," Reed ordered, cupping her jaw in his hand. "You defeated the resident alpha, Dr. Jones. Under pack law that puts you in charge."

Ariel shook her head. "Not a good idea. I took Hanuk down, but I didn't kill him. Regardless of what a bastard he was, I couldn't bring myself to kill someone who looked, smelled, and felt so much like you. Would you have killed Travis if he hadn't escaped?"

Reed nodded, his mouth tight. "Yes. I was willing to kill them before I stepped into the circle."

Ariel sighed. "I told myself I was too, but it didn't work like that for me. Killing Crane was easy. Killing Hanuk was not. I don't think I'm ready to kill twenty challengers to the alpha position over the years like Gareth said Matt has had to do. I can't even imagine what kind of challengers you've had to handle."

Her heart lifted when a ghost of a smile lifted the corners of Reed's mouth.

"Let's just say it was a few more than twenty. And yes, many of them were family members of one sort or another —unfortunately."

Ariel nodded. "So how do I make you alpha instead of me."

"Show your deference to me," Reed ordered, sighing in resignation.

"You don't sound too pleased. Don't you want to be alpha again?" Ariel asked. She frowned as she watched Reed shrug.

"Not really, but I don't want the pack to be under the control of another tyrant either. Unless you decide to stay, it might truly be time to look for an alpha outside of my immediate family—preferably one who might let me go off and live in peace."

Ariel looked at Brandi, who stood and shook her head. Hanuk was gone. She had killed him after all. Her sigh was long. She hadn't even taken their fight very seriously. Even now her wolf scoffed. It was the human side of her that rebelled against what had happened.

"I can't be the alpha, Reed. I can't do this—at least not right now. I'm sorry to dump this on you."

"It's okay. I expected this to happen. Kneel to me and lower your gaze until I tell you to rise again," Reed ordered softly, stroking her cheek with his hand again.

Nodding, Ariel knelt and bowed her head, keeping her eyes on Reed's shoes. She heard the whispering crowd muttering in shock. Moments later, Brandi and Heidi appeared next to her. They knelt and mirrored her actions without asking a single thing.

Reed lifted his head and looked around. "Any other challengers want to take us on?" he yelled.

From the corner of her eye, Ariel watched the circle of people shake their heads and lower their gazes to Reed.

"I declare myself alpha of the Black Wolf pack once again. I will choose a second later. These women are my family, and until their death, will be under the protection of this pack. The female alpha, Ariel Jones, retains the permanent right to challenge for the role of Black Wolf Alpha any time she is willing to come back and serve."

Reed watched until the pack members stood and nodded to him before slinking away. The majority of faces were filled with relief. He filed away the faces that had not been. He had no doubt Hanuk and Travis had been paying for the loyalty of those who carried out their so-called punishments. Persuading them to forget their old part-time work was not a job he relished taking on, but it had to be done.

When the rest of the pack had disbursed, he reached out a hand to Ariel. "Okay. You three can stand up now. It's all over. I'm the Black Wolf Alpha again."

Ariel kept a hand gripped tightly on her meager covering as Reed hauled her to her feet. Brandi and Heidi looked around. Both sighed in relief when Gareth and Ryan finally walked into the circle to hug them.

Ariel sighed too. "I have just one more question. How am I supposed to figure out where my clothes went out here?"

Reed chuckled. He was going to miss her. "You might find them back in the cabin. It was the last place you dressed."

She looked down at her naked feet. "Shit. I didn't even keep my shoes this time. This naked shifting thing is so not fair. I'm an alpha. Why can't I do this?"

Everyone exited the circle, laughing at her complaints.

Brandi eventually left Gareth's side and dropped back to walk with her as they hiked back to the cabins. "How did you get that bite mark on your shoulder? From where I stood, it looked like Hanuk didn't even get to touch you—not once. Your wolf was nearly twice the size of his, by the way. I loved it when you just stood on your hind legs and knocked him the hell out of the air."

Ariel reached a hand over her shoulder, trying to feel where the mark was. "Damn it, Matt."

Brandi laughed as she reached out and touched the spot with her finger. "It's here and shaped like teeth. Man, Matt just loves to mark you, doesn't he?"

Ariel growled in frustration. Matt was possessive, jealous, and wanted the kind of relationship she'd vowed never to have again. He was also supportive, caring, and the most generous, loving man in bed she'd ever known.

What was she going to do? She could one day be the Black Wolf Alpha—if she didn't end up the Gray Wolf Alpha's mate. That had bad pack politics written all over it.

She was probably going to be hearing from Matt soon and still didn't know what she wanted. No doubt Gareth would make a full report of the fight results before the day was over. If Reed didn't do it first.

"When I think about my life two weeks ago compared to today, it makes my head feel like exploding. Two weeks ago I was doing boring lab research and today I won a werewolf fight to the death. Why aren't you more freaked out about this shit?" Ariel asked.

Brandi shrugged. "Two weeks ago I was freezing my ass off in the Alaskan wilderness and watching Travis shoot Reed. The month before that I was sweltering in southern Florida helping take down a cocaine factory in one of the Keys. Frankly, getting turned into a kick-ass werewolf isn't even near the top of my bad-shit-o-meter scale."

"You're telling me it's all relative, aren't you?" Ariel accused.

"No. Why would I do that? I don't even know what the hell that statement means," Brandi teased.

Ariel snorted and then sighed. "It means my biggest problem is that Matthew Gray Wolf wants me to make a commitment to him —and his pack—and I'm not sure I'm ready to make it."

Brandi snorted in reply. "I hear Ryan's pressuring Heidi for a commitment too. I'm starting to think I drew the lucky straw with Gareth. He's being really decent and hasn't said one word about any sort of long-term arrangement."

"How can I even consider staying with him? Matt's insistence on making our relationship permanent has blown away every theory I had about the callousness of men. Do you think it's just werewolf males who take sex so seriously? I figured our female emotions would be a problem, not the guys wanting to mate us. That's why I gave you both the warning about not getting attached. I didn't want either of you to end up with a broken heart."

"I don't think I have a heart left to break, but thanks for looking out for me anyway," Brandi joked, punching her new friend lightly on the arm. She was pleased when Ariel laughed softly.

"Fine hard-ass. What about Heidi?" Ariel asked.

"Heidi's got a lot of experience and Ryan hasn't said anything yet. She's walking on eggshells right now. What about you?" Brandi asked back, lifting both eyebrows. "What are you going to do? You're the one the alpha wants and I hear Matt's pretty used to getting his way. I don't think he's going to be as easy to intimidate as Reed's grandsons."

"I know," Ariel said quietly. "I know."

SHE HAD SENT BRANDI AND HEIDI BACK TO WASILLA WITH THE GUYS, but chose to stay a while longer with Reed. She met the rest of his family during that time, which by her rough estimate made up at least an eighth of the total Black Wolf pack population. It was also quite startling to see his appearance closely replicated in many of his children and grandchildren. Reed said his family had always been large, but stipulated that they were very careful in making sure the pack took in new members, and therefore new DNA, whenever possible.

Travis and Hanuk ended up being just two of Reed's many male grandchildren. Amazingly, with them out of the pack picture, Reed's family accepted her as kin without even so much as a strange look. They made her feel welcome despite the fact her blondeness stood out starkly among those with native Alaskan blood running through their veins. It surprised her how little Travis and Hanuk's parents had grieved their sons' betrayals, but then she was reminded about how cruelly those men had treated their fellow pack members. It didn't take long to figure out Reed's family had disowned them long before she and Reed had shown up to challenge the toxic situation.

She roamed the village, mostly on foot, but several times in wolf form. Heads bowed when she passed no matter how she appeared. It was strange to receive such unquestioned respect, but her wolf puffed up under the attention, growling in satisfaction.

Reed stayed close when he could and she appreciated his support. Despite his reservations of being the Black Wolf Alpha again, it was obvious a feeling of calm and ease had descended over the pack. She watched Reed easing back into the role of elder, judge, and teacher. People regularly commented on his renewed vigor, and his more youthful appearance, but thankfully no one probed for reasons.

She had been there almost an extra week now. Matt was probably growling and pacing because she hadn't returned to him yet. She imagined him complaining to Gareth and the idea made her smile. It was the strangest thing to feel so close to a man in so short a time. After divorcing her ex, she hadn't even wanted to date. Now she wanted to go back and be with Matt, but at the same time, she feared what he would ask of her.

"Do you think my burning time is over, Reed? I haven't been desperate for sex in over a week."

Reed smiled at her honesty and her lack of embarrassment in talking to him. "Are you trying to find a logical explanation for why you want to go back to Matt? Or just looking for an excuse to return that takes the choice out of your hands?"

Ariel laughed. "Okay. I'm busted. My inner geek scientist says my intense longing for him is too strong for the short time I've known him. I want to go back, but I think my human side is restraining me."

"Well, I don't know if it helps your rationalization process any, but instead of human menses, you will come into mating heat every three months for the rest of your life. Being in heat is a lot like the burning time, only less easy to satisfy. It's part of the natural propagation cycle for werewolves and meant to lure a couple into making children. If you want to stay that long here in the pack, we can probably find you a male or two willing to help out when you get desperate. Females tend to abstain because even wolves have to take precautions to not accidentally conceive with someone other than their mates."

She heard Reed laughing at her heavy sighing. "Matt wants me to be his mate. He told me flat out when he snuck here to see me."

"Yes. I know he does. But what do you want?" Reed asked.

Ariel shrugged and sighed again. "A long relationship leash, no bite marks, and all the time I need to figure this out so I can make some clear decisions."

"I know you enjoy his company. What are your concerns? Are you afraid of Matt?"

She started to laugh at the question, but saw Reed was serious. Was she afraid of Matt? She could feel her wolf shaking her head.

"No. I'm not afraid of Matt. I'm afraid of myself. What if I can't be the perfect female he expects me to be? What if I need to do something important and he disapproves? I don't like the idea of having to fight him for control of every decision for the rest of my life. Last time I fought a guy for that kind of control, I ended up divorced and in Alaska being turned into a werewolf. I suck at rebelling."

When Reed put out his hand, Ariel snorted and curled her fingers around his.

"Now look at me," he ordered softly, and waited until she did. "At my age, I see into the heart of everyone I meet. Matt is a good man and he will never really control you, not even if you become his mate. He might use pleasure to entice you to stay with him. He might be kind and supportive and generous to influence your willingness to love him. But no matter what he says or does, you will always, always be a rebellious alpha on the inside. If your wolf decides you need to do something, and your human side agrees, Matt will not be able to stop you. You are mentally assigning him a power over you that I promise you he will never, ever have in reality."

"That's not how every werewolf I've met talks about mating. Even you said you forced your mates to accept you," Ariel said.

Reed laughed. "Now I am busted," he admitted.

"And this is why I'm so confused," she complained, looking away.

Reed belly laughed before defending himself. "I do have an explanation for you, Dr. Jones, but you might not like it. None of my mates were alphas. They did not feel threatened by the idea of being controlled the way you do. Most wolves are born to follow instead of lead, so they look for a leader, whether it is for their pack or their intimate relationship. This is not the case with you, Ariel. But you will have to learn this for yourself."

Reed paused until she met his gaze clearly.

"If Matt makes you unhappy in your relationship with him, your wolf will ruthlessly sever your mating bond to save you both. As unfair as it seems to your human ideas about marital commitment, only animals at the top of the food chain get to make those kind of choices. But you will have that choice because you are at the top. Despite your reluctance to lead, you have proven you are worthy—you know this—or at least your wolf does. These doubts you have about mating Matt are because you're adjusting to having a high level of personal power for the first time in your life."

"I want to be with him and yet I'm a little afraid of him. I keep going back and forth and the indecision I feel is maddening. But even though I've been fighting going back to Wasilla, I don't really think I have any choice. I'm only worried because Matt's warned me what's going to happen when I do. Next time I see him, I'll be getting more than a werewolf hickey. I don't know if I'm ready for that next step."

"You need to remember Matt says all that because he has grown up exercising his alpha side whenever it suited him. Your human upbringing trained you to be polite… and accommodating. Show him your wolf and your alpha side with no fear of reprisal.

Let him earn his way into your heart the old fashioned way. Your concern is the very reason two alphas so seldom mate. A constant battle for control can make for a tiring relationship, especially when you begin to raise a family. But I have faith you will use that logical mind of yours to figure out compromises as you two go along."

Ariel snorted. She hoped Reed was right, but more importantly, she wished she could feel it was true. "If it wasn't for Brandi and Heidi, I would just stay here and be your beta."

Reed belly laughed. "Then you and I would argue about everything. I'm too old to do that with you. Go argue with a younger man about life. I want a beta like Gareth, but two hundred year olds don't usually want to serve their pack. Matt got lucky."

Ariel gaped. *"Gareth is two hundred years old?"*

Reed nodded. "Yes. Matt is very fortunate to have someone so wise at his side."

Ariel ran a hand over her face and laughed around it. "I wonder if Brandi knows how old Gareth is."

Reed shrugged. "What does his age matter?"

A grin split her face. "I guess it doesn't if you're a werewolf."

They were quiet for a few minutes and then Reed let go of her hand.

"Stay one more night," he said. "Decisions are best carried out in the full light of day. Also, I need to get my mind wrapped around sending you away from me. I don't want you to go, but that's a selfishness neither of us can indulge in and be happy."

Ariel nodded. "I'll come back and visit often. And I'll bring the others. We'll come so long as we are welcome. You—where you are is home to us now. We talked about that while we were here. Brandi is the only one of us with anything to go back to in her old life, and even for her it's just a job. None of us really had family... until this happened. We're still a bit shocked that now we have each other and you."

"I think that's why you three mean so much to me. On some level I felt our link to each other the moment each of you went through your change," Reed said, rising from his seat. "Come. Let's get's something to eat. There's always someone willing to feed a hungry alpha... or two. I'm in the mood for some ham carved off the bone. Doesn't that sound delicious? It's one of my favorite meals."

Laughing about the possibility that she had inherited Reed's meat preferences, Ariel rose and trailed after him.

18

Somehow lingering to chat after a late breakfast the next morning turned into staying for lunch. By the time she actually started the drive back to Wasilla, it was mid-afternoon. Full of food and missing Reed, it was a very lonely drive alone for all those hours. It was made worse by her thoughts bouncing to Matt and away every ten miles or so.

It took her half of the drive to admit to herself how much she had missed Matt while they'd been apart. And not just for the outstanding sex. Making the long trip back in his truck, she realized what it had cost him in time and effort just to come see her for those few precious hours before the fight. He had pleasured her, bared his feelings, and then tucked her with well wishes before he left. That was more than being a lover—that was being a friend.

Maybe he was possessive and demanding and had many other trying personalities traits that she'd learn about as they got to know each other better. Was his collection of faults any worse than discovering over time that her human husband was petulant and selfish and petty? No man was perfect, but the plus column for Matt was full of good character qualities.

And the sex? Well, the sex between them was for her like having a freezer full of all her favorite ice cream anytime she got a bad craving. Matt typically gave her two or three orgasms every time he touched her, consistently satisfying her body. Even the first time had been spectacular. She was still feeling the influence of how right it had felt sitting in his lap afterward.

What if Reed was right about him not being able to control her alpha? If that was true, she had nothing to lose in committing to him.

Pulled from her thoughts by the sign heralding Wasilla, Ariel turned and pointed the truck down the main street of town. She slowed and stopped as she saw the leering guy—the one Matt had called Quentin—locking up the office.

She pulled into a parking spot and rolled down the window. "Hey, Quentin. Where's Matt?"

"Town hall meeting out behind Gareth's place."

Ariel narrowed her gaze. "Werewolf town hall or human town hall?"

Quentin snorted. "Which do you think? He's been mad all week about something. I think he intends to fix his mood by punishing Cheryl and her friends. At least he'll get it over with."

"What's he going to do to them?" Ariel asked. She'd like to kick Cheryl's ass, but she was concerned for the five women who had only offered moral support to her would-be murderer.

Quentin shrugged. "Matt will do what he thinks is best. He can't let a pack member go around doing what Cheryl tried to do to you. If he lets her get away with it, who would she try to kill next?"

"Good point. Are you heading out there? And do you want a ride?"

"Yes, to both. My place is near there and my truck is being worked on. Gareth was supposed to give me a lift home—but then this happened," Quentin answered, walking around to get in on the passenger side.

They drove three miles out of town until he directed her to turn toward a painted barn down a farm lane between two pastures. A few cattle grazed on each side. She saw a symbol on the flank of one.

"Whose farm is this?"

"Gareth's. Why?"

"Are these his cattle?"

Quentin turned to look. "Yeah, and that's his brand on them. He had to mark them a couple years ago when his new bull kept busting through the fence. His cattle kept getting mixed in with Mark LaFayette's bunch. Those brands have saved him a lot of arguing over what rightfully belongs to him."

Ariel snorted at the comment, but she had to admit it made sense—at least with cattle. "Are you married, Quentin? I mean, *mated*?"

"Why are you asking? I thought you belonged to Matt."

His surprise, and his assumption, had her snorting and laughing. "I wasn't asking about your dating status. I was asking in general. What makes you think I belong to Matt?"

Quentin shrugged. "The mark on your collar for one. Then there's the fact you still smell like him even though you've been gone for more than a week. But the biggest thing is that you're driving his truck. A man has to be deeply in love to let a woman drive his only vehicle."

Ariel belly laughed at his male logic. "You really think Matt's in love with me?" She smiled when she heard him snort.

"Everyone knows Matt's in love with you. He's never kept steady company with a female this long before. What we don't know yet is whether or not you love him back."

Ariel's smile widened as they neared the barn. "Well, I love him back—but I hate the idea of him thinking of me the way Gareth thinks of his cattle. Blame it on my human side."

Quentin must have thought her statement was funny, because he genuinely laughed.

"Your instincts seem to be pretty good about him. Matt's way worse than Gareth ever thought about being when it comes to his stuff. His name is carved inside his desk at the office *and* etched on the bottom of his chair. I've never seen a man so adamant about people knowing what's his. I can only imagine what form the need to mark might take with a female he wants other males to stay the hell away from. You have my sympathy."

"Thanks for warning me." Ariel smiled and got a smiling head nod in return. Quentin was turning out to be surprisingly nice. "So Quentin... what's the werewolf equivalent of a wedding ring?"

Quentin shrugged. "I don't know. Some couples wear rings, but they have to be real gold, not any of that cheap crap you get nowadays. As you know from Reed's situation, certain metals are poisonous to werewolves. Instead of wearing rings, most pairs just mark each other. People respect mating marks."

"So *pairs* mark each other? I hadn't heard that before," Ariel said. "Thanks for the conversation. I'm still learning and I appreciate the information."

"Okay. We need to be quiet as we head around back. If they've started, we don't want to interrupt."

Ariel nodded, thinking hard about what Quentin had shared as they walked.

Matt paced in front of the five crying women. "What you did was not some high school prank or college hazing. If Ariel had died, you wouldn't be standing here crying, you'd be dead too. There is no other way to look at this other than you were willingly helping Cheryl commit a murder. How am I supposed to trust you won't do something like this again?"

Their murmurs of apology and sobbing didn't even begin to appease him.

"Enough whining. I'm too angry to listen to your apologies.

You will all do a year's worth of community service—three times a week—beginning tomorrow. See Gareth for your assignments. Your schedule will be posted in the Sheriff's office. Now get out of here before I change my mind and do something worse."

Standing at the back of the crowd, Ariel crossed her arms as the five frightened, chastised women streaked past her without looking up to see who she was. Their fear of Matt literally stank on them and she didn't like knowing it was because of her. But she also thought they had gotten off pretty lightly considering Matt continued to look like a volcano about to erupt.

She watched as Gareth pushed her nemesis over to stand in front of a still pacing Matt.

"It has been three years since I intentionally took someone's life in order to save the pack. If Ariel had been as normal as any other member, she would be dead by your hand. That would have made my decision very simple, Cheryl. Since Ariel still lives, I am torn. You remain a potential threat to the pack because of your self-centered outlook. How can the pack trust you won't turn on one of them?"

"This was not about anyone else in the pack. I have only one complaint. The unnatural blonde alpha is not worthy to be the Gray Wolf Alpha's mate," Cheryl insisted.

"You have no idea who is worthy and who is not," Matt yelled in reply. "My mate is *my* choice—*and mine alone*, Cheryl. You have no say in who I choose. Neither does anyone else in the pack. And I tell you now—Ariel Jones is the only female I have ever in my life considered *worthy*."

Cheryl cringed from his anger, but lifted her chin. "Kill me then because I won't change my mind. I would rather be dead than see the pack be shamed by such a pairing."

Matt growled in warning and gave her a look that had her shrinking. "What does our pack need with a female as selfish and narrow-minded as you? The hardness of your heart is why you have been shunned by every male you've dated. Killing you would be doing the pack a favor."

"Can I do it?" Ariel asked in a loud voice, striding around the crowd. She walked forward and stopped on the edge of Matt's judgment ring. She was thankful Quentin had explained it to her as they watched. "I killed and unseated the Black Wolf Alpha a few days ago. I think I can handle killing one spoiled child who thinks she has the right to control other people."

Matt stopped pacing and crossed his arms as he stared. "Who's running the Black Wolf pack while you're away, Alpha Ariel?"

Ariel smiled and shook her head. "I gave the pack to Reed to run because I wanted to be with you instead. I figured you'd find something for me to do here."

Matt rubbed his nose, wondering how he could finish his detestable task with Cheryl when all he wanted was to sweep up the woman in front of him and run off with her. "I'm sure we can think of something to keep you busy. But right now I have to kill someone. Step back so you don't get blood on your clothes."

Ariel winced at his flat declaration. "How about you give me Cheryl's life for a mating present? I think I'd like a chance to change the way she thinks."

"Why would you want to save the life of someone who tried to outright kill you? You've killed several people yourself—one just recently—so I know you're not squeamish about death."

She shrugged at Matt's question, and his suspicions about her motives. She wasn't completely clear about them, but that didn't stop her from giving him her most imploring look. "I'm not sure why I want you to spare her life. I just do. Maybe it's one of those pesky alpha things you warned me about."

Matt snorted. "Cheryl has to be punished for her crimes against the pack. What will you do to punish her if I agree?"

Smiling, Ariel turned a wicked gaze to meet Cheryl's wide-eyed shocked one. She looked far more nervous facing her than she had with Matt. Both she and her wolf were pleased.

"Well, for starters, I think I'll buy Cheryl a book about improving her self-esteem so she doesn't need to measure her worth by the pack value of the man sharing her bed. Then after she reads the book, I thought I would quiz her on it. Maybe Brandi can think of something suitably obnoxious to do to her each time she gets an answer wrong."

"Reading a book? *That's* your idea of punishment for attempted murder?" Matt asked in disbelief.

"Don't worry, Matt. I'll make sure it's a *really big* book," Ariel replied.

A ripple of laughter and snickering ran through the crowd of pack witnesses. There was nothing like public humiliation to get a point made quickly. Cheryl blushed and hung her head, shamed by their discussion.

"Anything else?" Matt asked.

"Yes. I think Cheryl should have a front row seat for whatever part of our mating you need to make public with the pack. I want there to be no doubt in her mind, or anyone else's, that we are voluntarily choosing each other. Witnessing our mating will be a hard lesson about how life is full of surprises—bad ones and good ones. I know I've certainly had my fair share of surprises lately."

"Which category have you put becoming a werewolf into?" Matt asked.

Ariel smiled. "It's been a good surprise—mostly."

"And my mating proposal?"

"Definitely *good*," Ariel said, pleased when Matt smiled and laughed.

His smile fell away as he looked at Cheryl again. "I still crave your death, and if you give me another reason, I will have it. Be grateful I'm desperate enough to bargain your life in exchange for mating your savior. In addition to reading Ariel's book and taking her *quiz*, you will report to Gareth who will assign you to one year of community service work *at the jail*, even if it involves nothing more than sweeping out the holding cells. I want you to check in with the Sheriff *five days a week.*"

"Since her life is a gift to me, I guess it makes her my responsibility too. Can I step into the circle with her for a minute?"

Ariel waited until Matt nodded, then walked to stand in front of Cheryl.

"Matt is right about your elitist views. I am not an abomination, and neither are the other women who were created when I was. For now, I am a werewolf belonging to the Black Wolf pack. Soon I will belong to yours as well. I am *exceedingly* worthy to be your alpha's mate if he wants me. *Don't* make me carry out his wish to see you dead just to prove my loyalty to him."

She stared until Cheryl nodded and looked away.

"My public mating will be done tomorrow," Matt said loudly so everyone would hear.

Ariel turned and stepped out of the circle. "Sounds good to me. Can I be your werewolf-girlfriend-with-benefits until then?"

Matt smiled wickedly. "You can be whatever the hell you want, just as long as you be it in my bed."

"In that case, can I be your alpha?" Ariel teased.

"Oh, you are definitely *my* alpha," Matt teased back. "But I don't think you mean it the same way I do. I'll explain my definition to your logical mind later, Dr. Jones."

"How about you explain it now?" Ariel paused. "Well, after we drop Quentin off. I gave him a ride. His truck is in the shop. I picked him up on the way here."

Happy with the pleasant disposition of the female he loved, Matt slung an arm around her shoulders as they walked away. "You're a very nice person when you aren't fighting for your life. I have missed you, Ariel."

"I've missed you too. Let's go home and stop missing each other," she suggested.

Matt stopped walking and pulled her close for a scorching kiss, smiling when he released her.

19

ARIEL SIGHED IN HAPPINESS AS MATT FED HER ANOTHER BITE OF HAM. Great welcome home sex. A shared shower. Good food. What could be better than this? It was hard to believe she'd had so many reservations about coming back to him. She sat contentedly in Matt's lap, her legs draped over his as they talked.

"Don't you have any reservations about us at all?" she asked.

"Sure. I have thousands." Matt wiped his greasy ham fingers off on his spare shirt that Ariel was wearing, mostly just to hear her laugh. His smile was affectionate and his heart clenched in his chest as she sniffed the spot he'd made on her clothes and moaned in ecstasy at the smell.

"Mate me. I promise to feed you ham for the rest of our lives," he vowed.

"Stop. You're not distracting me with promises of food. Name one doubt about us you have," Ariel ordered. It took considerable effort, but she shifted her attention away from her delicious smelling shirt and back to his face.

"Okay. I'll name the biggest one. I know I will never have all of you. If something bad happens to Reed, you'll have to go back to the Black Wolf pack. As your werewolf family, they will always be part of your responsibilities, as much as Brandi and Heidi. Having to share my mate with so many others wasn't something I expected to have to do, especially not as alpha. I've had to do a lot of hard thinking and work on adjusting my attitude. I have accepted that even if you never lead a pack bigger than three, you will always be an alpha."

"What do you mean you never expected to have to share your mate? That sounds archaic in this day and age, even for werewolves. Were you planning to keep some female barefoot and pregnant, making your meals, and constantly at your beck and call?"

Matt laughed, but couldn't deny it. "Yes. Actually, I was. It is fairly common in werewolf relationships for the female to be subservient to the male."

Ariel rolled her eyes. "Someone as intelligent as you are could not seriously believe that kind of situation could ever work for us. What about the fact I might never be able to give you a family? Doesn't that bother you? It bothers me. It's not that I want babies, but I'd like to have the option."

Matt drew in a breath and let it out slowly. "Yes. I'm still working through our possible inability to make a family. So far, I have concluded that conception will be something me and your little nanos will have to work out. They seem to like me so far. They haven't removed my marks of possession from your body. It's like they somehow know I'm the best for you and your wolf. While you were gone, I decided a possible lack of children was a life risk I was willing to take to keep you with me. It is your company I want more than anything. Everything else in our lives will be a bonus."

Ariel bit her lip at his understanding and thought hard about how to explain her biggest concern. It was hard for her to put into words.

"I think what worries me most is there's so much we still don't know about each other. I really do have all those alpha urges you told me about. Did Gareth tell you how easy it was for me to defeat Hanuk?"

"Yes. I've heard the story of your amazing fight many times. No one who saw it will cease talking about it, no matter how much my blood runs cold every time I remember having to leave you alone to face it," Matt said.

"Matt—I wasn't even scared to fight—not for a single second—not even when I thought I was going to be taking on both Hanuk and Travis. Does it not seem a contradiction to you that the same bloodthirsty, fearless alpha is now sitting on your lap and letting you feed her ham? You really don't have to keep rescuing me from your jealous werewolf girlfriends, my evil cousins, and any future mad scientist who might want to dissect me."

Matt chuckled at her complaints. "Maybe I don't know what you're capable of, but I've always known what you were. Do you think your alpha side should worry me more?"

Ariel shrugged. "Maybe. If you make me mad, our fights are not going to be pleasant. In fact, I'm always amazed about how much leeway I seem to automatically allow you. It baffles me to feel nearly subservient with you when I would for damn sure kick any other male's ass for similar offenses. Can you explain why I feel this way around you and no one else?"

"Sweetheart, it's the simplest thing in the world. But actions are so much better than words."

Ariel saw the wolf in Matt's eyes seconds before his hot mouth claimed hers. Throat growling his possession, Matt's tongue demanded her arousal while his hands gripped her hips and dragged her flush against him. Her body instantly complied with his demands. Her hands ran over his chest in delight, rejoicing in his thunderous heartbeat. His fierce desire always thrilled her, no matter how many times they were together.

When he finally released her lips, she felt his sharp, dangerous teeth grazing her neck as they slid down her across her jugular. Her wolf didn't flinch from the contact even though her human side fully understood her life was at risk. If Matt had wanted to kill her, he definitely could have, and in a flash. But she remained still, literally frozen in place, while she waited for the male she desired to do whatever he wanted to her.

"Okay—just one more question. Where the hell do my survival instincts go when I'm with you?" she demanded.

"They're still there. They just aren't being felt because they aren't needed when you are safe in my arms. You belong to me," Matt whispered roughly, his teeth aching with the urge to mark her once and for all. "Your succulent body knows I adore it. Your scientific mind knows I respect your thoughts. Even your nanos know I mean you no harm. But I'm still waiting for your human heart to catch up. How long am I going to have to wait?"

Ariel bit her lip, thinking hard about it. "I'm not sure. If I belong to you, do you belong to me back?"

"Yes. I belong to you back. And you're the only female I've ever felt that way about. The feelings I have about you are so strong, they make any doubts I have fade away. What is left has turned into my absolute faith that we will adapt to each other. I cannot bear to think otherwise. I will do nearly anything to keep you in my life."

"*Matt...* " Ariel whispered his name and leaned forward, tucking her face into his shoulder. Her teeth sharpened in her mouth. Her wolf always made her strong. "I really like the idea that belonging works both ways. My wolf is feeling very possessive of you right now."

Matt's heart pounded hard at the news. "How possessive is your wolf feeling?"

"*Very possessive,*" she whispered. "I need you now. I need you badly."

Supporting her claim, her fingernails lengthened into claws. She used them to rip Matt's shirt to shreds in order to get to his skin.

"You can have me anytime and anywhere," Matt declared.

Wanting to save the rest of his clothes, he stood with Ariel clasped around his waist. Bracing her hips with one hand, he used the other to free himself from his sweats. When he sat down in the chair again, he lowered Ariel until his need of her pressed against her entrance.

"Take me in and make me yours," he pleaded. "It's what I want. I need you too."

Ariel groaned as Matt used his hands to help her hips find the perfect position. When he pulled her tight against his nearly naked chest, she slid down on him as he thrust up to get inside her. Together they created the physical bond they both craved.

One of his hands raked her hair back as he called her name in pleasure.

Ariel leaned forward and braced her hands on his shoulders to better meet his suddenly eager thrusts. "You're mine now," she whispered, nipping his ear. She circled back to his mouth, nipping his lips too. "I want you to be mine, Matthew Gray Wolf."

Needing more of him, she crushed his lips with hers and felt him quiver in response to her assertiveness as she bore down to meet his thrusts. His enthusiastic reactions told her everything important she needed to know about the man beneath her. They told her they were equals. Their relationship had that as a foundation.

She kissed and stroked and whispered his name. Eventually Matt stilled his movements, letting her take over completely as she rose and fell on him.

His half-lidded eyes stared at her breasts, enjoying the show.

"How possessive are you feeling now?" he demanded, his voice husky and full of joy.

"*Mine.*" Ariel choked out the single word, understanding what she was feeling at last.

Following a need greater than any she'd ever known before, Ariel pressed her weight down hard, clamping her muscles tight as she trapped Matt's erection inside her. Without any reservations, she leaned forward and sank her sharp teeth into his throat. When he yelled in surprise at her attack, she listened to her wolf and bit down harder, unwilling to let him loose in any way at all.

It was a moment like the one Reed had described. Instinct ruled her. She was acting from a knowledge greater than logic. Matt's erection throbbed within her depths while her muscles clenched around him ruthlessly. He was making half man-half animal noises and calling out her name. When her wolf growled in satisfaction over his struggles, Ariel completely understood... and agreed with her other side.

Her mind clicked off entirely when Matt stopped struggling and bent to her neck as well. His teeth sinking fully into her sent an indescribable amount of pleasure racing through every cell as the mother of all orgasms hit. She felt Matt pulsing in completion as he climaxed too, and still her body held on to him, not wanting to let go.

Time passed. She didn't know how much... or care. She was happy, satisfied, and complete.

Eventually, her wolf teeth receded and she gasped in surprise. Instinctively her tongue came out to lick over and around the indentations she'd made, healing them as Matt had done to her.

Then the magnitude of her actions hit her as hard as the big orgasm had. She moaned softly against his now marked skin, her human side suddenly unsure about how angry Matt was going to be about her show of aggression.

His hand in her hair gripped hard as he turned her face up to his. His mouth swooping down hard and hot on hers was a visceral shock even after what they'd shared, but she felt nothing but approval and gratitude in the kiss.

When her mouth was free again, she finally opened her eyes, willing at last to face what she'd done. Matt's gaze on hers was blazing hot. His arousal was banked, but the cinders of his lust were still burning. He was still inside her, a semi-firm reminder of what was possible. She shivered in anticipation of what he would do when the flames roared to full life again. It looked like her werewolf wedding night was going to be one where they couldn't get enough of each other.

Ariel sucked her bottom lip as she cautiously offered an explanation. "I don't exactly know why I did all that to you. I couldn't seem to help myself. Did it hurt when I bit you?"

Matt's smile was wide and wicked as he answered. "Yes. Alpha teeth are lethal. At first your bite hurt like hell, then it was incredibly blissful."

"Blissful?"

Matt gripped her tighter. "Yes. Mating with you was far better than any story I've heard anyone share about what happens. I've never had a climax last that long before. I didn't think you were ever going to let me find release. I'm still not sure what you did to stop it from happening, but... *damn*... I liked it."

Ariel wanted to chuckle at his description of her control, but her tired body couldn't manage humor. "Your bite didn't hurt me at all. It was glorious. It stopped time and I could sense every nuance of what was happening to us. My orgasm spun out as I felt yours. But tell me the truth, Matt. Didn't my aggression bother you?"

Matt snorted. "Are you serious? Not even a little bit. Your aggression thrills me. Your obedience humbles me because I have to work so hard to earn it. My wolf and I are thrilled beyond what I can describe in words to call someone like you our mate."

Ariel sighed. "Okay. So the bites... they mean we're mates now, right?"

Matt nodded. "Yes. Or at least our wolves are. I am committed to you like no other with all that I am. One day, I hope your human side accepts me just as completely as your wolf has. I know this has happened too fast for the cautious scientist in you. It is my goal to erase all her lingering reservations. Please let me. I love you, Ariel. All of you. No matter how complicated your life is."

She lifted a hand to his face. "I love you, too, Matt. I'll try to be the best mate I can be while I'm figuring out my crazy life."

Matt smiled. "That's all I can ask. Are you hungry?"

Ariel smiled as she shook her head. "Only for you. You make me insatiable."

"Best mating present ever—except for you biting me back."

Matt lifted her gently from his lap and held on until her legs were steady. He took her hand as they walked up the stairs.

"So what will we have to do for your pack tomorrow to make this official?" Ariel asked.

Matt grinned. "Nothing earth-shattering. But you need to wear something revealing. We both do. I want them to see my marks. I have to say your bite totally surprised me. Only one female out of every ten couples ever bites her mate back. You just became a unique werewolf statistic, Dr. Jones."

Ariel hung her head and sighed. "Biting you back surprised me too. It's not like I planned to do it. It just… happened."

"Do you regret it?"

"No. But I feel a little guilty, even if my wolf doesn't. She's… I guess I have to admit that she's just as possessive as you are."

Matt laughed at her admission, mostly because he could sense her honest shock. "Would you rather go back to being boring and predictable? I can't imagine someone as incredible as you ever being happy with that sort of life."

Ariel laughed as Matt dragged them both into the bathroom to shower.

2 0

GOING PUBLIC TO THE PACK WENT A LOT BETTER THAN SHE THOUGHT IT
would. Turns out, it meant Matt's family got to throw them a big
all-day party with lots of food. Matt's father looked nothing like
him, even though they sure acted like twins. When Nanuka had
caught her staring off into space, she had patted her arm and
kissed her cheek. She'd thanked her for the robe and gotten a
secretive laugh instead of an appreciative 'you're welcome'. She
made a mental note to keep an eye on Matt's stepmother.

Many times that day she'd wondered if the entire town had
come out to look at the marks on their necks. Nobody thought
twice about boldly pulling aside her or Matt's clothes to gawk
their fill. Before the day ended, she was very glad she'd taken
Matt's advice to wear the plainest white bra he'd bought her.

She'd also heard "congratulations" said a million times and
had responded with "thank you" an equal amount.

Her nemesis had reluctantly come to see them. Matt had given
Cheryl's embarrassed family no choice except to supervise. The
still angry woman looked at both their necks and nodded
solemnly, but walked away without saying a single word to either
of them. Matt's gaze had burned a mad hole in Cheryl's back as

she left. It was like the female who tried to kill her had a death wish.

But totally surprising her, it was Brandi and Heidi who gave her the hardest time about her officially mating Matt. They and their guys had followed her home to Matt's house, promptly dragging her outside in the yard for a private chat.

Heidi launched in before they had reached the edge of the yard. "Why did you do this, Ariel? I thought you said not to get too attached to the guys."

"Yeah, I'd like to hear this too. I thought you said the sex was just to get us through the whole female werewolf transition thing," Brandi declared, crossing her arms.

Ariel ran both hands through her rapidly growing hair. Accountability sucked. "Matt insisted we mate and I caved. Worse, I don't even regret it. Life can't be all about work... or problems. If anything happens to me tomorrow, I'll at least have spent my best days living with and loving a decent man.."

"Don't you mean a decent werewolf?" Brandi demanded. "Matt is not just a man."

Ariel sighed. "Yes. Okay. *Werewolf.* Matt's a werewolf. We're all werewolves. What's this inquisition really about? My werewolf marital status doesn't change your lives any."

Brandi kicked the dirt. "Of course it does. Gareth is getting more possessive. I have no intentions of staying with him. I have to leave. Or at least I want to leave. I want to go back to my job and find out who the hell was funding Feldspar Research."

Ariel shrugged. "So? Go—leave. I think it's a good idea. Just be careful and call now and again. I'll worry if I don't hear from you."

Brandi kicked the ground a second time. "I know. I guess I was hoping you'd go with me. I know Heidi wants to stay and work with Eva. Maybe I assumed the wrong things."

Ariel sighed. "Brandi, I'm sorry. I can't go with you. I like the idea, but I need to stay, and not just for Matt. I need to stay for Reed too. He needs me. And if anything happens to him, I'm kind of next in line to run the Black Wolf pack. Matt knows this is the case. I… damn it. I can't leave Alaska. I may never get to leave it again. Permanent responsibility is part of the whole alpha thing."

Brandi huffed out a breath. "Fine. I get it. I'm used to being alone anyway. I just thought… well never mind what I thought."

"No, don't say that. You thought right. We're friends… family… or whatever label you want to use for our connection. And if things weren't the way they are, I'd go with you in a flat minute. I mean it. I need you to believe me."

Brandi snorted. "Hell. Okay, sure. You don't expect me to hug you now, do you?"

Ariel laughed at the appalled look on Brandi's face. "You can skip the hug, but I expect you to be careful, call frequently, and come back alive. Those people you're going after are not worth dying for."

"Okay. Sorry I bitched at you. I'm sure you and Matt won't kill each other the first time you argue. And don't turn your back on Cheryl. She's evil. You should have let Matt kill her when he offered."

Ariel rubbed her nose. The action reminded her of Reed and she instantly missed him. She needed to borrow Matt's phone and call. "I'll deal with Cheryl. When are you leaving?"

Brandi shrugged. "Whenever. I need a ride to the airport in Anchorage and some cash until I get back to civilization again. Once I call in, I'll have to pretend I don't know you all for a while since you and Heidi want to remain deceased in the eyes of the world."

"Now you're scaring me. Can you stay a few more days until I get settled in?" She instantly relaxed when Brandi nodded.

"Yeah. Sure. I've waited this long. What's a few more days?"

Ariel turned to Heidi. "I already know what your major problem with this is. Ryan wants to mate you, doesn't he?"

Heidi crossed her arms and nodded.

"And how do you feel about Ryan?"

Heidi shrugged. "Confused. Resistant. But I don't want to end things either. I like him. He's amazing. I just want more time to find myself... I suppose. Since he found out about you and Matt, he has done nothing but talk about making things permanent between us. It makes my stomach hurt when I think about it."

"Sorry I set a bad example. What do you want me to do?" Ariel asked.

Heidi looked away and sighed. "Can you just forbid me to mate him?"

"I can. However, any control I have over your love life is nothing more than a mental illusion you're fostering for your own benefit. No one can tell your heart what to feel, not even the most bad-ass alpha."

"Just order me, Ariel. My willpower is not going to be enough. I need a good, solid reason to hold him off," Heidi declared.

"Fine—you cannot mate Ryan, or any male, until you are a hundred percent sure he's the right werewolf for you. When you're sure, you have my permission to mate whoever the hell you want. I expect you to take at least a few months to become sure." Ariel snorted when Heidi breathed out a ragged sigh of relief. "All better now?

"Much. I'll tell Ryan what you said tonight."

Hearing the back door open, Ariel turned to look toward the house just as Matt, Gareth, and Ryan came outside looking for them. She laughed when she heard Brandi grunt in irritation.

"Relax. They're not keeping tabs—not really. They're just checking to make sure we're okay. I don't like all the hovering either, but you'll make yourself insane if you let it annoy you."

"Gareth specializes in annoying me. It's his idea of foreplay," Brandi said stiffly.

"You just need to train him better. Guys will do most anything for you if they know there's sex in it for them at the end. Ask Gareth for a foot rub or a massage," Heidi suggested.

Ariel saw Brandi's indignant look pass from Heidi to her and back to Heidi. She couldn't imagine Brandi asking Gareth for a hug or kiss, much less a foot rub. Their coupling hadn't left much of an impression on the former agent.

Firmly pushing aside her escalating concern, she told herself that fixing Brandi's love life wasn't her problem to solve. Neither was putting a hiatus on Heidi's.

"Ladies, I have no answers, but I will be here if you need me. Right now I plan to enjoy my conjugal rights. I suggest you make the most of your situations while you can. You never know what kind of change tomorrow is going to bring."

Heidi's friendly, caring hug surprised her, but Ariel hugged back because it felt right to do so. She smiled as the most carefree female she'd ever met happily trotted off to the unsuspecting, and soon to be disappointed, Ryan.

Head down, Brandi stepped close to her which had Ariel raising an eyebrow. "Did you change your mind. You want a hug now after all?"

"Yes. I want a hug. Bite me," Brandi said, cringing at her enormous relief when Ariel laughed and pulled her into her arms. "I hate this. When did I start needing hugs? It's all Gareth's damn fault that I'm getting mushy."

Ariel grinned as she turned loose. "You still sleeping with him?"

Brandi nodded and sighed. "He doesn't give me any choice in the matter. If I sneak off to the spare bedroom after sex, Gareth just comes and gets me. No matter where I fall asleep, I always wake up in his bed. He's gotten good at ignoring my complaints about it."

Ariel smiled. "Gareth's practically tapping his foot with his impatience to take you home. I see him doing that all the time. I think it means he likes you."

Brandi huffed. "I better go. It's only for a couple more days. I can deal."

"Instead of 'dealing', try enjoying the attention. I'll see or talk with you tomorrow," Ariel called to Brandi's waving hand as she disappeared into the dark with Gareth.

Sighing with relief when she heard Gareth's vehicle starting, she turned to Matt. "Apparently I pissed off my pack when I mated you. Since when does an alpha need her pack's permission to do anything? I thought it was supposed to work the other way."

Matt chuckled. "They must have gotten over their mad pretty quickly. Both hugged you goodbye."

Ariel laughed and leaned against his arm. "We're an all-female pack. Hugging is what we do. It's sort of a biological imperative for us."

"I'm sorry, but I feel I must correct your assumptions, Dr Jones. You're not an all female pack any more," Matt said, pulling down the collar of his shirt. "See this? The pack alpha marked me as hers. I'm part of her pack now."

Ariel leaned forward and kissed her mark on him. It caused butterflies to flutter in her stomach every time she touched it. "That works for me. My pack could use a few good males."

Matt smiled. "I think you're going to get at least two more."

"That's what you think. Brandi's leaving in two days and Heidi made me forbid her to mate Ryan."

Matt's eyebrows shot up in shock, but when they lowered, he laughed. "I stand by what I said. I know both of those men."

"I personally wouldn't put a bet on them," Ariel declared.

Matt grinned. "Well, I would."

Ariel looked him up and down. "Okay. What kind of bet?"

"I want a child for each couple that mates for life."

Ariel barked out a laugh. "Ha! What will I get if they *don't* mate?"

Matt chuckled. "You will still get a child for each couple. There is no chance of me losing. I have great instincts about relationships."

Ariel laughed at Matt's bragging. "All I heard was blah, blah, blah and 'here honey—here's ten times more responsibility for you'. No bet, buster. We're using condoms when I come into heat, which thankfully will be several months from now."

"It will be two months and nine days—give or take a day. You should probably note it on the calendar in the kitchen if you want me to buy condoms," Matt said, taking her hand as he pulled her inside. They walked up the stairs to his bedroom—their bedroom —and he smiled the whole time thinking about how lucky he was.

"How can you know when I'll go into heat?" Her eyes widened when Matt pointed at his nose. "You can smell hormonal changes in me? I don't believe you."

"Fine. Run all the scientific tests you want. It won't change the outcome."

Ariel threw up her hands, far beyond embarrassed. Matt could smell her hormone shifts? That had to be impossible. "So how does this work? Am I supposed to come to you when I want to know the date of the next one?"

Matt grinned at her indignation and backed her up until her legs hit the bed. "Instead of using protection, many couples simply abstain during the female's heat cycle. I think we should practice all we can while it's still our safe time."

"*Safe time?* Did you make up all that stuff just so you could seduce me tonight?"

His answer was a husky laugh and a searing kiss as their bodies tumbled to the mattress. "I don't have to lie to get my way, Ariel. I'm an alpha. I can just take what I want. Remember?"

After all his teasing, his sensual dare was more than she had the power to resist.

"Big talk, Alpha. I've had your entire pack looking at my breasts all day. After that, I *dare you* to shock me," Ariel challenged, quivering in anticipation.

"Challenge accepted," Matt smiled, his teeth extending in anticipation.

Ariel laughed as Matt shredded the clothes from her body, and then squealed when he buried his face between her legs. The unleashed Gray Wolf Alpha sent her over passion's edge in less than a minute. Protests flitted through her mind, dying one by one as he adjusted her body into whatever position he wanted to use to torture her next. After the first three screaming orgasms, everything else became a blur of sensation after sensation.

She lost track of time again, but suspected his torment lasted for several hours. When her alpha finally tired of proving his point, he told her he loved her and fell into an exhausted sleep on top of her. There wasn't even enough energy left at that point to push him off.

Ariel promised herself that when she recovered from their sexual marathon, she was going to make Matt pay—one way or another.

But when he woke her with kisses and promises of ham for breakfast, all she remembered was spending a wicked night with her alpha mate alternately laughing and begging for mercy.

— **The End** —

NOTE FROM THE AUTHOR

Thank you for reading *Ariel: Nano Wolves 1.*

If you enjoyed this ebook, please consider leaving a positive review or rating on the site where you purchased it. Reader reviews help my books continue to be valued by distributors/resellers and help new readers make decisions about reading them. You are the reason I write these stories and I sincerely appreciate you!

Many thanks for your support,
~ Donna McDonald

Visit **www.donnamcdonaldauthor.com** to see a complete list of my books and to join my mailing list.

EXCERPT FROM BOOK 2

BRANDI: NANO WOLVES 2

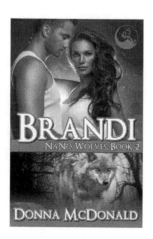

1

Brandi slid gently out of bed, careful not to disturb the male still sleeping quietly in it. She gathered up her jeans and slipped them on, sighing when they barely fastened. Gareth's cooking had been typical high-fat, mostly-protein guy fare. During her time with him, she had packed on a few extra pounds that not even their vigorous nighttime activities had kept off her butt.

Good thing she was leaving before the meager clothing supply she had purchased no longer fit. Her fake death had temporarily suspended her access to her normal accounts. She couldn't afford to spend any more of the emergency rations her field handler had wired to Anchorage for her. Money was not something she craved in large quantities, but she appreciated the comfort it could buy at times.

She pulled on the bra she barely needed before covering it with a faded t-shirt she had fished out of the donation tub in Matt's office. She would top the outfit off shortly with a new black leather jacket. Gareth had insisted she get the heavier coat to match the short, dark dyed hair he still professed to hate.

Lastly, she picked up her new Colt 911, acknowledging its welcome weight in her hand. Along with wiring her money, her handler had also express shipped a gun to a Federal Firearms License Holder near the Anchorage bank that had received her funds.

Both the money and the weapon had arrived five days ago, along with a plane ticket back to Virginia, a new burner cell phone, and a shiny new Federal Agent ID. A replacement driver's license and passport had also been included to round out her return to reality.

She felt a twinge of guilt thinking about the woman listed on all the various pieces of her identification. Each was proof to the world that Agent Brandi Jenkins had returned to the land of the living. She found her reluctance to use them ironic for several reasons.

For one, this was not the first time in her agent career that her death had been faked. Secondly, unlike the other undercover incident, this time she'd actually enjoyed being dead. All the rest of the reasons could be attributed to the man she'd left warming the bed she'd crawled out of this morning.

Since weapon holsters had never worked for her, Brandi hadn't wasted her scarce resources buying one. She checked to make sure the gun's safety was on before tucking the loaded weapon into the back of her snug-fitting jeans.

Finally, she turned to study the sleeping man in the bed. One of Gareth's silvered temples gleamed in the early morning light. Even asleep he looked confident and sure of himself, which he nearly always was around her. Whatever Gareth had done when he'd been younger, it had tightened his jaw and put a stubborn glint in his eyes, especially when things didn't go his way. Rather than putting her off, his grounded personality drew her in and tempted her to let him try and ground her, too.

In sleep, Gareth's body was sprawled over most of his king-sized bed. Though he wasn't a large man in girth, he still took up a lot of space. Maybe it was because every inch of him was honed, hard muscle and he knew exactly how to use it to his best advantage. His toned and taut form was admirable, and very appealing to her werewolf side, though she'd never actually told him. Compliments and revelations would have only complicated today further.

Brandi walked to the bed, looked down, and felt regret grab her by the throat harder than it had when she'd made her phone call earlier in the week. It was a bad, bad idea to feel this way about a temporary lover, but she couldn't kid herself about not liking Gareth. Because of her uncharacteristically high regard, she owed the man a real goodbye, not the typical sneak-away she did to most of her bed partners when the time came to exit their life.

Reaching out her hand, she shook Gareth awake, stepping back in case he woke up reactionary. "Gareth... it's time for me to go."

Gareth groaned and pried one eye open. "*Go?* Does that mean last night didn't change your mind? What kind of sexual bliss does it take to content you, woman?"

Despite how sexist Gareth sounded, Brandi chuckled at his complaints. He was protective and argumentative and demanding. But it was nothing she couldn't handle... and she still really liked him.

She lowered herself to the edge of the bed, hip checking him until he moved his toned ass over enough to make a space for her. "Great sex doesn't have that effect on me. Sorry, Stud. I'm shipping out today."

"Damn it. I don't want you to go." Gareth shifted a little more to let her lean in his direction. "I think you should call your boss back and tell him you've changed your mind."

Brandi smiled. She reached out a hand and ran it over his face. "We had a good run, didn't we? You saw me through my transition, and I'll always be grateful for that. But I have to go back to where I started this adventure. I need to see if I can get to the bottom of it."

Gareth lifted his hand and cupped her breast, enjoying the feel of her instantly peaked nipple through her shirt. Her reliable reaction to his touch meant she was already his as far as their wolves were concerned, but persuading her human side of that fact was not going to happen in the next ten minutes.

"I'd like to get to the bottom of you again," he whispered.

Her companionable snort of laughter over his boob grab was worth suffering the uncomfortable glare she also sent his way. Just once he'd like to touch the prickly woman and know for certain she'd welcome it. They'd had a lot of sex over the last couple of months, but never once really made love to each other. It had taken him most of that time just to get Brandi to sleep an entire night in his bed.

And now she was leaving him. How the hell was he supposed to just let her walk out his door? Especially since he knew exactly what she was heading back to deal with? Gareth cursed himself and life in general. It didn't change things, but it gave the frustration writhing inside him a voice.

"You'll come back to see Ariel and Heidi, right?"

Brandi nodded. She was pretty sure she would. Those women were part of her now in a way she didn't really understand, but had finally stopped trying to. Wherever those women chose to live was going to be a place she'd have to return to now and again. They were like family... an intimacy to other people she was not used to having, but had decided she didn't want to give up.

Gareth's voice was sleepy rough as he sighed, and at the same time, soothing to her soul. Her fingertips travelled over his bristled jaw to his talented lips.

"Maybe I'll even come back to see you, Gareth. I've never done that with a man before, but I guess there's always a first time."

Gareth grabbed her wrist and used it to lever his body upright until he could wrap his arms around her. For once, Brandi let him without resisting. He sighed as he hugged her close. "Damn it. It took you long enough to admit you liked me."

Brandi chuckled into Gareth's shoulder. "Is that your jaded way of saying you actually *want* me to come back and see you?"

Gareth pulled back and put a hand into her hair, yanking softly to get her gaze to meet his. "Do you want me to admit how tempted I am to tie you to the bed and keep you here with me forever?"

"Gareth... don't."

"I know. You asked me not to go there, but you know I don't want other women anymore. I just want you. And I know you want me back, so spare me the friendly lies you've told the other guys when you left them. I know how it is between us... and it could be better."

Brandi laughed as she hugged him tight. "What woman wouldn't want you? Your between-the-sheets talents are immense and you're a decent guy outside of bed. But I still have to go. I have things to do. We've talked about this many times."

Gareth snorted and tugged harder on her hair. She let him show his dominance and didn't fight his efforts. It crossed his mind to capitalize on her concession and show her just how serious he was about keeping her. His fangs tingled in his mouth just at the thought.

He refused to believe Brandi was leaving him for good, even though no amount of wolf mating rightness was going to change the woman's mind about what she felt was her duty. Hadn't he suffered the same guilt enough to know?

Brandi didn't love him yet. Or at least she had herself convinced she didn't. It was the primary reason he'd made his phone calls within hours of hers.

"Come back to me," he ordered softly. "I don't want this to be over between us."

Brandi leaned in to cover Gareth's mouth with hers, surprising both of them with the spontaneous action and the fierceness of it. She rarely initiated intimacy, but in that moment, it seemed the thing to do. If this morning was the last time she saw Gareth, she wanted him to know he would always be special to her. She broke their kiss and pulled back to look at his face one final time.

"You're one of the few men I've ever liked in my life. Maybe I will come back to see you, but don't wait for me. I'm not one of those women who make promises because I know I can't keep them. You do what you have to do. I'll be doing the same. We'll see how it goes when our paths cross again."

Gareth dropped his hands and turned her loose. After losing two other important females in his life, he wasn't someone who made promises either. Brandi's connection to him was his greatest quandary… and his Achilles heel as it was turning out.

"Go then," he said roughly. "Take care of yourself."

Her mouth on his a final time had him growling soft and low when she broke off the kiss. Gareth stayed in bed as Brandi rose and walked briskly out of his bedroom, his house, and his life. The moment his front door closed behind her attractive, tough-as-nails ass, he was calling himself all kinds of a fool for not telling her everything he'd been holding back.

2

GARETH SIGHED WHEN HIS ALPHA GAVE HIM HIS BACK. NORMALLY such an action would have upset him enough to be disrespectful and provoke his leader's wrath. Today he understood why the man looked away from him, and even agreed with his open show of disapproval. But he couldn't waste his time worrying about Matt's feelings, pack protocol, or werewolf politics. All he could think about right now was what he had to do.

"I told them to land the Osprey in the road in front of the house, so if you're going to look for them, keep watch in that direction. The plane has some new technology they're testing, so it might be cloaked. I don't know who they're sending to collect me. Since I was hitching a ride, I didn't get to make any special requests for friends."

Matt snorted at Gareth's attempt to placate him. "I don't know why you felt you had to call in those meddling bastards at all. We would have helped you, Gareth. All you've done by contacting your old organization is open the pack up to dealing with whatever shit storm comes out of this. When Brandi finds out the truth, she may shoot you."

Gareth shook his head even though Matt wasn't looking at him.

"This is bigger than what the pack can handle... I *feel* it, Matt. I called them to come get me so I could keep the shit storm away. You know that's how it works."

Giving up on convincing Matt of his honest intentions, Gareth turned and stared Ariel down which was not easy. The female Alpha was more than a little intimidating. Her sharp mind made her natural Alpha aggression all the more formidable. Plus at the moment, she was both angry *and* afraid for someone she cared about. It was the worst combination of emotion to deal with in any female.

He lifted his chin. "If Brandi calls, don't order her home, Ariel. If you force your Beta to come back here, she'll hate you and her life—as well as me."

Ariel glared and shook her head over the order. Who knew a person's physical absence could cause such an empty hole inside her? She certainly hadn't known it would be like this when Brandi left. She doubted Brandi had known it either.

She had known precisely the moment Brandi got on the damn airplane in Anchorage because every hair on her body had quivered in alarm at her Beta's departure. A wild-eyed Gareth bursting into Matt's house an hour later had eerily validated her sense of Brandi heading into danger. Now she was livid at herself for not having listened to her instincts more before she'd agreed to let Brandi go back alone.

"All I have is some sense of impending trouble. I'm almost ill with worry for her," Ariel declared, yanking on her hair.

Her mate turned from his post at their picture window and raised his eyebrows. Ariel read the censure in his direct gaze and shook her head over another damn life lesson.

"Let me guess... this debilitating anxiety about Brandi is just another pesky Alpha problem, isn't it?" She watched Matt nod and wanted to punch him. Her mate's small smile told her he knew it too.

"Your worry for your Beta is not as overwhelming as it would be for me in these circumstances, but it is not something you can set aside. Whatever your instincts are telling you is without doubt the reality of Brandi's situation. It must in some way be addressed. Sending Gareth to see to her safety is an appropriate action to take."

"Damn it. I should have gone with her myself. She wanted me to go—expected me to. With Reed taking over his pack again, it was just bad timing for me to leave Alaska," Ariel declared.

"No—it was never your place to go," Gareth declared. "You are her leader, but I've come to realize she's mine to protect. I knew it on some level the first moment I saw her. I did as good a job ignoring our connection as Brandi did, but the difference is my complacency stops today. You have my word, Ariel. Whether Brandi returns to Wasilla or stays where she is... I will be at her side from now on. I am her mate."

Ariel snorted. "*Her mate?* Brandi doesn't think that way about you, Gareth. She doesn't feel that way about you either. I don't think the woman has ever allowed herself to love anyone."

"Forget love—Brandi doesn't let herself feel anything—period. But I couldn't force her to stay here just so I could teach her. That was never going to work. She's... " Gareth paused, swore, and raked a hand through his hair.

"She's... *what?*" Ariel prompted.

"Brandi's like I was a hundred years ago, and just as green about what's important. I understand what makes her tick even if I don't like it. Being around her is like seeing a mirror of my past. Brandi's all about duty and little else. One way or another, she was going to find a reason to go back to her job."

Ariel flexed her fingers, making fists and releasing them. She wanted to beat up on something or someone. It was her default reaction to mental pain since her conversion into an Alpha werewolf. Her eyes flashed when she heard her mate growling at her show of angst in front of a pack member.

"Listen to Gareth. Getting worked up and angry won't help

Brandi… or us," Matt said firmly, turning back to the window and crossing his arms.

Ariel glared at Gareth without knowing why she was so angry at the calm man. There was no clear enemy for her to hate, so maybe Gareth was just a handy target. But when she spoke, she turned and directed her comments to the only man she'd ever met besides Reed Black Wolf who seemed to intuitively understand her internal conflict.

"I watched Brandi coldly kill a man she considered a threat to us when we escaped from Randall Crane. Since I had just killed two before that, who was I to pass judgment on her actions? I admit I put it behind me and forgot what she was. But no matter what kind of life the woman has led, nothing could have adequately prepared her to deal with a scientist doing what Crane was doing. He abducted and experimented on us without a shred of remorse. My gut says Crane's benefactors have found out about us and know what we are."

Gareth watched Matt nod in agreement with his mate, but his friend and leader thankfully didn't say anything to confirm her suspicions. Matthew Gray Wolf was a solid rock. When he'd returned home to Wasilla after his retirement, Matt's pull on him had been something he couldn't ignore. Being the pack's Beta had been the last damn thing in the world he had wanted… or needed at the time. But Matt had calmed a side of him he'd had a hard time living with after all he'd done.

He looked away from the honorable man he served to stare down his equally honorable, but less-in-control-of-herself mate. "My gut says the same, Ariel. I think Brandi is in trouble. That's why I've decided to go after her."

At the window, Matt barked out a triumphant laugh and pointed. "There they are—those sneaky bastards in their black suits and dark glasses. They think they're being so stealthy. Why the hell did you call in the half-ass cats, Gareth?"

Gareth grimaced. They weren't cats. They were panthers—well

part panther. They were also highly trained and had very sensitive hearing. He hoped like hell Fallon and Lars weren't listening too closely to Matt's voice which had a tendency to project well beyond the walls of his house.

Sighing over drama he didn't want, but couldn't avoid, Gareth fished the keys to his truck out of his pocket and held them out to Ariel, who frowned but took them.

"What are these for?" she demanded.

"Mechanical parts freeze up fast here. Drive my truck while I'm out of town. I called in a favor to get to the lower forty faster than a commercial flight. With luck, I'll get there around the same time Brandi does. The people she works for are going to want to find out about what happened to her. I just hope she's smart enough not to tell them what she's become."

Ariel snorted, but walked with Gareth as he started toward the door. "I didn't have a clue about werewolves before Crane experimented on me. From what I gathered from Brandi and Heidi —they didn't either. I guess I'm glad you're going after her, but who's going to be Beta while you're gone?"

Gareth stopped for a moment and grinned. "Matt will tell Quentin he's standing in for me, but you'll be the one doing any real helping if it's needed. Quentin's young for a werewolf. He tends to choke when he has to do something unpleasant."

He opened the door and started out, then stopped and stepped back to Ariel. He put his arms around her and hugged, ignoring her surprise. When the distrustful female pulled away, he laughed at the stunned expression on her face.

"I forgot what it was like wanting someone to approve of me... or trust me. Other than Matt, I typically don't give a damn what anyone thinks. It was hard enough when I found out I wanted approval from Brandi. Now I discover I want it from you too."

Ariel frowned. "What form do you expect my approval to take?"

"Let go of the anxiety you have about her. Give Brandi's care over to me—at least while I'm gone. I'll be in touch with you and Matt as soon as I can to give you some sort of status about what's going on."

Ariel nodded, unable to give him the words, but she had already moved into acceptance of what Gareth said. Glancing at Matt, she saw him still glaring out the window.

She looked back at Gareth. "They have slow human heartbeats, not rapid shifter ones. What the hell are they, Gareth?"

Gareth sighed in resignation. He'd kept the truth quiet all these years, but now it was finally coming out. "You're right about their human heartbeats, Ariel. They're not full shifters... just damn close."

"You're telling me Crazy Crane wasn't the only mad scientist doing experiments, aren't you?" Ariel demanded.

Nodding abruptly, Gareth closed the door behind him, shutting out Ariel's shock. There was no time to wonder why he'd blurted it all out like that. Maybe it was because he knew Matt wouldn't keep any truth from the female sharing his life. His Alpha was the only creature alive who knew about his former job... and what he'd done because of it. All most of the pack remembered was he'd disappeared for about forty years, then suddenly came home and taken his place as Beta. It was mostly the truth.

Right now he couldn't worry about what effect his revelation might have had on betrayed scientist, Dr. Ariel Jones. He also couldn't concern himself with what Matt was going to have to deal with when his intelligent mate put it together and started hammering him with questions.

Instead of keeping peace between his pack's mated Alphas, he had to save the fledging werewolf he'd accidentally fallen in love with. His personal epiphany after she left this morning had knocked the complacency right out of him.

The sense of dread he currently carried about Brandi's situation was all he had energy for.

3

BRANDI SHOWED HER BADGE TO THE GUARD AT THE CHECK-IN DESK. His eyes widened at the bypass code on it, but he politely ushered her around security and through the express lane. She didn't often have to come in to the main office and knew she was unrecognizable as the woman who'd visited last time. Fortunately, all that was necessary for the guard to know was that she had earned the three digit code gaining her fast entrance today.

Four more guards stood straighter as she neared her target destination. She stopped outside the office per protocol and pulled her gun from the back of her jeans. She held it in the air while suffering a silent pat down from two of them.

Efficient hands slid down and between her legs. She thought she heard a low, frustrated growl nearby. Her thoughts went instantly to the male she'd left lying in bed early this morning, which elicited a snort about her imagination obviously working overtime. What did it say about her that she missed Gareth already?

Brandi glanced around as she tucked her weapon back into its place, feeling silly when all she saw—and smelled—were human men doing their jobs.

One of the two guards who hadn't felt her up finally opened the door for her. She walked inside the room and shook her head as the man behind the desk swore and stood.

"Black hair sucks with your complexion. Nice jacket, though. The shades make you look like you stepped out of a spy movie."

"I decided to update my agent image after I woke up naked and strapped to a mad scientist's gurney. Obviously, the guy didn't get what I was from the park ranger look I had going on in my backpacking clothes."

"I see. Where's the mad scientist now?"

Lies and rationalizations sat easily on her tongue just waiting to be said. All the mental rehearsal she'd done on the plane ride was now going to pay off.

"Randall Crane's ashes are spread across Anchorage. Thought you said investigating Feldspar was going to be a vacation?"

Flashes of their past hit her when she was treated to her handler's full-wattage smile over her sass.

"I don't believe I used that exact term… "

Brandi laughed then. "I got damn lucky when someone cut loose a wolf Crane had captured. A shit show happened during the rescue attempt and the resulting commotion gave me the first opening I'd had to escape. Weird thing was I barely got my ass out of the damn building before the whole place exploded. Who do I have to talk to around here to get a new handler?"

"Holy shit, I've missed you, Brandi. You're the only person with nerve enough to talk like that to me. I half expected the person coming in was someone trying to use your identity. Whoever faked your death did a damn good job."

"Me die? You know me better than that, Lane."

"I thought I did. Why did you wait so long to contact me?"

Brandi snorted. Now the questions were getting real. "Why are you asking me something so obvious? It's certainly been a while since I landed in your hot seat."

"One—I wanted to make sure you were really alive. And two—

I wanted to personally hear what the hell happened. Now take the hot seat and start talking. Who the hell tried to kill you this time?"

Brandi sighed as she slid into the chair across from him. She noticed Lane sat back down too. Though she sometimes worked with supervisors in the field, Lane Nelson was her handler and the man she ultimately answered to about assignments. He was also the one who decided where she went next time... and what she got to do.

As she mentally ran through what she intended to share with him, a part of her couldn't help noticing he was just as handsome as ever. Once upon a time...long ago, before Lane's promotion to the position he now occupied, he'd been her preferred bed partner. The man had been talented between the sheets and had asked little in return for his generosity. Their relationship had been for physical relief, pure and simple, but his performance was always well done. Plus, he'd seemed to care about being discreet, something she'd learned to value in her line of work. Out in the field, she had sometimes even missed him.

Well, she had before Gareth.

As if summoned, thoughts of last night ran through her head. Lane's presence didn't cause a single familiar flutter. Not that those kind of flutters happened all that much for her.

Well, they happened with Gareth routinely, but she figured her increased libido was just a werewolf thing. Everything physical was more intense since her conversion. Her craving for raw meat was the only aspect she hadn't yet learned to enjoy. But better sex? That was a real perk, which was interesting since she wasn't feeling the slightest inclination to assuage her now stronger urges with the still handsome and proficient male sitting across from her.

Brandi barely fought back a sigh over her mind taking a conversation time-out to conduct a sex comparison in the middle of a debriefing. It was just one more way Gareth had changed her. She was officially female.

"The bottom line of what happened is Crazy Crane tried to kill me and failed. After Feldspar's wolf retrieval team tagged me, I got locked in a cage for more than a week. From what I pieced together of the timeline, they executed my faked death while I was locked up. All around me were an assortment of captured wolves in cages just like mine. It was like being held in a zoo. Gradually, the wolves started disappearing, like one or two a day. Later I discovered they were being dissected and thrown out in the trash. At the end of my time, the bastards came back and tagged me with the tranquilizer gun again. I woke up several hours afterward, strapped down naked on a medical gurney."

"What exactly were they planning to do to you? Assault you?"

Brandi shrugged, snorted, and set her gaze on her hands. "No. They didn't touch me, unless you count Crane's leering assistant feeling me up as he checked the straps. He and Crane talked like I was going to be part of some sort of experiment. I kept expecting the two of them to pull out a scalpel and slice me open like they had the wolves."

Internally wiping away sweat when she finished, Brandi knew she was bypassing Lane's questions as best she could. Instinct warned her to say as little as possible about knowing the scientist's real motives. It was odd to now feel such instinctive distrust for a man who had sent her on many dangerous missions. So much had changed for her—it was hard to accept all at once.

"Who broke the wolf out?"

Brandi ordered her mind back to the conversation. "One of the scientists who worked there. Crazy Crane and his assistant tried to stop it from happening. It didn't work out well for any of the people involved. I think the scientist may have ultimately killed him. Crane had given me a sedative and was dead by the time I woke, got loose, and found him. I took his vehicle keys from his pocket and next thing I knew the place was on fire. The building blew all to hell as I was driving away. I ended up wandering around for a while in Crane's stolen jeep. Don't worry about car jacking charges. I scraped the vehicle identification number from both the window and the engine. I also destroyed the plate to cover my tracks."

She winced inwardly when Lane ignored her teasing, looked away, and started tapping his pencil again. She narrowed her eyes as realization hit. He was fishing for information. It looked like the distrust she was feeling went both ways.

"So where have you been all this time, Brandi? Your death was registered a couple months ago."

Brandi blinked in mild shock over Lane's extreme nervousness as he asked the question. What the hell did Lane know? Or think he knew?

"I've been staying with someone I met just outside Anchorage. Given my headaches and mind wanderings, I figure I had some sort of undiagnosed concussion going on. I made friends with some of the locals and just laid low while I investigated Feldspar's meltdown. A few days ago I gave up and decided to call in for help, which is why I'm here."

She watched Lane nod, but his jaw was tight.

"Look Lane, I don't know what kind of Intel you got about what happened, but all signs of Feldspar's previous existence got completely erased just days after the shit storm passed. The ground was practically vacuumed during cleanup. That means evidence of my capture story is nil. The dead wolf bodies are long gone and nothing of interest is left in Anchorage. I came back here to pick up the pursuit... or at least that's what I want to do. I want your permission to keep looking for whoever was funding Crane."

She watched Lane nod absently as he started tapping his pencil more rapidly on his desk. She'd never seen him actually use his tapping pencil for writing. The noise he was making was especially annoying to her sensitized werewolf hearing. She had to restrain herself from snatching the torture device from his fingers.

But it wasn't just the pencil tapping that bothered her. Her senses suddenly went on a four alarm alert. Lane smelled funny—like adrenaline funny. Now why would her long-time handler—

the man who put her in Anchorage to begin with—be generating those chemicals just talking to her?

Then she noticed Lane was staring at something over her shoulder. She turned and looked in the same direction. Only the closed door met her gaze. She turned back and gave him a confused look… mostly on purpose. She was on edge and wanted to know what information he was keeping from her.

"Expecting company, Lane?" Brandi frowned when Lane shrugged and looked away. Her inner alarms went off again… and were even louder.

"When I passed along your story, some interesting individuals got wind of it. So the short answer to your request is yes—you get to keep investigating this situation. Whatever Dr. Randall Crane was doing with those wolves, it was a hell of a lot more than just studying them. You don't kidnap and hold a federal agent hostage without having a bigger agenda—one worth risking jail time in his case."

Brandi blinked a couple times at Lane's conclusions before nodding. "I agree. Someone was financially backing Crane's kookiness because he kept talking about earning two more years of funding. He liked to brag about how smart he was and how famous he was going to be."

Lane's derisive snort made the hair on the back of her neck stand up. It was all she could do not to turn around and look at the door again. The only reason she didn't was because she didn't want to reveal her intuitive apprehension to him.

"You're going to get to look into the matter further, only you're going to have a partner helping out. The powers above us have sent an expert down the food chain. In fact, the man they sent says the two of you have already met."

Brandi shrugged. "Maybe. I think I've worked with just about every department here at least once."

"No. You've never worked with this one," Lane said quietly, but firmly. "This department is different. No one knows what they do—not even me. Yet ironically, they were the ones behind wanting to send an experienced field agent to investigate the wolf abductions. Your need for a break made you the right choice in case things got crazy—which they obviously did."

"Wait. You sent me into that crazy shit blind and let it crash on me? If you would have told me what you were after, I might have taken different precautions," Brandi exclaimed, her gaze raking Lane's toned body. It was funny how sexual attraction never could make up for a man being an outright ass.

"It wasn't my choice. Orders were to let you observe what was there to see. The only survivors found after the explosion were two confused lab technicians. Both vaguely remembered seeing you and two other women just before the place blew. We found a record of your vehicle accident, but no body was found among the charred metal. There were no traces of the two other women either. One of them was a scientist on Feldspar's payroll—probably your wolf rescuer. We don't have much on the other female. Our assumption is both burned to death and their remains were removed by whoever Feldspar paid to do cleanup. What we still don't know is *why* such extreme measures were taken to destroy all evidence at the building site."

"I wondered that myself. I didn't find a glass beaker shard, a piece of metal cage, or anything of value where the building used to be. I also checked the wooded area surrounding the place. There were a few emptied shell casings... nothing more."

"But you got away."

Brandi shrugged. "Sure. You know me—I'm pretty hard to kill. So when do I get to meet the expert I'm supposed to work with? I'm kind of anxious to get started looking before the trail gets any colder. Alaska is a very boring place, Lane. I'm ready to have something to focus on."

"The expert is just down the hall. I tucked him away until I made sure you were really you. Are you sure you're up to seeing him now? I could make him come back tomorrow if you want."

Brandi shrugged again and frowned at his odd offer. "Why wouldn't I be ready now?"

"No reason, I guess."

She watched Lane tap a number on his intercom. When the person answered, Lane looked at her as he gave the order.

"Agent Jenkins is ready. Send our guest in."

When Lane stood, she did too. They both turned to the door when it opened. She smelled him before he entered.

"Travis Black Wolf." She spoke his name flatly as she glared.

"In the flesh. Hello, Agent Brandi Jenkins."

"Why are you here, Travis? What the hell is going on?" Brandi demanded.

Travis ignored her questions and her glare, glancing between her and Lane. Finally, she heard him snort.

"I would say that's kind of obvious, wouldn't you?"

"You work here… like *here*?" Brandi demanded, unable to believe she was seeing him.

"Yes. Welcome to your past and my present," Travis said sharply, frowning at Brandi's wounded gaze on him. "I only figured out after I got here that we worked for the same organization… just very different branches."

Brandi shook her head as she ran a hand over it. She turned to Lane. "How much do you know about Travis? He's not what he seems. I know for a fact he tried to murder his grandfather. I know because I helped prevent him from doing it."

She heard Lane snort before he turned a glare in Travis' direction. "Hiring cold-blooded murderers is nothing new around here. Nobody from his department is ever what they seem to be."

"What is this *really* all about, Lane?"

Her boss ignored her query and continued to stare at Travis. She rubbed her nose. Some competition thing was going on between the two men… something she'd walked into blindly. Did Lane already know what she was? She was still pondering how much Lane knew when he spoke again.

"Okay, Black Wolf. I want answers and I want them now. You want me to believe you just conveniently lived near Feldspar and found my wounded agent without reporting it to me?"

Travis shrugged. "That area is near the place I consider home. I was studying Feldspar's activities, just like your agent was. What was going on there sounded like something my department needed to look into so I made a few calls. Though no one seems to have informed her yet, Agent Jenkins now knows too much to stay assigned to regular duty in your area. I'm sure my handler has gone over all that with you. I'm surprised you didn't see fit to cover it with her."

"Oh hell no. I'm not *your department's* anything. I work for Lane. That's final." Brandi narrowed her gaze on Travis as she spoke. She listened to the steady rhythm of his heart. The traitor was telling the truth about his motives... or at least as much of the truth as Travis wanted Lane to know.

She looked back at Lane, scanning her handler's angry face for clues about who she could trust. If Lane had any idea she and Travis were werewolves, it didn't show itself in any fear he felt.

"You wouldn't have watched my agent without investigating her background. Why don't you tell me why Brandi is so interesting to your group?" Lane ordered.

She watched Travis' gaze hold Lane's without flinching. His presence here didn't mesh with her memories of watching his ass exiting the alpha challenge ring to get away from fighting Reed. The last time she'd seen him, Ariel had just killed Travis's cousin and Travis himself had been running away from Reed like the coward he truly was inside his agent suit.

"Brandi showed up in Wasilla in a lab coat. She had no ID whatsoever. And she wasn't talking to anyone. It took me a bit to match her up to the blown up truck and missing person. By that time, I'd guessed enough of her story to report it. We agreed only to me delivering that information to my handler and to you... which I did. The decision to recruit her was not my choice."

Lane shook his head. "Brandi was never supposed to be abducted in the first place. You were supposed to keep anything from happening to her."

Brandi's gaze came back to Lane... her betraying ass handler. "What am I missing here, Lane? I'm not stupid or deaf—but this is making me feel like both. What the hell was I really doing in Alaska? It's past time to come clean with me."

She watched a muscle ticking in Lane's jaw. His anger was escalating. The more calm Travis acted—the madder Lane seemed to get. If she hadn't wanted information so badly, she'd have found their pissing contest entertaining.

"Travis Black Wolf's handler is the one who talked me into sending you up there. I'm going to make some calls. Watch yourself with this guy in the meantime. You probably already told Black Wolf too much."

Brandi nodded as she turned and looked up into Travis' steady gaze. His expression gave nothing away to Lane, but his eyes were speaking volumes to her. What power did Travis have in her organization? Did Ariel and Heidi's fates hang on how she handled this surprise?

Glancing back at Lane, her gut warned her about letting Lane find out the real truth about what happened. She wondered why Travis hadn't already told him. That would be a question for when she got him alone.

"While you talk to the top, I think I'll have a chat with Mr. Expert here. He probably has a lot he wants to tell me, don't you, Travis?"

Brandi smirked when both men snorted at her sarcasm. Damn it, her life hadn't even taken a side trip in Alaska. The most interesting men always ended up being deceitful, manipulating assholes. Why was that?

Some days it was barely worth getting out of bed. That was especially true today. She should have just crawled back on top of Gareth and let the world go on without her. If she had realized she was returning to a job that had screwed her over royally, she might have done just that.

Brandi shrugged as she looked at the attractive young male watching her intently. She could tell he was a bit nervous, probably because he'd seen her kill his and Hanuk's beta in the fight ring. According to werewolf sociology, she and Travis were related as well as being packmates. But Travis Black Wolf certainly didn't seem like family to her, no matter how much he smelled like Reed.

"Come on. Let's get something to eat while we talk. Airplane food sucks."

"Absolutely. Lead the way... I'm still new in town," Travis said, opening the door.

She could feel Lane staring a disbelieving hole in her back, but refused to let herself be bothered anymore by the emotions of either male. Whatever was going on, she would find a way to deal with it herself.

When the needle entered her hip on one sharp jab, Brandi swung instinctively to grab it, but it was far too late.

"You fucking bas..."

She heard Lane calling her name in alarm as her limp body fell neatly into Travis' waiting arms. Blackness claimed her as Travis laughed in her ear.

4

When Brandi woke, she was strapped to a medical gurney. Déjà vu washed over her, making her feel stupid and inept. The one consolation was her clothes were still on this time.

Looking around the room, she saw sinks, IV stands, and extensive lighting mounted on movable fixtures. Science had never been her favorite subject in school, but everything she was seeing pointed to the fact she was in another freaking lab.

"*Shit,*" she swore, staring at the ceiling and feeling like six kinds of a fool.

She was going to kill Travis Black Wolf's betraying werewolf ass, maybe even before she found out what the hell he had really been doing in Lane's office. She didn't for one minute believe he was just another agent like her.

She wiggled her wrists and found them bound securely. Squirming, she felt pain where Travis had stabbed her with a giant hypodermic needle full of knock-out juice.

When the door opened, she turned her head to glare at the person who entered. Her wolf strained inside her, wanting to attack. Brandi snorted and tested the restraints on her wrists again. They were canvass and strong, but not nearly as strong as she was now. A tall, thin man wearing glasses and a falsely apologetic expression approached the bed. She could practically hear him rehearsing his lines before he spoke.

"Hello, Agent Jenkins. I'm Dr. Santiago. I'll be doing the research on your hybrid conversion experience. It would save us a lot of trouble, and you a lot of drugs, if you decide to cooperate with our investigation. I apologize for our rather unorthodox methods of recruitment. We weren't sure you would go along with an official transfer. Your previous handler has reluctantly, but finally, agreed to release your contract to us."

Brandi snorted and looked at the ceiling. "You must be smoking something really good to think that makes any sense to me at all. Being drugged, apprehended, and strapped to a gurney for scientific examination *does not* qualify as a work transfer. You've merely made me your prisoner, Dr. Santiago. I don't intend to be one for long."

She saw him hug the computer tablet to his chest and ponder her like a strange bug he'd pinned to a display board in biology class. Dr. Santiago was just another version of Crazy Crane. Fortunately, he was also human and easily killed, whether she used her wolf or not. Her gaze narrowed on his throat as she contemplated ripping it out. Her wolf danced inside her, ready to help. Brandi decided she just might let her.

"Most come to us with some reservations about working for our department, but I'm afraid you have no choice, Agent Jenkins. Your physiological changes preclude your agent service being conducted elsewhere."

Brandi smiled. It made her examiner visibly nervous just like she hoped. "Okay. Since I'm strapped down and you're not, I guess you have a point. What do I get if I agree to become your test subject?"

Santiago sighed. "You're not my test subject and I am not Randall Crane, Agent Jenkins. I have no wish to make more of you. I just want to see what he's done in your transmutation and figure out how to counteract it."

Brandi snorted. "Who are you trying to bullshit, Doctor? If you're successful in reversing what happened to me, wouldn't you automatically learn how to create more?" She watched him shrug at her conclusion. His smirk combined with his non-answer made her furious. Angry heat spread through her.

One minute Santiago was looming over her. She heard him call out just before his tablet tumbled to the concrete floor. She landed on top of him in wolf form with all four paws pressed into his chest. She growled low and bared her teeth to his wide, frightened gaze. The smell of his urine suddenly filled the air. His complete terror didn't satisfy her or her wolf enough, but she knew smelling his blood would. She opened her mouth and bared her teeth again, preparing to close them around his neck.

When the door opened a second time, complete shock instantly robbed her of her blood lust. Morphing back to human form, Brandi never even felt the familiar pain of changing. The buzz of nanos working under her skin went mostly unnoticed as she stared in shock.

"*Gareth?* What in hell are you doing here?"

Gareth rubbed a hand over his jaw as his gaze took in the dangling straps Brandi had broken when she'd shifted. "Would you believe I came to rescue you?"

Brandi snorted and fisted her hands. "You're too late. I found out my handler was the one who sent me to Feldspar, only it was to investigate Crane—not the wolves. The dipshit who just pissed himself here intends to change me back. I was about to make sure he doesn't get the chance to practice his mad scientist skills on me."

Gareth rubbed a hand over his head. "I see that... but you can't kill him, Brandi. He works here."

"I won't be loud. I can do it quietly with my bare hands and no one will know. I don't need my wolf to end his miserable, needle-probing, dissecting ass."

"I know. Sound carrying is not the reason you can't kill him. Dr. Santiago a scientist... and he works for our side."

Gareth walked into the room cautiously and closed the door. He could smell the adrenaline still pumping through her. He could also smell her happiness to see him. *What a mess. What a fucking mess.*

Reaching down, he extended a hand to the man on the floor and helped him up.

"She... she... surprised me," Dr. Santiago stated.

Gareth nodded as Santiago positioned himself behind him for protection. "I know. She wants to kill you and is trained to do it in more ways than you're used to dealing with, Doctor. I suggest you wait until you have Agent Jenkin's full cooperation before doing any testing. It takes her a while to come around to new thinking."

"Very well, Agent Longfeather. I'll just leave you to your... debriefing... of our new recruit while I go change. Good to see you again. Hope you're enjoying your retirement."

Gareth nodded as the doctor hustled around him and out the door. When his gaze returned to Brandi's, her arms were crossed and her eyes were on fire. Santiago had unknowingly revealed all the secrets he'd been hiding from Brandi in his comments. The error he'd made in waiting was now glaringly obvious.

"Holy hell. You're in on this shit too. If I had my gun on me, I swear I would shoot you without giving it a second thought." Brandi ran a hand over her head as she glared. "Between Lane, Travis, and now you, I've had about all the damn back stabbing I can take. Is Matt an agent too?"

Gareth shook his head. "No. No others from our pack. Just me. I didn't know Travis was an agent until the day you left. When I called in, I was told he had offered to help induct you. I was told to stand down and let it happen as planned."

Brandi snorted. "Induct me into what exactly? Does our

government have some kind of secret society that collects the misfit creations of its power mad scientists?"

She studied Gareth's guilty expression while mentally gauging what it would take to get around him and out the door. She had no idea what waited beyond it, but she was not going down easily again. In fact, if she could help it, she was not going down again at all.

Brandi watched a somber Gareth nod and frown.

"Our department is a monitoring service for human hybrids of any kind. Each newly discovered hybrid is researched and studied so a strategy can be developed to handle them in case they go rogue. There are many other hybrids like you, including those whose experimental situations didn't turn out as well. They're all in the database of this organization. Hybrids are chipped so they can be tracked if they escape."

"*Chipped?* You mean *I'm* chipped... like a fucking vet clinic does to a dog or cat?" Brandi shook her head and groaned. "I swear my taste in men gets worse every year. We slept together for two months, Gareth. I even told you the truth about what I did for a living. Do you know many people I ever disclose my life to? None, Gareth. None. Because the only man I ever told before you used the information to try and have me killed."

Gareth sighed. "I know. You told me. I wish now I had told you about this, but I couldn't bring myself to do it. I knew it was going to be like this when you found out. I guess I was being a coward, selfishly wanting to keep you to myself. I'm sorry, Brandi. I should have warned you... or something."

"*Or something?* Lane sent me to Crazy Crane and delivered me up as a test subject. You let me come back here knowing damn well I would be collected as a lab rat the moment I arrived. And now, thanks to you—and fucking Travis—these crazy shit scientists already know all there is to know about me. I bet you guys told them about Ariel and Heidi too. Have I got everything about right, Agent Longfeather?"

Gareth rubbed his jaw. "I didn't know the part about your handler setting you up, but that doesn't surprise me. That's how most agents get involved in hybridization experiments. Only a few have volunteered."

Brandi turned, grabbed an IV stand, and deftly swung it in Gareth's direction. He ducked of course, but she had anticipated his block, and his defensive reactions. When he dove at her to wrestle the IV stand from her grasp, she quickly released it to his hold. Catching him off-guard, she grabbed his free arm and twisted it behind him until she had enough leverage to put Gareth on the floor. The IV stand clanged on the concrete as it fell from his grasp and rolled away from their bodies.

If Gareth had changed into his wolf during any part of their struggle, it might have been a different fight altogether. She figured regret was making him careless. She wasn't going to let it do the same to her.

"Pay attention here, Gareth. This is how agents break up with each other."

She raised his head and sharply slammed it back down on the concrete floor of the lab. Gareth's sudden stillness beneath her knee was her safe signal to climb off his back and move quietly to the door. She opened it, peeked out, and saw two tall, blond men talking to Travis across the room. With all the noise her tussle with Gareth had caused, she had to believe the room was soundproofed. Whoever was running this place obviously didn't want other employees hearing the screams of their unwilling test subjects.

She rubbed the spot on her ass where Travis had shoved the needle as she glared at him through the crack. Thank God she never shared Ariel's conscience about taking out Reed's family members. If she ever got the traitorous werewolf alone again, she was going to take Travis out once and for all. Reed had plenty of children and grandchildren. One less clone of him wouldn't harm the Black Wolf gene pool. Plus, Reed would probably kill Travis himself if he knew he was putting his whole pack at risk.

She glanced back at Gareth still face down on the floor. A trickle of blood seeped out from under his forehead. She was still too mad at him to regret her actions in taking him down, but something unfamiliar was tugging at her heart.

Shaking her head over her uncustomary compassion, she grabbed a handful of gauze from some sort of nearby prep tray and knelt to slide it under his forehead. No doubt Gareth would heal and come after her eventually. Hopefully by then she would have gotten away without leaving a trail.

Standing once more, she pondered how best to handle the situation. She felt around on her body for tender spots that might be hiding a tracking chip. Gareth hadn't confirmed the presence of one in her, but he had heavily insinuated it. Had that been done before she'd gone to Alaska? If so, why hadn't Lane known where she was? Or had he?

Rubbing her face in misery with each downward spiraling thought, Brandi decided waiting around was no way to constructively handle this. Walking to the door again, she opened it just wide enough to peek out. The two blond guys were still there, but Travis was now nowhere to be found. Telling herself it was a good thing, she shook her head and pondered how to play her escape.

Decision finally made, Brandi finger-combed her hair back into its normal shaggy chaos and walked out of the lab room confidently, heading straight for the two blond guys. Smiling, she waved as she got closer. "Hi. I'm Agent Brandi Jenkins—newest recruit—I guess. Where did Travis go? I wanted to talk to him." She sniffed the air. "What are you guys?"

"We are very handsome... and my name is Fallon... just Fallon. This is Lars... my partner. He is less handsome, but passably good-looking if you like his type. He is lucky I have bad vision."

Brandi laughed at the guy's teasing, but it wasn't really a joke.

Fallon was incredibly handsome... but then so was Lars. They were both quite striking... and Nordic sounding.

"You are Gareth's woman... his new mate?" Lars asked.

Though usually in perfect control of her reactions, especially while trying to escape captivity of any sort, Brandi couldn't prevent her mouth from dropping open at his query.

"*Mate?* Are kidding me? Gareth is good in bed, but he's also a lying bastard. So no... we're not mates. Right now, we're not even friends."

Fallon chuckled before he turned to Lars. "He didn't tell her about this. Now she is mad. He is still silent and strong... and just as stupid as ever."

When Lars huffed indignantly, it made her chuckle at the dynamic between them... before she caught herself.

"If I were her, I would be mad too," Lars declared. "Did you hurt him when you fought just now?"

Brandi bit her lip. Damn. An open fight with these two did not mesh with her need to get away. "I don't think so. Gareth's head is too hard."

Fallon burst out laughing. "I like you already. The mighty Gareth... felled by a female. This I must see happen sometime."

"Does Gareth need medical attention?" Lars asked.

Brandi reached out and patted his arm. "You are a very good man, Lars."

"No. Do not tell him that," Fallon protested. "He has the big head already."

Laughing, Brandi took a step back. "So... are you two going to let me go?"

"Depends. Are you going after Travis? He said he was returning home and Alaska is very far away. You would make it a very expensive chase if we had to collect you from there."

Brandi shook her head and sighed. "Then I guess I'm not going back to Alaska just yet. It's tempting to go kill Travis Black Wolf's betraying ass, but I suppose it can keep until next time. But I do need some time alone to think about what kind of shit pile I've landed in here."

"I hear much anger between your words. Your friends in Alaska... they are quite safe. You keep them that way by willingly being here," Lars declared quietly.

Brandi blew out a breath, not happy with the advice, but she felt the truth of it in her gut. "Did you guys get the same deal from the people in charge?"

Fallon and Lars exchanged long looks before they both shook their heads.

"Not exactly. We are special... *two of a kind*," Fallon declared.

Brandi snickered at Fallon's bragging. "Well, I made creepy Dr. Santiago piss himself a few minutes ago. How much trouble am I going to be in for it? He announced he was going to reverse engineer me and my animal side didn't react well to the news."

Fallon snickered then covered his mouth with a hand to laugh. Lars smacked his arm. Brandi grinned. Friendships formed quickly and lightly had always suited her well. She was glad to find such friendships here because she'd surely made some whopping mistakes trusting people in Alaska.

Fallon shrugged as he spoke. "Santiago is a little fish scientist. You need to see the big fish. I don't know how he will feel about your intimidation methods."

Brandi lifted her hand. "Fine. Let's get the introduction over with and see what he says. Point me in his general direction."

She saw Lars shaking his head. "What?"

"You might want to give that some thought first. His name is *Sheldon Crane*—as in slightly better scientist brother of *Randall Crane*. I believe you have already had the pleasure of Randall Crane's acquaintance."

"Brother? Well, fuck me for being a complete idiot," Brandi exclaimed in anger, running both hands through her hair as she groaned in disbelief. She had only been in Virginia a matter of hours, but she already knew who had most likely been funding the man who experimented on her. It had been her own damn government—the government she'd served most of her life already. Could she have been anymore blind?

Fallon gave her a wicked smile. "Unfortunately, I cannot accept the lovely offer of enjoying your body. You are very attractive, but you smell too much like Gareth."

"You would cheat on me with a *wolf woman*?"

Lars landed a hard punch on Fallon's shoulder which had Brandi reluctantly chuckling again, despite her shock.

"Hopefully Gareth's stink will wear off after a while," she declared.

Lars snorted. "Why bother trying to remove it? Gareth will just put it back. He only came back for you. After what happened to his last mate..."

Brandi saw Lars wince when Fallon punched him—and hard.

"*Paska*! I was not going to tell her all the man's secrets, Fallon."

Brandi looked between the two of them, wondering what Fallon had stopped Lars from revealing.

Not that it mattered.

What mattered was keeping Ariel and Heidi safe until she could figure out how to deal with what was going on. These two acted blasé about her staying, but their unsteady heartbeats told her it was best not to run. She imagined they wouldn't hesitate to do what was necessary to retain her when they felt the urge.

"It's okay, Lars. Gareth's past is none of my business. But I guess I need to go wake him up if I'm staying."

"We'll help you. I can carry him. I've done it many times before," Fallon declared.

Following her instincts to gain all the sympathy she could, Brandi nodded as the three of them headed reluctantly back to the lab room. With nowhere else to go in Alexandria, she was going to need all the allies she could get where she was. Lying, traitorous, bastard ones would have to be included.

"Guys... I have an apartment... *shit*. Or at least I did. Can

Gareth and I get a lift there to see if my key still works for it? I need time to sort this out."

"You are taking Gareth home with you instead of to his hotel?"

When Lars looked surprised at her seemingly abrupt change of mind, it made her laugh. "Yes. I'm just going to put Gareth to bed, see that he heals, and then make him help me tomorrow. Trust me... what we had in Alaska is over now... completely over after he lied to me."

"But what if it is not over for Gareth?" Lars asked.

"Trying to change my mind would not be wise unless he has a death wish. I do not forgive betrayals." She heard Fallon chuckling and turned to face him. "I'm not joking, Fallon."

"Of course not. You are a dangerous lover. I can respect that," Fallon declared with a smile.

Brandi smiled back at the flattery, appreciating Fallon's observation, even though the words were offered with a good deal of sarcasm. "Yes. I suppose I am a dangerous lover. But I'm also a great friend."

"Good. We need more of those, even if they are wolves," Lars declared.

"Hey—I like being a wolf. It's better than being a... being a... " Brandi sniffed as they opened the lab room door. "You're some sort of exotic cat."

Lars laughed. "So our noses mean we have no secrets from each other, eh? I like this idea. Tell us... is Gareth a wild man in bed? Fallon and I have often wondered."

"*Gareth? A wild man?*" Brandi burst out laughing. "No. Gareth's just proficient. He gets the job done. Better than some men at least."

Fallon and Lars both chuckled at her less than sterling summary of Gareth's bedroom talents as they lifted the still unconscious man from the floor. They positioned him over Fallon's shoulder. Then out they all trekked out again, heading down the long hall to an elevator. Brandi assumed it would take them to a parking garage.

A familiar figure in a white coat walked towards them. When he passed by, Brandi growled low in her throat. She had to fight the urge to howl and break his ear drums when Dr. Santiago flinched and jumped in alarm. The tablet he clutched flew from his grip and went skittering down the hallway floor. The nervous doctor scrambled after it. She snorted at his fright and grinned as they walked on through what turned out to be a mostly empty building.

As they stepped into the elevator, Fallon and Lars were speculating about whether or not the man would have to go change clothes again.

Brandi told herself she shouldn't feel so proud.

Want more info? Visit the web page for Book 2.

EXCERPT FROM BOOK 3

HEIDI: NANO WOLVES 3

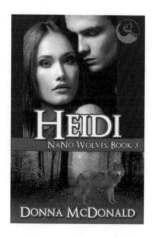

1

Heidi sighed and climbed from their still warm bed as she watched Ryan pace the confines of her room at the inn. Though she'd never seen her lover's animal side in reality, it was easy to see the restless wolf prowling inside the even more restless man. Ryan continued complaining as he dressed.

She went to the bathroom to wash her face, but left to the door slightly open to be polite.

Ryan's blind persistence about the state of their relationship left no room for her to express any feelings of doubt she still had. She felt pressured by his constant demands for more than she wanted to give at that moment. Was she fond of Ryan? Yes, of course. Did she love him? Her answer was always a big "I don't know" which was the core of her problem, and more than enough reason to slow things down.

She was tired of fighting and trying to get him to see she needed time, space, and the freedom to figure things out. Instead, they'd been having this exact argument every day since she'd finally found a way to move out of the inn and into her own place. Not that she'd found her perfect sanctuary to live in yet, but apparently her intention to do so was more independence from her than Ryan could handle. He insisted she had to live with him and refused to hear anything to the contrary.

"Tell me the truth, Heidi. Do you want someone else in the pack? I know you see nearly every male come through the healing center at some point."

Heidi fisted a hand on her hip and glared at her jealous lover. "How many times are you going to ask me that stupid question? One possessive werewolf is more than enough for any sane woman to want to deal with. You know you're more than enough male in bed. Some nights you barely let me sleep, Ryan. What more could I want?"

Ryan growled, unable to hold it back. "If I'm so great in bed, then why won't you talk about moving in with me?"

Heidi snorted at the sound. It took more than a bunch of growling to intimidate her these days. Ariel and Brandi growled constantly. She wasn't immune yet, but she was damn close.

"I'm not going to move in with a man just because of great sex. I've had my share of sleeping with men and the ghosts of their former lovers. I think we both need some space to work through things before we can talk about any sort of real future."

"Fine. I'll buy a new bed, one I never shared with any other female. See? Ghosts all gone. Problem solved," Ryan said, lifting a hand.

Heidi shook her head. "Are you not hearing my words? Closure is about a lot more than a piece of furniture, Ryan. You're not just going to slide me into your mate's old house and make me an echo of a dead woman—wolf—*whatever*."

"That doesn't make any sense. My mate's been gone for years now. I'm ready to mate again—*with you*. Come live with me and change whatever you want," Ryan insisted.

Heidi growled, the sound rumbling in her chest as it surprised her. She seemed to growl a lot when she was aggravated. "I don't know who I am yet, so there's no way you could know if I'm right for you. I need time to figure things out, not constant pressure. That's not unreasonable given all I've been through, now is it?"

Ryan huffed out a breath and then snorted. "I know you went through a lot being changed into a werewolf, but your pack mates have both adapted and taken mates. Why can't you?"

Heidi swallowed the hurt she felt at being unfavorably compared to two women she greatly admired. "In case it has escaped your wolf senses, I'm not Ariel or Brandi. And if you think their lives are a bed of roses with their so-called mates, they're not. They make things work on their own terms."

"Mating is simply two people wanting to be together. It doesn't have terms," Ryan said firmly.

"You're twisting my words because you're not hearing what I'm saying. I can't fight with you every day, and also be calm enough to do the healing work at the center. I need time for myself, and… and my Alpha said I could have it. One way or the other, I intend to create a living space where I can grow into the person I was meant to be. Right now I don't see that being with you when all we do is argue."

"Is that your final word on the matter?" Ryan asked, tugging on his coat and hat.

Heidi nodded tightly. "Yes. Whether you understand my reasons or not, I'm taking the time I need to sort myself out."

"Fine," Ryan said, marching out the door and slamming it behind him.

"Fine to you, too!" Heidi yelled, knowing his werewolf hearing would pick up her sarcastic echo.

She was still glaring when the door suddenly opened again. Her whole body relaxed when she saw it was Brandi. Her pack mate and friend came in and perched on the edge of her bed.

"Trouble with your Calder triplet of choice?" Brandi asked.

Heidi snorted. "I should have just picked stupid Junior, but no, I had to pick the needy, serious one."

Brandi chuckled. "I passed Ryan as I came up the stairs. He looked upset."

Heidi grabbed two handfuls of her hair and yanked as she growled loudly. Brandi's laughter had her releasing her inner bitch who was still seething mad at him.

"I will not be pressured into becoming Ryan's mate. I don't even need Ariel's directive against it anymore. He's made me so mad now that all I want to do is stay the *Hello Pete* away from him."

"*Hello Pete?*" Brandi repeated, laughing at the phrase. "Is that how you swear?"

"Yes. I was raised in a conservative town," Heidi explained.

"Me too," Brandi said. "But it didn't fucking take in my case. The military wiped the rest away."

Heidi snickered. "You think I'm a big wimp, don't you?"

"No." Brandi rose and walked close enough to put a hand on Heidi's shoulder. "No, you're definitely not a wimp. A wimp would never have run with us that day. A wimp would have turned herself in to the authorities by now. You are hell and far from being a wimp."

"Yeah? So what am I then?" Heidi asked, her confidence frayed. "I wish someone would tell me, because I sure as the sun shines don't know."

"You're going to be whatever the hell you choose to be, which is what I always see in my visions of your future. And speaking of visions... that's why I'm here this morning. Can you call Eva and come out with me instead? I need to check on something I saw last night."

Heidi's anger disappeared as fast as it had built within her. She'd always seen her ability to set anger aside as a gift, but it had sometimes made her an emotional doormat. There had to be something in-between the two extremes. There just had to be.

She nodded and grabbed a jacket from the closet. Eva would

have to understand because the needs of her primary pack came first.

"What did you see in your vision?"

She watched Brandi run a hand through her now shoulder length hair that she had to cut every five days. It was a big change from the short, choppy bob Brandi had worn when they met. For reasons none of them could explain, their nanos chose certain aspects of their personal appearance to tweak. Brandi's nanos evidently liked her with long hair. Gareth did too, but then wasn't that true of all males?

"I don't know if what I had was a vision or just a very strange dream. I couldn't tell this time. But if I don't go see the place I saw in my head, the wondering over it will drive me crazy."

Heidi nodded to show her acceptance. "Okay. Let's go. I'll call Eva on the way. Is Ariel going with us?"

"Of course. She's downstairs waiting now."

The helicopter blades still whirled quietly overhead as Katarina Volkov ducked and ran under them. She did not turn to look at the dead pilot she'd left on the ground, nor did she lift her middle finger to salute the blasted flying machine. She wanted to do both, but did neither because there was no time to vent her frustration in the usual ways.

She'd killed the pilot to escape. What was done—was done. Now all she could do was run before the pilot's boss came back.

The silver collar her captor had put on her was still doing its job very well. Although it had kept her from shifting to a wolf, it had not drained her determination to flee when she saw the chance. Her handsome abductor would not be happy to return and find his expensive pilot dead. The one he called boss on the phone would not be happy either.

Of course, if she ended up dying in her escape, she would be the least happy of all... which she was smart enough to know could still happen. The collar burned her neck so badly it felt like she was choking. Perhaps it was all in her mind. She was still woozy from the drugs they'd used on her when they'd stolen her from her modest professorial home at Moscow State University.

If she could have shifted to a wolf, it would have improved her weakened condition, but wishing for the impossible would not help her survive. It was up to her human form and that was always a bit of a challenge in dire circumstances.

Curse her luck with men. Her handsome abductor possessed hair of midnight black and eyes like green jewels. Waking to see him standing over her had seemed a fantasy come true until she noticed his eyes held absolutely no delight. He gave her some water and eventually some food. Then he drugged her again, jabbing the syringe into her arm with no remorse at all.

He'd even refused to give her his name and brusquely told her she didn't need to know.

Her inner wolf had worked hard to push away the drugs from her organs because she woke up to find the plane resting on the ground. She listened to her captor tell the pilot how he had to go into Anchorage. The idea of escape seemed destined once she knew where she was. The pilot's attempt to accost her had provided the last motivation her wolf side had needed to find the energy to strike.

Alaska was not her motherland, but it was close in many ways. She decided if she didn't die, she would run. She would run across Alaska until she found the pack that the visionary, Nicolai Vashchenko, had joined during her grandfather's time. Before her father had banished her, the grandfather she'd liked had filled her head with tales about him, tales her mother had often punished her for repeating.

From Russia to Alaska, Nicolai had roamed across continents until he'd found a new pack—one that appreciated his gifts of prophesy and second sight. Once settled, he'd sent word back to one or two friends that he was doing fine. He did not care enough at that point to tell the family who'd shunned him. He also did not tell the woman who'd said she loved him, but had no faith in his calling.

Giving up on Nicolai, her grandmother had eventually taken another mate, Katarina's own grandfather, which is why she now existed. Yet her grandmother had not given her grandfather a mating that was a whole love. It was Nicolai Vashchenko's name on her grandmother's lips when her final breath left her. Only after Katarina was fully grown did she realize her grandmother's deathbed utterance had broken what was left of her grandfather's heart.

Yet why had it surprised? Even as a child, Katarina had known her existence came from one heartache chasing after another. Her mother conceived her without a true mating and her biological father refused to admit she was his. In her pack, giving birth to a female Alpha was mostly seen as a curse on your family.

Perhaps it was true.

No one had stepped forward to claim her as mate or to help her defend her right to rule the pack. But everyone had supported her father in getting rid of her.

Her father hated her. She knew for truth because he'd said so often and with great passion.

She'd seen surprise—and what she wished was pride—in her father's eyes only once. His sons by a female not her mother were not borne Alphas, but both had attempted to be one to please the unhappy male who sired them all. She'd emerged the victor from their public attack only to be immediately sent away in shame.

Shunned, Katarina had gone to nearby Moscow and resigned herself to live among humans until her destiny changed. She had lacked Nicolai's courage to venture so far from what she'd known all her life... and she secretly hoped to be missed and asked to return. Years passed though—over fifty years—with no changes. She'd heard nothing from her pack in all that time, other than a brief message telling her that her biological mother had died. She'd grieved alone and then she'd gone on.

Until the day a handsome wolf had taken her from her home.

Katarina slowed her jog as her vision blurred. Her throat tightened painfully, obstructing her breathing more than ever. Her wolf urged her on, saying help was close, but how would her wolf know such a thing? Her monthly shifts had never been enough to appease the restless animal inside her. Unhappiness had eventually turned inward to become unpleasant traits like irritation and impatience with everyone. She fought a daily battle to push away the despair of being alone.

Humbled by the true possibility of death, she found herself praying Nicolai's Alaskan pack might find and help her, but life had taught her prayers often went unanswered. After years of no werewolf company but her own, she'd come to her own conclusions about the hierarchy of her species. Alphas got discouraged just like regular pack members. They were just hard-wired not to show it, which was the only reason her protesting feet still carried her forward. It was the one thing about herself she trusted implicitly.

A jolt of electricity shot through the collar and the blazing pain stole what was left of her bravery. The rising black behind her eyelids overshadowed her deep disappointment in herself for not succeeding in her escape. She thought wistfully of her grandfather's home in Balashikha. She thought of Moscow, St. Petersburg, and all the places she'd miss in her motherland when she was no more.

No one was coming for her. No one cared. She'd lived alone. Now it seemed she would die that way as well.

On her knees, Katarina called once more to the spirit of her grandmother's true love. She did so in English, which might have been the language of his new people. In either case, it was the only other one she half-way knew.

"Nicolai Vashchenko in the great ever after, I ask you to meet me on other side," Katarina whispered.

Gritting her teeth, she screamed, but it only came out a croak. Her hands stung like fire as she made one last attempt to rip the silver collar off before she hit the ground.

2

Ariel drove them in the SUV Matt bought for her so she wouldn't have to shift and run everywhere she needed to go while he was busy in town. Brandi sat in the passenger seat pointing out turns.

Heidi's comfort level with the two women still amazed her even after all the months that had passed since their turning. They said "let's go" and without questioning, she climbed into vehicles with them and just went. Why? She wasn't sure. Reed told her innate trust was just a natural part of pack mentality.

Brandi pointed up ahead. "There... see that grove of trees off to the right. There's a field just beyond it. I think there's a path from the roads to the woods. Pull along the edge if you can't find a place to park."

Ariel glanced at her excited Beta. "Thought I was the Alpha in this group."

"I have three words for you," Brandi said, her smile widening as she pointed a finger at her own chest. "Agent. Bossy. Visionary." She reached out and patted Ariel's shoulder. "Don't worry, Doc. You're still the smartest among us."

"Is that sarcasm?" Ariel demanded, trying not to laugh.

In the backseat, Heidi decided Brandi was like a werewolf GPS. The woman never got lost, and even when madder than Heidi had ever seen anyone get except Ariel, Brandi always remained in control. She secretly longed for just a little of that emotional cool— or whatever the quality was.

Ariel pulled off the road into a grassy lane and put the vehicle against the edge as much as possible. "That's the best I can do. If someone comes along, they'll never get by us."

"Not likely. From the looks of things, this road hasn't been used in ages. I'm guessing three years or more," Brandi said, walking ahead of them.

Heidi zipped up her jacket and stuck her hands in both her pockets. She matched her stride to Ariel's. Brandi walked quickly ahead, soon disappearing among the trees in her hunt.

"You and Ryan have a bad morning?" Ariel asked.

Heidi sighed as they walked. Guess everyone in the inn had heard at least part of their fight.

"I've worked enough hours at the center to get my own place. Apparently healers earn their living differently than normal people. The rest of what I take in will be in store credit and donations. Basically, I have accounts with money in them all over town. It took me some time to get used to that sort of bartering goods for my services, but I'm ready to own it now. Several people are even looking out for the perfect house for me."

"I'm guessing Ryan doesn't like you being so independent," Ariel said.

Brandi sighed. "I don't know what his problem is. It's like Ryan wants me to be completely dependent on him. Maybe he thinks it gives him a convenient excuse to keep suggesting we move in together. We've been having the same argument for a month now. I want... space. I need time to figure myself out. He wants a commitment I'm not ready for—that I may never be ready for."

Ariel shrugged. "Then you should take all the time you need."

Heidi nodded. "I know. I'm going to take the time, no matter how mad Ryan gets at me over it."

Ariel reached out an arm and let it rest lightly around Heidi's shoulders. "If he truly loves you, he'll deal with letting you find your way."

"Do you think he really loves me?" Heidi asked.

"Don't you?" Ariel asked back.

Heidi sighed and shrugged. Ariel moved her arm and Heidi instantly missed the comfort of it. Her need for her Alpha's approval was strong. "All I know for sure is that sex and love are two different things."

"Don't you mean two parts of the same thing?" Ariel asked, putting her hands in her coat pockets to keep them warm. "When my human marriage starting falling apart, my husband and I lost our sex life first. He rationalized it by saying I was boring in bed. Maybe I was at that time. Whatever the case, divorce soon followed for us. But I can't even imagine having sexual issues with Matt other than his intention to make me pregnant if he can. Our life is balanced with our mutual need of each other. I think this is the way it's supposed to work."

Heidi put her hand on Ariel's arm and made them both stop. "But he knows a baby might not even be possible. Are you sure Matt's trying to get you pregnant?"

Ariel nodded. "Yes. He makes no secret of it. Luckily, I've only been in heat that one time. He was supposed to tell me when it happened, but he conveniently forgot until the third night I'd kept him up and busy. He obviously didn't think my human self-control could hold out during that phase, but changed his tune after I slept in his guest room for the remaining two nights of the cycle."

Wide-eyed at the news her Alpha was sharing, Heidi let her hand slip away. "Eva and I talked about werewolf heat cycles. I haven't had one yet. Brandi thinks she may have had one when she and Gareth mated, but no babies resulted. Do you think Brandi would tell us if she got another cycle?"

Ariel chuckled. "Yes. Us... Gareth... and whoever else upset her while it was happening. It makes PMS look like a small headache. When it happens to you, you're going to know, Heidi. Unless some scheming male tells you that you have the equivalent of a werewolf flu. If Nanuka hadn't come by to visit, I might never have known the truth. She glared at Matt and didn't back down or leave until I'd processed what was happening for myself."

"Wow. He must want children very badly," Heidi whispered as they started walking again.

"Or he wants to prove my scientific theory about it being impossible is wrong," Ariel suggested.

Heidi sighed again. "Are all males just controlling jackwagons?"

"*Jackwagons?*" Ariel asked, chuckling over the term.

Rolling her eyes, Heidi picked up her pace. "Yeah. Yeah. I know my swearing sucks. I'm a wimp."

Ariel laughed loudly. "You are hell and far from being a wimp. You may be behind a bit in your personal evolution, but that doesn't mean it's not happening. You saved my life when it was supposed to be impossible. Who knows what you're capable of doing? Cut yourself a break and just be happy to be you, honey."

"Thank you, Ariel." Heidi launched herself at her Alpha who laughed as she pulled her in for a comforting hug.

Brandi's yell and subsequent swearing had them both pushing away from each other to run in the direction of her voice.

"Hey, I found her! Ouch—damn silver! You sorry ass motherfuckers. Shit, that hurts like a mad bitch."

They cut through the trees and brush in the short stretch of woods separating the road from the grassy field behind it. They found Brandi bent over something hidden in a bunch of tall grass.

Heidi was almost completely out of breath by the time she stopped running. Her Alpha was hard to keep up with when she was moving at top speed, even in human form. She dropped to her knees beside the woman Brandi had rolled over. The werewolf was medium height with a curvy, no-nonsense kind of female build. A mile of long, reddish brown curls had been woven into a braid and slung over one shoulder to fall down the front of her.

She wore a silver collar around her neck, which had left burn marks against any skin the silver had touched.

The three of them looked up at the same time and stared at each other. Shared memories of their time with Crazy Crane precluded the need to talk. Someone had made sure this woman couldn't shift. The question was... why?

Brandi dug out her phone. Seconds later, she said in a rush. "Gareth, check on the kids. Tell Jesse and Marilyn that someone may be after them. The kids know the drill to disappear and stay gone until they hear from us. We found the collared female werewolf I dreamed about and someone's obviously..."

Interrupted by a loud growl, Heidi watched Brandi hold the phone away as Gareth yelled through the connection, and then she pulled it back to her ear.

While Brandi argued with her mate, Heidi examined the woman. Did Ryan really expect her to jump into mating madness with him? No thank you. She needed a much calmer life and she intended to have one—even if it meant living alone.

"Gareth—if you'll shut up for a minute, I'll explain. I didn't tell you about the vision because I thought it was a damn dream. Stewart didn't say anything this morning, and you know he always does when I've had a real vision. I couldn't stop thinking about it though, so I talked Ariel and Heidi into taking a little road trip with me just to check. Now I have to go because this person I've found may actually be dying. Next time don't freaking yell at me when I call and need your help. Okay. Good. I love you too. Check on the kids."

Brandi flipped the phone closed. "Gareth should be grateful he's so good in bed because most of the time he's hell to live with outside of it. Him and his stupid cows drive me fucking crazy on the best of days. Cattle farmer, my ass. Controlling werewolf bastard is more like it."

Ariel cleared her throat and looked over Heidi's bowed head. "Ix-nay on the astard-bay stuff, Brandi."

Heidi grunted in disgust. "Pig Latin? What am I? Two?" She shook her head as she tried to ground herself to the earth as Eva taught her. "Could I please have some quiet so I can concentrate here? I may have to shift if I can't get centered as a human."

From the beginning, Eva had taught her to diagnose without shifting. They did a meditation to call her wolf power up without becoming a full wolf. What she hadn't told Eva is that her nanos scrambled anyway, preparing her body for the transmutation whether she went through with it or not. Using the power of her wolf sent a million ants crawling just under her skin. She'd often had to learn to ignore their clamoring to fix what wasn't broken.

Heidi held her hands above the woman's midsection. "She has bruising on her spleen and two cracked ribs. I'm also sensing there's some internal bleeding which could kill her. Seems like she had to fight to get away from whoever had her. The internal bleeding is bad news, but the real problem is that collar. It's keeping her wolf from helping. We need to get it off."

"I tried to break it," Brandi said, showing her wounded fingers. Silver caused what looked like third degree burns on all werewolves.

Heidi looked at Ariel, who just shook her head sadly. Ariel couldn't do it either. "We'll have to take her to Eva. She has tools to remove the collar safely."

Now it was Heidi's turn to shake her head. "No. She's fading too much. I don't think she has that long. But I have a theory about how to get it off."

"Her breathing is getting more shallow. Better try something fast," Brandi added, still crouching by the woman.

Nodding again, Heidi rose to her knees, leaning over the

woman. She closed her eyes, but instead of calling her wolf, she called to the human side of herself. She thought about being a human teenager. Her best friend at the time had given her a sterling silver necklace with half a heart that fit like a puzzle with the other half her friend wore. She mentally put on the silver friendship necklace again, envisioning the silver chain resting comfortably around her neck. Her nanos went on high alert for the task, scrambling so hard under her skin that they made her wince in pain.

"What is it? What are you doing?" Ariel demanded.

"Shush," Heidi ordered, not opening her eyes. "I'm fine. I'm talking to my nanos."

Then she opened her eyes, reached behind the woman's neck, and felt for a clasp. The silver was cool to her touch. She unclipped the latch of the collar, amazed that it came undone so easily. The woman gasped, rolled to her side, and coughed as she fought to breathe normally again.

Ariel pulled off her t-shirt and held it out. Heidi dropped the silver collar in the middle of it. They watched the woman open her eyes and stare at them.

"Shift to wolf so you can heal," Heidi ordered.

"Collar," the woman said hoarsely.

"It's gone now," Heidi answered. She also nodded to emphasize it was true. "You're safe with us. I promise. Now shift to heal."

Nodding briefly, the woman crawled to her knees and morphed into a stunning silver wolf, quite surprising since her human coloring was just the opposite.

"Is it me or does she remind you of someone?" Brandi asked, watching the large wolf walk around.

"Her wolf is an unusual color for around here, but everything else looks like she could be one of Reed's pack," Ariel supplied.

Heidi raised an eyebrow as she watched the silver she-wolf now attempt to run. Empathy had her remembering how it felt to let your animal side roam freely. Her nanos instantly scrambled again, changing her body back to werewolf. She accepted that now as just normal. It had felt strange being completely human again anyway, even for such a short time. How strange it had felt had surprised her. Her wolf side made her stronger, wiser, better. That was evident in her healing work.

The last of her resentment about her fate drifted away on the breeze blowing by them all. It was one of those moments you treasure quietly and tuck away inside you as profound. Heidi sighed as her gaze came back to the silver wolf who looked at her and whined.

"You're fine. I'm a pack healer. You can trust what I say. Shifting should be enough to get you functional again. Do it a couple more times."

Heidi turned to see Ariel and Brandi looking at her instead of the werewolf they'd just rescued. "What?" she asked, slightly uncomfortable with their intense interest.

"You sound just like Eva when she's giving orders," Ariel finally said.

Heidi smiled, and then she laughed. "You always say the nicest things to me, Ariel."

She swung her gaze and grinned at Brandi, nearly smirking—okay, maybe completely smirking—over her Alpha's compliment. "Want to say something nice to me as well?"

"No," Brandi said, fighting her twitching mouth. "I want to know how in hell you removed that silver collar without burning your fingers to the bone."

Ariel chuckled. Heidi's smile for both of them was wide. "Healing secret," Heidi declared.

A naked woman walking up to them wearing only her shoes interrupted their private conversation. The size of the silver wolf seemed out of proportion compared to what the small female looked like in human form. They stared, each fighting her own reaction to seeing such big breasts on someone shorter than any of the three of them. Unable to fight off the urge, they each looked down at their own much smaller breasts and then back at the stranger's.

Brandi looked off and said nothing. Heidi bit her lip to stop herself from giggling when Ariel covered her mouth with her hand to keep from laughing. The woman facing them didn't seem embarrassed a bit, just uncomfortable to be standing there nude in front of them.

"Forgive please my nudeness. Clothes are back on plane they used to steal me. Soon the handsome one will come. We go now so I do not have to kill again, yes?"

"Kill again?" Brandi asked carefully.

"Yes. I kill pilot who help steal me from home," she said.

"Are you Russian?" Brandi asked.

"Some would say. Mostly I am werewolf without country or pack. My name is Katarina Volkov. My thanks for you to save me," she said.

When Brandi spoke to her in her native language, Katarina lifted both eyebrows, but answered back. Then she held up a hand. "No wish to be rude. I speak English to honor all those the great Nicolai sent to rescue me."

"Nicolai?" Ariel asked, her brow furrowing.

Katarina nodded. "*Da.* Nicolai Vashchenko, great werewolf who left his pack and found a new home in Alaska. I prayed to him to help me. He sent you."

Brandi laughed. "Actually..."

Ariel cleared her throat and shook her head. "I've heard that name before. Nicolai was a visionary like Brandi. He joined the Black Wolf pack and knew Reed's grandfather. Are you looking for Reed?"

"Reed? Who is this Reed?"

"He's the Black Wolf Alpha now. His grandfather was Nicolai's friend—I think."

Katarina nodded. "Reed," she said again, letting it settle in her mind. "Is good name, yes?"

The three of them nodded in answer.

Ariel smiled. "We're part of Reed's pack too… and we also have our own just the three of us. To complicate matters further, two of us have taken mates in the Gray Wolf pack as well."

Katarina snorted. "Is very complicated."

"You're safe with us, but let's get back to town," Ariel said, turning the way they needed to go. "I have some spare clothes in the car you can wear. They might be too big for you, but they'll beat being naked and cold."

Katarina sighed and fell into step beside the tall, blonde Alpha. "This is for me—how you say—great humiliation. Shift then—no clothes. Just shoes. Always."

Ariel snickered. "Welcome to the club, Sister."

"Club? What is this club?" Katarina asked.

Heidi giggled. "Ariel shifts and loses her clothes too. She only keeps her boots. Brandi and I get to keep our clothes."

Katarina elbowed Ariel. "You are Alpha. Why you allow them such disrespect?"

No longer surprised when any werewolf immediately knew what she was, Ariel shrugged. "These women are more than my pack. They are my friends. I disrespect them back when the mood hits me."

Katarina nodded. "Understood. Nice to have pack. Better to have friends."

"Yes, it is," Ariel agreed.

3

"IT'S NOT FANCY, BUT IT'S CLEAN AND FAR ENOUGH AWAY FROM THE heathens that you should have a modest amount of peace."

Heidi smiled at her pack mate and friend. "What are you talking about? It's every bit as nice as the room at the inn. I had credit built up for several more weeks, so I was happy to let Katarina have it. Poor thing fell asleep as soon as she hit the bed. I appreciate you and Gareth letting me stay with you for a while."

Brandi waved the thanks away. "It's no problem having you here and we have plenty of room. The kids have their own barracks now—I mean, wing of the house."

Heidi giggled at Brandi's slip. "Is being a mother harder than being an agent?"

"Only by a factor of a hundred. Lately it's been made worse by my absentee mate who has to periodically get personal with his cattle. Apparently, it's breeding season. Gareth lets the bull into the pasture, then stands there to make sure he treats the cows right. Yes, I mean that in every sense of the statement."

Heidi laughed. "Bet Gareth comes home in an interesting mood on those days."

Laughing herself, Brandi made a face, but smiled when she thought about it further, and then shrugged. "I won't deny it. I'm just glad we have our privacy back. We get a little loud sometimes."

Silence descended as their conspiratorial laughter faded guiltily away.

Brandi's head suddenly lifted in alarm as she strained to listen. "I have to go check on them. This much quiet is not good with those three."

Heidi waved her away. "Go. I'm fine. The only things I have to unpack are what I pulled out of Matt's donation bin. Everything I own is all in the one bag I brought with me. I've been too busy at the Healing Center to go shopping."

Brandi nodded absently as she jogged away.

Heidi snickered as she looked around the inviting guest room. It was impossible to think of Brandi choosing the homey decorations, so it had to have been Gareth that chose the lavender patchwork quilt and decorative pillows.

Though both her pack mates offered their homes to her, staying with Brandi and Gareth had seemed a better choice than staying with Ariel and Matt. The dual Alphas would never leave her alone to ponder her next step. Whereas Brandi would probably forget she was around, like she did just now when she took off in a run to check on her hybrid werewolf kids.

If only Ryan could be a little more like that. Would he *ever* leave her alone long enough to figure herself out?

Her sigh was loud as she thought of the man she was avoiding. She missed sleeping with him, but he had to understand that she needed time alone—time to think.

What did she want out of this strange new life they all now had in freezing cold Alaska? Was she never going to go to the beach again? Never visit a park? Never go see a ball game?

The last thing she had time to deal with was figuring out how to be mated. Intuiting what was going on inside a person who was hurt or sick still overwhelmed her.

She was fond of Ryan and they had great chemistry. However, chasing physical chemistry from the lower forty-nine to Anchorage was what had stranded her jobless and penniless several years ago. It had not been fun and games to work as an escort just to survive. She didn't regret what she'd done to get by. She regretted being so desperate for love that she'd followed her stupid boyfriend to Alaska where he left her stranded.

Life taught her the hard way that great sex was not the same as real love. Love was... well, she wasn't sure what it was, since she had never found it. Her birth family hadn't exactly been populated with women in solid relationships. Becoming a werewolf hadn't changed the fact that she'd been born and bred to be a weak-hearted human female.

"Which is exactly why I need time to figure this whole werewolf thing out for myself. I don't want to keep being that kind of person," Heidi said aloud, sighing as she carried her single bag of belongings into the room.

"Stop fretting, Ryan. Brandi told us Heidi really likes you. That woman wouldn't say it if it wasn't true. Gareth's mate is simply not that kind of person."

Ryan frowned at his mother. "Why is that good news? Great— so Heidi likes me. Is that what I should want in a mate, Mom? Should I want the woman I love to merely *like* me?"

He yelped at his father's hard tap on the back of his head with a rolled up newspaper.

"Liking your mate is just as important as the bedding, son. I know I've told you boys that since you discovered your man parts were for more important things than pissing in the snow. As the oldest child in this family, you should be the one setting the proper example for your two younger brothers."

Ryan glared as he mulled over their reasoning. He ran a restless hand over his face. Why did no one but him realize that he'd just lost the second woman he'd ever loved?

"I don't see how being born a mere two minutes before Carson and barely four minutes before Dillon makes me the oldest."

"You came out first. That's just the way it works," his father replied.

Ryan glared even harder when his mother laughed at their argument. "I don't know why I'm here. You two are no help at all."

"Well, your father and I don't want to make you more unhappy. You can always go stay with your brothers until Heidi comes around," his mother suggested.

Ryan huffed out a breath. "No. I can't. They're messy and irritating. I need my own space."

Marilyn rolled her eyes before eyeballing her son. "Then why can't you see Heidi wants that for herself."

"Because I know I'm supposed to be with her," Ryan said, glaring back at his mother.

"Speaking of personal space, I thought you were looking at the Holton's property that's for sale. It's past time you got yourself a different place to live, boy. Where you are holds too many memories for you."

Ryan shrugged before sighing in defeat. "I have to wait until my current house sells before I can buy. In the meantime, Heidi refuses to spend the night in a place where I've slept with another woman. She's moving some place without me."

His mother's laugh had him glaring again. "What's so funny about that?"

She shrugged her shoulders. "I don't blame Heidi for feeling that way. She doesn't want to be a replacement for a dead woman. Any woman would feel the same."

Ryan spread his hands. "Which is why I'm selling the freaking house, but these things take time. The realtor said the house was more likely to move quickly if I wasn't messing it up on a daily basis."

"You never messed anything up in your life," his father said. "You're just a little hard-headed… nothing bad though."

His father's faint praise brought a smile to his mouth. "Well, I've messed up my relationship with Heidi. How is it my fault she turned out to be my mate? I never wanted to get so attached to her."

"You think that way because you're a smart man… ouch, Mari. I wasn't talking about me and you," his father protested, rubbing the back of his head where his mother had smacked him.

Their mock fighting brought on a real smile. Ryan sighed as he laughed. "I have to share Heidi with her work. Is that enough torture?"

"Torture? Her work is very important, Ryan. A healer like Heidi is a very worthy mate to care for," his mother said.

Ryan nodded. "True, but Heidi would be a worthy mate for me even if she was nothing more than a store clerk. The healing will always put a demand on her time and energy that I won't be able to fight against. The best I can say is that it truly brings her joy to help people. I just sometimes wish she was like a regular werewolf female. I hate having no idea where I stand."

"You're a worthy mate too, Ryan. I can see why you waited for her to come along before dating again. I think that was a smart move for you," his father said.

The unexpected comment caught him off-guard. Ryan nodded. "Heidi is the first woman to interest me since Claire died. If I get lucky, Heidi will be my last woman. Thanks for saying that though, Dad. It means a lot to me. I never planned on wanting to take a mate again at all."

"You're a good man and a good wolf—all your mother and I could have asked you to grow up to be. Now your brothers…

Dillon and Carson still need a bit more work. All we can do is pray the right females come along."

Brandi panted from exertion as she turned her face from where it was hidden in the pillow. It had almost smothered her, but it had kept her from screaming. Gareth had been in rare form this evening. His rumbling soft growl as he reluctantly slid out of her from behind was just more solid proof. In certain moods, the man was nearly insatiable.

She stretched and gathered her pillow into her arms, sighing and getting comfortable. Gareth wrapped an arm around her and then slid one muscular thigh over the back of her legs.

He idly rubbed her butt with interest, which sent her giggling. "Aren't you supposed to be an old man?"

It was all she could do to stifle her response as Gareth nipped her shoulder sharply. He'd been a gentle, thorough lover during her burning time. He'd been an aggressive, demanding lover when she'd rejected him. Now he could turn that aggressive side on and off at will, and did so just to mess with her. She'd bet money on it.

She rolled her head and smiled at the low-lidded, lust-filled look he gave her. "I'm not complaining, just curious."

"You've been very introspective lately. What's that about?" Gareth demanded softly.

Brandi held his gaze as he idly rubbed his fingers over her rounded, but very toned ass. Muscle tone without workouts was one of just many werewolf perks to her way of thinking.

"I don't think I've ever been introspective in my life," she answered.

"Well, you are now," Gareth said. "Out with whatever it is you're brooding about. Don't make me get rough with you. The kids have gotten used to you yelling at me, but we have a house guest. Heidi might actually come investigate if we start fighting."

Another giggle escaped before she could stifle it. Damn the man. "The three hoodlums we're raising nearly set the house on fire this afternoon. You watch your cattle getting it on all day and come home to me horny as hell, which I have to deal with no matter how tired I am. And now I've got a depressed pack mate bunking in my guest room. What kind of problems could I possibly have to be introspective about, Gareth?"

"Are you whining about getting laid so well? Or just mad I didn't give you that fourth orgasm you were straining after?" Gareth demanded.

Brandi raised up on her arms, whipped her pillow out from under her head, and smacked it over Gareth's face. Leaning over him, she put her weight into it, pretending to smother him just to prove she could. His laughter used up a lot of his air, and before too long she found herself flat on her back. Now Gareth was the one panting as he glared down at her.

She arched an eyebrow. "Let's get something straight, Longfeather. I do not whine. I inform you of my emotional status. You need to make me feel better like you promised. My life is hard and it sucks to be me right now."

Gareth sputtered with laughter as his head fell to his mate's breasts. "I swear I love you like no other. This is about Heidi, isn't it? Because if it's about the kids, you're shit out of luck. They're getting smarter, bigger, and stronger every blessed day. I can't stop that process. They're thriving here."

Brandi snorted and ran a hand through Gareth's hair. "I can handle the kids, but I have no idea what to say to Heidi. She seems so confused."

Gareth moved down and kissed Brandi's stomach. "You say nothing. You hug. You pat. You stand by until she figures it out. There is nothing to do but stand guard."

"Is that official Pack Beta advice?" Brandi asked.

Gareth nodded against the soft skin under his cheek. "Yes. It's also friend advice. You can't make her decisions for her. All you can do is stand by her side while she comes to terms with her own power. Heidi is undergoing an evolution within herself—something you and Ariel breezed through without even realizing it was happening."

Brandi's sigh filled their silent bedroom. "Okay," she said at last. "Any chance I could get that fourth orgasm? I could use the distraction."

Gareth laughed softly as he kissed his way down.

4

SHE WASN'T FINDING ANYTHING CRITICAL, SO HEIDI LET HER MIND drift around while her hands looked for answers. Direct touch told the best story of a person's body, and she was grateful to have gained permission for this check.

The woman on the table lay very still as her hands moved gently from spot to spot, but Heidi could practically see the wheels in Katarina's mind turning and turning. The Russian Alpha's energy was driven to act, to solve, to do something.

Lying still must be a strenuous exercise in control for her. Ariel's energy looked very similar to Katarina's. Come to think of it, Reed's energy did as well.

She smiled over the realization that it must be an alpha thing. Her life seemed full of Alphas needing her care.

"My body hurts, but is not important. I make big problem between Ariel and handsome Matt. They fight over me."

Heidi snickered. "I'll let you in on a little secret, Katarina. Matt is trying to get Ariel pregnant. *That's* what's causing their problems. You're just a safer thing for them to argue about in front of people."

Katarina laughed softly. "Is good to hear," she said.

Heidi smiled and nodded. "Don't worry. They'll be fine."

"You have good soul, Heidi the Healer."

"Thank you," Heidi said, warming to the woman. She smiled down at her and this time held the Russian Alpha's gaze. "So do you. Your energy is very clear. I've found that usually matches a person's conscience."

"*Spasibo*. Life hard, but I not become bitter. Very proud of that."

Heidi walked around the examining table. Katarina watched her with curious eyes.

"Why Ariel not want babies of sexy Gray Wolf Alpha?"

Heidi laughed softly and shrugged. "I have no idea. I'm sure they'd both make great parents."

"So we gamble over it, yes? I put money on Matt."

Heidi laughed for real, the loudness of it surprising her. "You'd bet on Matt? Don't tell Ariel. She'd get mad at you."

Katarina nodded. "Why? Must bet to win. He has starry eyes for her."

"Starry eyes, huh?" Heidi repeated, grinning at the description. "Yes, I suppose he does."

Katarina nodded. "Like your sexy wolf have for you."

"My wolf? I don't have a wolf," Heidi denied.

Katarina touched her nose. "No can lie to this. You smell like him. He smell like you."

"Thanks," Heidi said with an eye roll. A sigh of resignation slipped out after. It irritated her into frowning. "Ryan is just a…" She went silent looking for a way to describe their relationship.

"Mistake?" Katarina suggested.

"No," Heidi admitted, feeling instantly chastised. "Ryan was not a mistake. I like him just fine. He's just… pushy."

Katarina laughed and it too echoed in the room. "Your wolf has dick. All dicks like that. Push is good sometimes, yes?"

Heidi rolled her eyes, but grinned. "Yes. Push is good sometimes." She stepped away from the she-wolf. "Okay, Katarina.

Your insides are still bruised in your human form, so take it easy for a few more days."

"Nothing easy for me," Katarina declared, scooting off the table. "But you help me buy food for stomach, yes?"

Heidi laughed at the question that really was more of an order. Ariel was the least demanding Alpha she'd met so far, including Reed, who routinely told her what to feel. "I guess I could do that. I have to catch a ride home with Brandi's mate in an hour though."

"*Spasibo.*"

"Does that mean thank you?" Heidi asked. She hung up the white lab coat stolen from Feldspar and pulled on the jacket she'd worn to work that morning

"Yes… and is polite," Katarina added.

Heidi nodded as they headed out the door.

Wasilla had two food stores. One was mostly dry goods and dried food that would last for months. The other was a combination of bait shop and refrigerated storage, but it was the only one where you could buy something frozen you could warm up in a microwave.

Ceiling height refrigeration units lined the store walls broken only by a freezer or two. Aquariums full of feeder fish and other forms of bait ran down the middle.

Heidi wrinkled her nose at the fishy smell and now understood completely why Gareth insisted on going to Anchorage to shop. Feeling like the most squeamish werewolf who ever lived, she put her eyes on the ceiling as the store owner scooped two feeder fish out of a tank and handed them over to a couple of older male werewolves as a snack.

Though she heard the bell above it sounding, Heidi didn't look at the door when it opened. Instead, she turned and walked back to where Katarina peered into a refrigeration unit with a frown.

"Need some help?" Heidi asked.

Katarina shrugged. "English is hard and I need practice. I read slow."

"Tell me what you want and I'll help you find it."

Before Katarina could answer, someone said her name.

"Heidi? Is that really you?"

Heidi turned and met the startled gazes of two of her former escort customers. Her wolf squirmed in her gut, uncomfortable around the predatory males. She rubbed her stomach in a warning for her animal to stay out of sight.

"Erwin... Larry. How are you?" she asked, not knowing what else to say.

This was a situation she'd feared happening, but at least she did have a strategy for it. It was the same one she'd used on all the customers she hadn't wanted to be too friendly with as a working girl.

"Everyone thinks you died in the fire at that science lab place," Erwin said.

Heidi shrugged. "I did. Can't you tell?"

Both men laughed at her flippant answer. Katarina mumbled something ominous in Russian and started forward until Heidi yanked her back. Her hands shook at the amount of courage it cost her to restrain the Russian Alpha.

"No, Katarina. Please. I... got this. Trust me."

Katarina crossed her arms as she backed away, but continued to glare at the men and her. Great. Now she had a pissed off Alpha to deal with as well. Her hands shook a little harder at the thought, but she made fists until the quivering eased up.

Larry lifted his chin at Katarina and Heidi sighed about what she had to do.

"Who's your new friend, Heidi? She's awfully cute too. How about Erwin and I buy you two a drink? We can talk about old times. Maybe have a little fun after. What do you say?"

The bell above the store door rang as it opened again. This time her wolf howled in welcome to the man who entered. She looked up and met Ryan's gaze across the room. "No, no, no," she said. But shaking her head did not slow Ryan's momentum as he wove through the growing evening crowd who'd come looking for dinner.

Knowing she had little time left before things got ugly, Heidi stepped close to the two men and put a shaking hand on each of their exposed throats as if caressing them. Her voice was urgent and insistent.

"Listen to my words. I'm not the woman you think I am. I just look like someone you used to know. My husband is coming over to us and you're going to apologize to him for harassing me."

Hoping there'd been enough time for the suggestion to take effect, Heidi dropped her quivering hands and stepped back just as Ryan appeared at her side.

"These guys giving you grief?" Ryan asked calmly, glaring at the two smaller men in front of him.

Heidi swallowed nervously as Erwin and Larry held up their hands to Ryan. They both laughed nervously.

"Man, I'm sorry. Your wife looks like a woman we used to know. We didn't mean any harm," Erwin said.

"No, man. We didn't do nothing to her, just embarrassed all of us," Larry added.

Ryan's brow furrowed at their profuse, overdone apologies. "Fine. Get your business done and get lost."

Heidi swallowed nervously when they laughed at his orders to leave, but was glad they also scrambled to do as he said. She could see why Ryan would make Matt a good second when Gareth stepped down. Ryan was a lot like his father, and Jesse Calder was not the kind of man many dared to cross.

Sighing internally, she kept her face stoic as her possessive werewolf lover turned to study her.

"What did those guys say to you?" he asked.

"Nothing important enough to share. I was the one who lied

and told them you were my husband, but don't read too much into that part of my story. You were just a quick excuse to get rid of their unwanted attention."

Ryan snorted, but a grin crept across his face. "The husband part is more truth than fiction. I hope one day you see that."

"Don't start," Heidi ordered.

Then she turned and met Katarina's puzzled gaze. She turned back to Ryan with a flushed face. Katarina's kidnapping was being kept quiet for now. She saw no reason to tell Ryan and worry him more.

"Uh... Ryan? I don't think you've officially met Katarina Volkov. She's a visiting Alpha from Russia. Someone she knows joined Reed's pack. He's coming down tomorrow to collect her. I'm keeping her company in the meantime."

Ryan nodded and spoke to Katarina in a stilted version of what Heidi could only assume was grade school level Russian. Katarina seemed to understand him though. She spoke slowly back to Ryan in her language, but her curious gaze kept returning to Heidi.

When Ryan's gaze drifted to Erwin and Larry checking out, Heidi lifted a finger to her lips, hoping to gain Katarina's cooperation. Katarina's head nod relieved her, but she had to work hard to emotionally ignore the giant questions lighting the Alpha's eyes. In her panic to stop Ryan from attacking the men to defend her, she'd forgotten all about Katarina watching her every move.

Ryan's gaze finally came back to her. She smiled softly at him, reaching for the kind of calm she used when healing. She needed it quite often when dealing with her demanding werewolf lover.

"Gareth was looking for you. Eva said you went shopping with a friend. I told him I'd find you and bring you out to his house. Can I buy you and Katarina some dinner first?"

Sighing, Heidi nodded. "Sure. That would be great, Ryan. Thank you. Katarina is staying at the inn while she's in town. I gave her my old room."

Katarina's gaze bounced between the two of them. To her

credit, the intense, talkative Alpha somehow kept from blurting out what Heidi had managed to completely hide from everyone in her new life.

But now she had to confess her special skills to her Alpha before Katarina confronted her about what she'd seen her do.

Want more info? Visit the web page for this book.

OTHER BOOKS BY THIS AUTHOR

ALIENS IN KILTS

Matchmaker Abduction

Nate's Fated Mate

Shades Of Darcone (coming soon)

CYBORGS: MANKIND REDEFINED

Peyton 313

Kingston 691

Marcus 583

Eric 754

NANO WOLVES

Ariel

Brandi

Heidi

Reed (coming soon)

FORCED TO SERVE

The Daemon Of Synar

The Daemon Master's Wife

The Siren's Call

The Healer's Kiss

The Daemon's Change

The Tracker's Quest

MY CRAZY ALIEN ROMANCE

ABOUT THE AUTHOR

After 35 years of doing everything else for a living, Donna McDonald published her first novel in March of 2011. Fifty plus novels later, she is living her own happily ever after in life as a full-time author.

McDonald's work spans several genres, such as contemporary romance, fantasy, paranormal, and science fiction. Romance and romantic elements abound in her work, but she claims humor as the most common element across all her writing. Addicted to making readers laugh, McDonald includes a good dose of comedy in every book.

For More Information…
www.donnamcdonaldauthor.com
email@donnamcdonaldauthor.com

Made in the USA
Columbia, SC
29 August 2023

22183792R00174